Backstabbers

Mike Roche

Resort Readers Publishing

Copyright © 2022 by Mike Roche

All rights reserved.

This book is a work of fiction. Names, characters, places and incidents are either products of the author's imagination or used fictitiously. Any resemblance to actual events, locals, or persons, living or dead, is entirely coincidental. All rights reserved. No portion of this book may be reproduced in any form or by any means, electronic or mechanical, without written permission from the publisher or author, except as permitted by U.S. copyright law.

Cover design by Stuart Bache and The Books Covered Team

ISBN: 979-8-84-247429-5

Contents

Dedication		VII
Introduction		VIII
1.	Chapter 1	1
2.	Chapter 2	5
3.	Chapter 3	8
4.	Chapter 4	11
5.	Chapter 5	13
6.	Chapter 6	15
7.	Chapter 7	17
8.	Chapter 8	20
9.	Chapter 9	25
10.	Chapter 10	29
11.	Chapter 11	32
12.	Chapter 12	36
13.	Chapter 13	40
14.	Chapter 14	42
15.	Chapter 15	47
16.	Chapter 16	48
17.	Chapter 17	51
18.	Chapter 18	53
19.	Chapter 19	57
20.	Chapter 20	59

21.	Chapter 21	62
22.	Chapter 22	66
23.	Chapter 23	69
24.	Chapter 24	72
25.	Chapter 25	75
26.	Chapter 26	78
27.	Chapter 27	81
28.	Chapter 28	84
29.	Chapter 29	87
30.	Chapter 30	90
31.	Chapter 31	93
32.	Chapter 32	96
33.	Chapter 33	98
34.	Chapter 34	100
35.	Chapter 35	103
36.	Chapter 36	105
37.	Chapter 37	109
38.	Chapter 38	112
39.	Chapter 39	114
40.	Chapter 40	117
41.	Chapter 41	119
42.	Chapter 42	121
43.	Chapter 43	124
44.	Chapter 44	127
45.	Chapter 45	129
46.	Chapter 46	131
47.	Chapter 47	134
48.	Chapter 48	136
49.	Chapter 49	139
50.	Chapter 50	142

51.	Chapter 51	146
52.	Chapter 52	151
53.	Chapter 53	154
54.	Chapter 54	156
55.	Chapter 55	158
56.	Chapter 56	164
57.	Chapter 57	165
58.	Chapter 58	167
59.	Chapter 59	170
60.	Chapter 60	172
61.	Chapter 61	175
62.	Chapter 62	177
63.	Chapter 63	179
64.	Chapter 64	180
65.	Chapter 65	185
66.	Chapter 66	187
67.	Chapter 67	190
68.	Chapter 68	193
69.	Chapter 69	196
70.	Chapter 70	201
71.	Chapter 71	205
72.	Chapter 72	208
73.	Chapter 73	211
74.	Chapter 74	214
75.	Chapter 75	218
76.	Chapter 76	223
77.	Chapter 77	225
78.	Chapter 78	227
79.	Chapter 79	230
80.	Chapter 80	232

81.	Chapter 81	234
82.	Chapter 82	239
83.	Chapter 83	241
84.	Chapter 84	244

Also By Mike Roche	247
About The Author	248
Afterword	249

For my Brothers and Sisters, still out there, still in harm's way. Especially, my female partners like the fictional Kate Alexander, who always had my six. Stay safe.

Introduction

I set this novel in Tampa, Florida. I use the Tampa Police Department as a delivery vehicle for the story. With that said, I took some creative license in the operations of the department for simplicity. I derived the characters from an amalgam of people that I have encountered throughout my forty-year law enforcement career in different cities and many agencies. I hope you enjoy.

Chapter One

The stain of death could never be washed away. Officer Erin Gifford looked through the windshield as the wipers cleared the deluge. She pulled to the curb under a towering oak tree and could see a man pacing on the front porch of the two-story Victorian home. The porch light silhouetted his image.

With a marathoner's body and a short pixie style cut, Gifford looked over at her rookie officer, Rick McMahon, who had the enthusiasm of a golden retriever puppy on a tight leash. As he unbuckled his seatbelt, Erin grabbed his shoulder.

She told him, "Listen to me. That man up there is Melvin Storms. He is one of the fiercest defense attorneys in Tampa. If he is rattled and pacing, that means we are walking into a shit storm. Stay close and don't say anything. Understand?"

"Yes ma'am"

"Don't call me that. I am not your mother."

The two officers sprinted to the porch, dodging as much rain as possible and splashing through the puddles. Water droplets rolled off their coats and splattered on the porch. Despite coming face to face in the courtroom, the skilled litigator did not recognize Erin. She could see his face was as pale as his long, white mane.

Erin gave a tug on her gun-belt and asked, "Mr. Storms, you called to report a homicide?"

He held out his cellphone without speaking. Erin read a text message from Dom. "I screwed up and I am sorry. Please take care of my affairs and the estate according to my wishes. Good bye my friend."

"Okay, who is Dom and whose home is this?"

He shook his head in disbelief and said, "Dominic Marchetti. This is his house. As soon as I received the text, I came over. There was no answer at the door or his phone. The door was locked. I ran around to the back door, which was unlocked." He sighed heavily and combed his hands through his white hair, coming to rest on the back of his neck." I walked in yelling Dom's name and

Carol, his wife. There was no answer. Then I found Dom in the front office. Dead. Murdered! Oh, my gosh." He turned away and exhaled.

"Why do you think this is murder?" Erin realized she was the one asking questions of the attorney.

Storms turned towards the officers and closed his eyes hard as if to block the memory. "There was a gun on the floor."

A second patrol SUV pulled up. Officer Ray Cruz arrived on the front porch. He shook rain off his jacket like a wet dog.

Erin said, "Melvin, have a seat here on the porch pointing to a white porch swing. Officer Cruz will keep you company. Myself and Officer McMahon will look. How many family members does Marchetti have, and did you hear anything inside the house?"

"It's Dom, Carol and their two children, Megan and Ethan. When I saw Dom, I ran. I wasn't listening."

"Okay, thanks."

The two officers stepped in muddy puddles as they walked cautiously down the side of the house. At the edge of the rear of the house, Erin stopped, listened, and looked around the small backyard and the detached garage. They preceded in silence to the back steps. Erin looked at her enthusiastic rookie and said, "McMahon, we don't know if someone is still here or not, or if in fact this is a murder-suicide. There is a possibility that there is someone still here, so be careful. We treat this like a whodunnit murder. There will be a lot of eyes on us afterwards." McMahon nodded excitedly. Erin rolled her eyes and pulled out her pistol.

She made note of the time for her report, and pulled the glass door open and yelled, "Police! Anyone home? Police! Announce yourselves!"

Silence. Erin wiped her feet as well as she could. She could see the footprints of Melvin Storms tracking through the kitchen. The light from the appliance clocks provided some ability to see. She turned her flashlight on and beamed it down the hallway from the kitchen. A crack of thunder jarred the house.

They stepped quietly and were careful not to cross her feet to maintain her balance, but the creaking wood floor gave their movements away. Erin stopped and listened. Nothing but the sound of rain hitting the house. She continued towards the front door and peered into the front office to the right. She motioned for McMahon to stay like an obedient dog.

Erin walked towards the body of who she presumed was Dominic Marchetti. Slumped in the chair, his right arm hung to the side. A pistol on the floor under his hand. His graying face had a bullet hole in the temple. There was no point in checking the obvious. He was a dead.

Erin moved towards the stairs and nodded to her partner. She provided hand signals to McMahon that Mr. Marchetti was dead. She first pointed and then gave a thumbs down.

She looked up the stairs and pointed her gun towards the top. She once again yelled, "Police! Anyone home?"

She provided hand signals to McMahon to follow and be quiet. She turned off her flashlight until they reached the top. Each step groaned and protested as Erin and McMahon made their way up the dreaded staircase. Her hand braced her ascent on the smooth wood banister. Officers hated going up the steps, which left them in an exposed position with nowhere to hide. They called it a fatal funnel. Once at the top, she scanned the landing and motioned for McMahon to follow.

Erin turned on her flashlight and lit up the bedroom doors. She walked into the room at the head of the stairs. She could smell a pleasant perfume. The beam from her flashlight illuminated the bed. The person who Erin assumed to be Carol Marchetti was lying on her bed, motionless. A white tank top was like a sponge soaking up a circle of blood surrounding what appeared to be a bullet hole. Her graying complexion was also a highlighter of her death.

The officers scanned the rest of the room and bathroom. Nothing gave an indication of a robbery. The left side of the vacant bedside was disorderly, but an organized mess.

They moved past the right side of the stairs and entered the next room. Neither officer was prepared for what they would witness. There, laying on his back, was the motionless body of ten-year-old Ethan Marchetti. A single bullet through his chest and the associated blood stain. Officer McMahon's previous enthusiasm had departed as he made the sign of the cross.

The last bedroom was Megan Marchetti, the fourteen-year-old daughter. Again, as in the previous two bedrooms, nothing appeared out of place. Meghan still in her final resting place of her bed, a bullet hole in the chest. McMahon made the sign of the cross again.

After checking the rest of the upstairs and determining that no one was there, Erin holstered her pistol and looked back at McMahon. "You good?"

"I'm... ah... not sure."

"That's okay. I'm not either. This is fucked up. You might want to reconsider going back to that seminary. Better to pray for protection from evil than come face to face. Who kills sleeping kids? That's just fucked up."

"Very disturbing."

"Okay. We have to notify the sergeant. He can make the calls to notify the shift commander, crime scene, homicide, medical examiner and we need another couple of units for crime scene integrity. Now we have to secure and preserve the scene."

Chapter Two

The clap of thunder shattered the darkness. Kate felt the thumping of her racing heart. Her eyes glanced for danger as a flicker of lightning bathed the room in a quick burst of light. As Kate rolled over to check the clock, her cell phone began chirping. She answered on the first ring, "Alexander."

"Kate, this is Lieutenant Sullivan. We have a nasty one for you. Sergeant Stewart asked for you to be primary and the rest of the squad is also getting a jingle."

"The rest of the squad?"

"Yep. Four dead. An entire family. Could be a murder-suicide, but it's still early. The PIO and the M.E. have been notified."

"Okay, text me the address. Thanks."

Kate pressed end and sighed. The pelting of the window followed another flash of lightning. She felt a warm bundle next to her. She patted the outside of the duvet and felt the impression of Brittney cocooned under the covers. Kate smiled, knowing that her daughter, not thrilled with the storm, had sought refuge in her mother's bed.

Kate stepped into the bathroom and closed the door. The flash of light from the fixture was a shock to her conscience. She splashed cold water on her face, brushed her teeth, and threw some powder on her cheeks. She slipped into her ready clothes that she had selected the night before. She pulled her brown hair into a ponytail and stepped out into the darkness.

Peeling the covers back, she admired the angelic face of her daughter. Kate cradled her in her arms and carried her into her mother's room. She felt that her eleven-year-old was getting heavy. Her mother, already sleeping light from the storm, sat up and looked at Kate, who was bathed in the glow from another bolt of lightning. The thunder rumbled in the distance.

"I'm sorry, mom. I've been called in. The rest of the night, I will be gone. I found Brittney in bed with me. The storm no doubt scared her." As she laid her daughter on the bed, she kissed her forehead and whispered, "I love you."

She kissed her mother's cheek. Her mom responded, "I love you, sweety. Be careful."

Kate kissed her mother and said, "Always."

Kate stepped into the kitchen, brewed a cup of coffee to go from the Keurig, grabbed a mint-flavored Cliff bar from the canister jar, and headed out into the night. She sprinted for the car through the steady rainfall and jumped into the car.

Detective Kate Alexander steered the black Dodge Charger down the wet street towards the address provided by the Lieutenant. She peered through the windshield as the wipers swept the raindrops across. The gray, two-story Victorian style home stood like an angry sentry on top of a small hill. The red brick chimney stood out tall above the roof. Kate thought this house and the entire gruesome scene she was about to enter belonged in some horror movie.

She pulled the hood of the raincoat over her head and grabbed her portfolio, along with a small blue towel. She sprinted up the street and bolted up the stone stairs for the shelter of the covered porch. Kate tossed her hood off, opened her jacket, and showed her gold detective's badge to Officer McMahon. She announced her name to the young officer, who looked ashen.

Kate slipped the cloth booties over her shoes. She slid the raincoat off and left it on the porch. The veteran officer that Kate recognized greeted her in the entryway. Kate said, "Hi Erin."

A sullen faced Erin Gifford said, "Hello Kate. This is bad. In all my time in the service and in the department, you never get used to the sight of children being the victims of war or crime."

"Okay, tell me what we have?"

"Family of four. The Marchetti family. Two children, ages ten and fourteen, shot once in the heart. They are both in their beds. Their mother was also found shot once in the heart. No signs of a struggle. Mr. Dominic Marchetti is in the office. Shot once in the head. Appears to be self-inflicted. We found the weapon at his side on the floor. A suicide note is on the printer, not signed."

"Okay."

Gifford opened a small memo pad. "We received the call to meet a party for a death. We arrived and met Melvin Storms, the attorney. He said he received a text from Marchetti that read, 'I screwed up and I am sorry. Please take care of my affairs and the estate according to my wishes. Goodbye, my friend.' Storms drove over here and could get no one to answer the door or the telephone. The backdoor was unlocked. No evidence of forced entry. After CSI cleared the kitchen, I moved Storms inside. He is waiting for you at the kitchen table."

"Okay, Erin thanks. Is that your partner out there?"

"Yeah, he was a seminary student. He might want to rethink that change of careers. I thought I was going to have to get a barf bag for him."

"Remember when we were young and naïve?"

"That's too far to remember."

Kate patted Erin on her arm, and they both chuckled.

"Erin, can you give me a quick sketch of the floor plan?"

"Sure. Nice house. He was a commodities broker. Looked like he was doing well, but who knows?"

"You are right."

"Office to the left, living room to the right. Kitchen and dining to the rear. Hall bath under the stairs. Upstairs is three bedrooms and two baths. The master is facing the stairs."

"Thanks Erin."

"Sure. I would rather be in here than out in that mess." As she pointed outside.

They both ducked at the crash of thunder that made the glass rattle in a nearby curio cabinet.

Chapter Three

Kate walked into the office of Dominic Marchetti. His sagging body was seated in a chair. His head was slumped backwards. The man's feet were naturally flat on the ground, not showing any signs of a struggle. He was wearing dark slacks and a white dress shirt that was no longer pristine.

Leaning in towards the body, Kate looked at the wound. She observed the tattooing and stippling around his temple, indicative of a gunshot wound from a gun fired close to the entry wound. She would have to wait for the autopsy, but it did not appear that the barrel was pressed against the head. In contact wounds, you could see the searing outline of the gun and a star wound from the exploding gasses when the barrel was pushed against the skin. With the stippling or tattooing from gunpowder showed that the gun was fired from close range but not against the skin.

She could see what appeared to be a slightly larger exit wound on the opposite side. Skull fragments, brain matter and blood spatter collected on the wall next to the chair and the left shoulder of his formerly white shirt.

The Glock model 17 – 9mm caliber was on the ground underneath where his hand dangled. Kate asked the crime scene tech, Dee Hanna, if she had finished photographing. The short-haired blonde Dee said, "Yes. This is a horrible scene with the kids upstairs."

Kate valued the input from Dee, an experienced homicide detective in her day, who returned as a CSU tech after retiring from the police department. Kate slid her hands into a pair of blue latex gloves and said to Dee, "With kids, it's always horrible and senseless."

Dee nodded in agreement. Kate noted Dominic's watch was on his left hand, indicating he was right-handed. That matched the wound on the right side of his head. Kneeling down, Kate looked on the trigger hand to see if there were any obvious traces of blood blowing back on the hand. There appeared to be a few specks in the webbing between the thumb and first finger. There was always blowback. Kate could not see any on the white sleeve cuff or the wrist.

She expected a little more, but under microscopic examination, they could see for certain.

Once the gun is fired into the brain, the hand provides no resistance to the recoil of the weapon as it tends to flip out to the right, away from the body. The limp arm hung on the outside of the chair. Kate picked up the weapon and ejected the magazine. She pulled the slide back far enough to see another round had been chambered, as semi-automatic guns will do.

Again, in a suicide, the hand provides the support and resistance for the slide to eject the spent shell, extract a new bullet from the magazine, and deliver it to the chamber so it is ready to be fired again. In some suicides, the lack of resistance of the hand results in a round not being chambered. They sometimes blame a weak wrist on new timid shooters on the firing range and resulting in a failure to feed the next round into the firing position. She called Dee to photograph the round in the chamber and the magazine.

Kate now looked over at the suicide note in the printer. She read the contents, "I am terribly sorry for all that I have done. I wanted to spare them the humiliation of my disgrace and suicide. I ask God to have mercy on their souls and to please forgive me. Dom"

Kate read it again. Not much in there. He doesn't describe what he had done. He doesn't speak with familiarity with his wife and children. He refers to them in the collective "them." It was just a hunch, but she thought the note was just a little too sterile and light on details for a final farewell. Most notes were deeply personal, expressing remorse and extreme discomfort. Not this one. She asked Dee to bag it and send for fingerprints and DNA. Since it was on the printer, it should be pristine, with no one touching it.

Leaving the note on the printer was odd to Kate. Most people committing suicide would want to make sure the note is closer to the body to ensure that it is discovered. Most suicides did not leave a note. In fact, only about thirty percent left a note.

There was also an absence of family photos and a drink next to the body. Many victims of suicide needed a little liquid encouragement to compensate for extinguishing their body. Many would also hold or have the image of loved ones as a last vision before they leave forever. There were family pictures on the wall. Perhaps that was good enough. None of these conjectures were absolute, but it gave pause with the setting that could show a staged crime scene.

She asked Dee, "Have you ever worked a staged suicide on the job or CSI?"

Her lips pursed and said, "A few. That's something you see more in the movies or crime fiction. I've had more the other way of trying to conceal a suicide."

"Yeah, I agree." She hoped this was not her first staged scene.

She looked around the office. The cell phone was sitting on the desk. She did not want to touch it for fear of corrupting any fingerprints on the nonporous surface.

The bookshelves were filled with books on economics, politics, and what appeared to be the entire collection of books by Stephen King, Michael Koryta, and Joseph Wambaugh. Those were his escape and recreational readings.

Photographs captured happier times with the family on vacations around the world. The smiles provided no insight into the horrors inside this once happy home.

Kate turned to Hanna and said, "Hey Dee, make sure you process the keyboard and the cell phone for prints and DNA."

"Sure, no problem."

"Would you obtain a soil sample from the side yard, the rear along the walking path? Then we need one from the yard next door as a possible control sample to show uniqueness."

Dee's face showed intrigue. "I have never grabbed soil samples before. But I like where you are going with this."

"I haven't either. I would think there is a uniqueness to the soil. As muddy as it is, I am hoping if this turns into a murder, the suspect will have the soil on their pants and shoes. I'll call the FDLE lab to see if we can do it."

"I like it."

Chapter Four

Kate ascended up the angry stairs of the foreboding home. Her shoes echoed on the creaking wood steps. She thought there was no way someone climbed these stairs without drawing attention. At the top of the stairs, she took a deep breath and turned towards the first room on the left.

She illuminated the room with her Surefire flashlight. She did not want to touch the light until someone had dusted it for fingerprints. The ceiling fan rotated the air. The room was in a disarray. The floor was littered with clothes and footwear. Posters of local sports teams and athletes were thumb tacked to the white walls.

In the full-sized bed was the body of a young Ethan with a short-cropped haircut. A single gunshot wound in the heart. His white t-shirt showed burns from a close proximity gunshot wound. Kate could see the sheets and mattress under the lifeless figure had absorbed a large blood pool. He had not moved from the time of the initial shot. There was no evidence of a struggle, just a messy kid's room. She jotted a few notes of her impressions.

She now walked into the Megan's room. The fourteen-year-old seemed to be asleep. In the flashlight's shadow, the girl resembled Kate's own daughter Britney, whom she had left just an hour ago in a slumber. Kate shook her head in disbelief and her eyes looked upward for strength.

This girl would not be waking up to play on her PlayStation, listen to music or trading texts with her BFF. Kate could see that this victim suffered the same fate as her brother. There was a contact gunshot wound to the left chest. The blood pooling under the body also showed there was no movement after the discharge of the weapon.

Kate stood in silence, studying the innocent face of the lifeless victim. Despite her veteran presence in the homicide squad, she could not understand what would possess someone killing a young teenager. The child's face projected innocence and a future that would never be realized.

Kate looked around the room and digested the images of the decor. On the wall next to the bed was a poster from the Game of Thrones. Kate thought of her old partner Frank Duffy in how he would've made some dark humor connection between the poster and the death of this child. But even Duffy had his limits. With children, there was no tolerance for dark humor.

Kate stared at the somber silence of the girl's face while she envisioned the happier times giggling at the excitement this girl had for life. Her mind drifted to her own daughter Britney and the innocence of her youth, which had been scarred by the tragic death of her father and Kate's husband. Thunder rocked the house and shook Kate into consciousness.

Kate picked up an iPad, pushed the start button. Being locked, she used the child's finger to open the screen, and a game appeared, perhaps Minecraft, but Kate was not sure. She minimized the game and hit the message icon. A pang of guilt crept into her as she felt like a voyeur examining someone's darkest secrets. As she scrolled through the text messages and email inbox and sent messages, she only noticed the innocence of youthful chatter and gossip between friends. Those same friends who would awaken to the horror and reality that one of their friends had been brutally murdered. Kate blew a lungful of air through pursed lips to control her emotions.

Chapter Five

She walked out of the room and turned to the right, towards the master bedroom. Kate entered the final death room. The bedroom looked like most formal bedrooms. They furnished it with large clunky walnut furniture in a four-poster bed.

One thing that Kate noticed, the polarization of order within the bedroom. The room appeared to mirror their personalities. On the left side of the bed and the surrounding area, the room resembled the disheveled nature of Mr. Marchetti. The floor and the dresser nearest to where Dominic slept were littered with discarded clothes. On the night stand several nonfiction books on economics and financial magazines and periodicals.

Carol Marchetti's side of the bedroom was pristine and well-organized. She, like her two children, laid in bed on her back with a gunshot wound to the chest. There appeared to be no struggle, and she died where she was shot.

What struck Kate was that all three victims appeared to have been in a state of slumber when they suffered the fatal gunshot. Despite the loud clapping of thunder throughout the evening, she still felt a gunshot inside the home would've awakened at least one, if not all, of the victims. It was also unusual that all would be on their back. Quite often, people were side or belly sleepers. It was unclear as to the order of succession of deaths. Only the killer could answer that question.

Kate entered the restroom. The flashlight illuminated her face in the mirror. It cast an eerie image, almost a hallowed look. She thought she looked older. Her face was tougher, with a few more wrinkles. But that's what will happen to a young woman's face who endures the premature death of her husband, and her life as a homicide detective in a major metropolitan city. Examining these grisly murder scenes, especially with innocent children that had so much in front of them, would rob anyone of their youth. It was left up to her to become their voice, to seek justice and answers to these violent acts and to prevent them from ever occurring again.

She looked at the counter. The right side was neat and orderly. The left sink area was cluttered. The toothpaste tube opened, the brush on its side. The shaving cream lid was on its side and the razor was upside down. There was no organization. She looked in the trash and did not notice anything relevant. She opened the medicine cabinet. A few bottles of over-the-counter medicines, and one prescription for cholesterol and another for blood pressure for Dominic. In a society dependent on prescriptions, their cabinet was light.

Kate deliberated the tragedy of the murderous rampage. This beautiful house surrounded by majestic oak trees in a grand neighborhood, owned by an apparently successful businessman and occupied by a beautiful, sweet family, was the setting for a morbid scene and hidden secrets.

What had occurred in their personal lives was a cataclysmic shattering of their once peaceful existence, and what would intrude such horror into their lives? Did Dominic just snap and decide to take his entire family with him? Kate knew no one ever snapped. They become consumed in an emotional negative vortex, which builds like a cauldron of discontent towards life. Or was it something much more nefarious? A suicide and murder in appearance, but was actually a calculated and senseless murder. All good homicide investigators considered all possibilities.

Chapter Six

Refocusing her attention, Kate walked down the steps. She and Erin nodded at each other. There was nothing to be said after seeing the images that would steal away into the memory for the rest of her life. Kate wondered down the hall to the kitchen. She looked at Melvin Storms messaging his white-haired scalp. He looked up at her. His face provided recognition but was void of emotion. Melvin Storms was one of the most feared attorneys in Tampa, but on this night, the murders had stripped his confidence to the core.

Pulling the chair out, Kate sat across from Storms at the kitchen table. Her mind drifted to thinking of a few hours earlier, the happy family sat at this same table and enjoyed their last meal together. How much premonition did any of them have about the horrors ahead?

"Hi Melvin." As her hands steepled on the table.

"Detective Alexander."

"I am assuming you knew the family."

"Ahh… yes… ahh, terrible."

"How did you know Mr. Marchetti?"

"I've known him for years. We frequent or did frequent the same social circles. We were in the same Gasparilla Krewe."

"Why did he reach out to you specifically?"

"I was his attorney and friend."

"Why don't we start from the beginning and tell me the what and the why?"

"The why? Why would anyone kill their entire family? What in the hell would cause someone to kill their children? Oh God. This is horrible."

Kate patted his arm. "Yes, it is."

Melvin took a deep breath and blew his lungs out like he was chasing the demons away. "The storm was interrupting my sleep. I heard a text come in. I looked at it and saw that it was from Dom."

"You mean Dominic Marchetti?"

"Yes." He raised the phone up and extended his arm out to read the screen as Kate came closer and looked over his shoulder. She read the text, "I screwed up and I am sorry. Please take care of my affairs and the estate according to my wishes. Good bye my friend."

"What did you think this message meant?"

"He was in trouble. Since he is dead... I suppose I can provide you with the details." He bit his lip, shook his head, and continued, "He worked for Hercules Investments. He was a genius with money. He made a mistake and moved some money into an account for his mother that belonged to Hercules."

"So, he embezzled the money."

"Well, he was planning to pay it back."

Kate put up her hand and said, "Melvin, I know he is a friend, but you are not in court, and we need the truth and not some defense strategy."

Melvin hung his head and looked up at Kate. "I just don't understand. We were in negotiations with Hercules to repay the money. I did not know he was so dejected."

Officer Gifford sauntered into the kitchen. Kate looked over at Erin as the officer spoke. "Sorry to interrupt, but I've got some snot-nosed political ass wipe demanding entrance. He said he is with Senator Thorland's office. I told him I didn't care if he was the Senator, no one enters a crime scene. I get the feeling he doesn't like to be told no."

Melvin spoke up and said, "Oh, that is Rodney Upton, Senator Thorland's chief of staff. I called him. He is a good friend and knows Dom."

Kate said, "Melvin, I'll be right back. Erin, I would like a witness and some backup."

"Girl, I've I got your six. You can count on me."

Chapter Seven

Kate scanned over the youthful chief of staff. She caught a whiff of cologne. He was set for breakfast at the club wearing a button down pin-striped shirt, pressed khakis and white soled casual shoes. His hair was neatly combed, and a neatly groomed beard. Kate figured there might be shaving cream behind the ear. Who gets dressed like they are going to a country club, but instead going to a murder scene at 4:00 am? Kate had an immediate distaste. "Yes, can I help you?"

"Yes, I am Senator Thorland's chief of staff, Rodney Upton." As he handed his business card to Kate. "Mr. Storms requested my presence."

Kate nodded, looked at the card, and said, "How is it you know the Marchetti family?"

"We are friends. We are in the same Gasparilla Krewe."

Kate started to say that Dom would not be throwing beads off the float this year, but held her sarcasm. "What can you tell me about his current state of mind?"

"I talked with Dom a few weeks ago, prior to his current dilemma with Hercules. He seemed well grounded. In fact, he told me a story about an old friend who had committed suicide, and his wife was so distraught that Dom had to hire someone to take care of her and provide emotional and physical support for months until she could get a grasp. After that ordeal, I was surprised he would choose suicide, but perhaps that may have planted a seed that germinated a perverse idea. I am afraid that experience could have provided a motive to this tragic incident."

"Did he seem depressed?"

"He was always a little moody."

"Moody?"

"Like the stock market he invested in, his mood was up and down. He was a bit eccentric, like many intellectuals."

"In what way?"

"He preferred to drink at dive bars and eat at off beat restaurants. Some places I did not feel comfortable."

"I could see that."

"He would give out hundred-dollar bills to the homeless and the panhandlers. He carried a Star Trek lunch box and ate a sandwich at his desk. Then he might go to Berns Steakhouse and order a 10-ounce filet and spend a few hundred dollars on a bottle of 2005 Chateau Valandraud Saint Emilion. I am not sure that you are familiar with that class of wine." He flashed a contented smile.

Kate nodded, recognizing the put down. "Having taken some French while I was at Duke, I am familiar with the Boudreaux region of wines. By the way, you placed the accent in the wrong place on Emilion. It's actually pronounced like A-mil-yon. The "N" is mostly silent." His smile dissipated like a deflating balloon.

She continued with another question. "Do you think he could have suffered from some mental health impairment?"

"I'm not a psychologist."

"I understand, but do you think he could have been depressed or bipolar?"

"I really don't want to make any judgments outside my field of expertise."

"Which is?"

"Politics."

"Of course it is. Thank you for stopping by and I will tell Melvin you stopped by."

"On behalf of the Senator, I would like to provide comfort to Mr. Storms."

"That will not happen. This is a crime scene, and this is my field of expertise. No one enters this area without my permission. You would not want to be called as a witness because everyone written on the log is subject to be called as a witness in court."

"Detective..."

"Alexander."

"Yes, Detective Alexander, I don't care for your tone."

Kate placed her hands on her hips and said, "Rodney, I am not conducting a favorability poll. This incident, as you describe it, is the murder of an entire family. Two children died a tragic death in this house. I just examined their lifeless bodies. That is my only concern in identifying the motives and killer. I don't care who is offended by my tone, as long as I obtain justice for those children. Have a nice day Rodney, and you can leave now. If we need anything else from you, we will be in touch."

The two officers turned their backs on the political aid and walked inside. Once inside, Erin Gifford extended a fist bump towards Kate and said, "I am glad you have not softened your Kick Ass Alexander attitude."

"Frank Duffy told me more times than I could count, what is the definition of Irish diplomacy? That is to tell someone to go to hell in such a way as to look forward to the trip."

"You left Rodney with his pants around his ankles. He has no pride left. By the way, how is Frank?"

"He is a train wreck. Some are self-inflicted, but you throw in the shooting, his wife's death and a lot of Irish whiskey and it is a volatile mixture. Time will tell."

"Well, he would be proud of you. You took Rodney down a couple of notches."

"He deserved it. We have four bodies in here and he is acting like this is some political rally. He can shove his sensibilities up his and his Senator's ass. Besides, I didn't vote for him, anyway."

"I did not know that you were such a connoisseur of wine."

"I'm not. It could come out of a box, and I wouldn't know the difference."

"I heard that. I'll let you do your thing and check on my pale-faced rookie. Let me know if you need anything."

They turned towards the sound of the engine of the car starting and the headlights blinking on. The tires on the wet pavement made swooshing noise as they watched Upton drive away in a black BMW SUV past the house.

Chapter Eight

Kate said, "Hey Erin, the weather has probably slowed them down, but the rest of the squad should show up soon, including my new partner, Cody Danko."

"You mean Good Night Danko?"

"Huh?"

"Yeah, that's his nickname. Couple years ago, he and his partner rolled on a call to a robbery in progress at a convenience store up in the Heights. Danko's partner, Troy Fletcher, goes through the front door and Danko goes around back and enters the rear. So, Fletcher confronts the bad guy, who has grabbed a little girl and threatens to kill her. The bad guy didn't know Danko was coming up behind him. Danko put one round right through the brain stem and dropped him like a bag of cement. According to Fletcher, Danko looked down at the bad guy and said, "Good night, asshole." So, the legend was born. Since then, he has been known as Good Night Danko."

"Oh Sure, I remember that story. I didn't realize that's who it was. Sounds like a solid guy to me."

"He has a solid reputation. I heard he did time in the Afghanistan and was in some hot zone trading lead downrange every day."

"Well, I'll be looking forward to meeting Mr. Cody 'Good Night' Danko." The two officers chuckled as Kate turned and reentered the somber death house.

Kate pulled out her telephone and called Sergeant Alfonso Stewart. After one ring, the soft-spoken Stewart answered with an upbeat and alert tone. "Al, it's Kate. I'm here at the scene and it's a bad one. Four dead, including the husband, wife and two children. It appears to be a homicide-suicide by the husband, but I'm not convinced. I'll bring you up to date when you arrive."

Stewart said, "I should be there in a few minutes."

"Okay, see you then."

Kate then called Fiona Quinn, who was the on-call assistant state attorney for Hillsborough County. Kate liked Fiona, who she admired because she had a toughness highlighted by her skill and beauty. Unlike the Sergeant, Fiona Quinn had been sound asleep and answered with an impaired voice. Kate described the horrific scene and was told by a more alert prosecutor that she lived in Hyde Park and would be there shortly.

As Kate disconnected the telephone call, she heard a light knocking on the front door. She stepped over and pulled the door open and met her new partner for the first time. She could smell the robust aroma of caffeine. His chiseled face had an easy grin, holding two cups of coffee.

"Hi Kate, I'm Cody and I understand we're riding together. Since I didn't live too far away, I thought you might enjoy a little caffeine boost to start the morning."

She took the one from him and felt the warmth radiated through her hands. She took a sniff and enjoyed the robust aroma. Cody reached up and combed through his blonde waves, shaking the moisture off. He wiped his hand on his jacket and said, "I didn't know how you take yours, so I took the liberty of putting some cream in the coffee, and I have some sweeteners in my pocket." His hand reached into his police windbreaker and pulled out an assortment of artificial sweetener packets and sugar packets.

Kate smiled and said, "You come prepared, don't you?" She reached into the palm of his hand and selected her sweetener of choice, unbleached sugar. "Thank you very much. That was kind of you." Kate and Erin traded smiles and winks at each other, as if Kate had just scored the quarterback as a date for the prom.

Kate said, "Cody, this is a bad one to take your training wheels off. We have four dead in separate murder rooms. It's a husband, wife, daughter, son. The initial appearance is a homicide-suicide. I have my doubts, but we will discuss that more later. The possible shooter and deceased is Dominic Marchetti. His attorney received a text from him. His attorney is Melvin Storms, and he is sitting back in the kitchen."

"The Melvin Storms? He is a big hitter?"

"Yes, I have some history with Melvin. I don't know whether you remember when Rollins was shot chasing after the bad guy. The shooting occurred at Melvin Storm's home. So, he has a different appreciation for the police after we saved him from Shugart killing him."

Cody leaned in towards Kate and in a hushed voice said, "I remember that one, and I certainly remember your family being taken hostage. I'm glad it ended as well as it did and that you are able to take care of business. I'm new at this, so if you don't mind, I'll just be your shadow."

"Okay shadow, follow me. I'll take you on a tour when the others arrive. Until then, we can interview the attorney." Kate. took a sip of the coffee and nodded with pleasure. "You are my hero."

After Kate escorted Cody through the hall, they entered the kitchen, which had been cleared by the crime scene unit. "Melvin, I am sorry for the interruption. Melvin, this is Detective Cody Danko. Detective, this is Melvin Storms. The two exchanged handshakes and Kate said, "Senator Thorland's aid stopped by and wanted to provide support. I sent him on his way."

"He can be a little.... enthusiastic."

Kate nodded in agreement and asked, "Tell me from the beginning, after you arrived here."

"I parked out front and ran up to the porch. The light was on. I rang the doorbell rapidly a few times. I then knocked and knocked. There was nothing. I called him again on my cellphone and got his voicemail. The same for Carol. I tried the door, and it was locked. The backyard entrance is on the right side of the house. After walking down the side yard, I knocked on the back door and tried to open it, and it was unlocked. I walked through the kitchen and called out their names, and I received no response. When I looked in his office, I saw Dom and..." He paused and took a deep breath, "... he was dead. I saw the gun on the floor next to him. I hurried out and called 911 and waited on the porch."

"Okay, did you move anything?"

"No. Nothing."

"Did you see any other footprints coming from outside through the kitchen?"

"No, but I wasn't looking either. It was dark."

"Tell me about Dom? Any mental health issues?"

"Kate, I learned a long time ago not to play psychiatrist. Many people suffer from various ailments and are on meds or in therapy. I've had many clients that surprised me. Someone could easily label Dom eccentric. His personal life was unconventional. He probably had a genius IQ. He was a collector of oddities and if it wasn't for Carol, he would probably be a hoarder."

"Any history of suicide attempts or threatening considering the position that he was in with the fraud allegations?"

"No never. In some ways I would say that he was relieved to having been fired. He didn't feel like they appreciated him. He had another job offer."

Cody stepped from being the shadow and asked, "Excuse me, Mr. Storm. How was his marriage? You said that perhaps they appeared to be maybe the odd couple in their differences?"

"She certainly was his anchor to his meandering ship. She was clearly the CEO of the house. My wife was once told by Carol that her life had always been very vanilla. Being married to Dom brought all kinds of colorful and interesting toppings, creating a marvelous sundae."

"Thank you, sir. Just one more question. Are you aware, or could there have been any infidelity in the relationship?"

"Now, I'm going to sound like one of you cops on the witness stand. Not to my knowledge. I had no reason to doubt their love. They truly were opposites that attracted and clung like magnets."

Kate gave a smile of appreciation to the new detective. She recalled the days of being a new detective and being terrified of speaking up, surrounded by experienced investigators. Especially being the lone female in the squad. For most females in police work, she felt testosterone sometimes impeded the thought process for the male ego. Females had to work harder and smarter to win over their male counterparts. Cody showed restraint and only asked a natural investigative question. She was warming to the new partner. He certainly won brownie points with the coffee.

Kate took another sip of coffee and asked, "Good question, Cody. Melvin, tell me about this embezzlement?"

"He was quite brilliant with managing money. He had an MBA from Wharton. Apparently, he was making some high-risk investments in commodities to gain further favor with the Stimpson brothers, who owned Hercules. He also had an account set up under his mother's name, which he failed to divulge. The Stimpson's found out he had been misappropriating winning trades to his mother's account and losing trades to the Stimpson's house account."

Kate said, "Not the way to win favor with your employer."

Storms nodded in agreement. "It pissed him off when he was not promoted and that they took his knowledge and skill for granted."

"Famous last words."

"When they discovered the impropriety, they threatened to report him to the SEC and strip him of his license. We were attempting to negotiate a repayment and not reporting him. He was going to his mother for a loan to cover the losses."

"Why not sign the proceeds over?"

"He had spent a good portion of the funds."

"On what?"

"He wouldn't say."

"Who were you dealing with at Hercules?"

"The compliance officer, Jennifer Bartsch."

"Who was his mother?"

"Valerie McCormick"

"The writer?"

"Yes. There is some bad blood there and she would not help him."

"Bad blood?"

Melvin gave a half shoulder shrug, "The typical mother and son drama. I don't know the specifics. He had another revenue opportunity that would pay off the debt."

"How."

"Another job opportunity and he said that he could reach out to his in-laws for a loan."

"Now, let me ask you, are you aware of anyone who would've wanted to kill Dom?"

Melvin shook his head and said, "No, not at all. He wasn't like a ruthless businessman or Wall Street trader. He was more like the absent-minded professor who was quirky and goofy. There may have been some people that would become impatient with his eccentricities, but I don't know anyone that would want him dead along with his entire family. I really believe that he was terrified of losing everything and that he was terrified that his family would suffer from the alienation and humiliation. Just so senseless. Senseless."

"Yes, it is. One last thing. Do you know if Carol Marchetti has any family?"

"I know she was from the Philadelphia area. They met while he was studying for his graduate degree. I'm sorry that I don't know more."

"We have not made it public yet, but we did find Carol, Megan and Ethan dead upstairs."

He dropped his head, and his body quivered. Kate gently patted his shoulder as he began to sob. He finally inhaled and sighed heavily and looked at Kate. "Thank you for telling me."

"You are welcome, Melvin. I am sorry for the loss of your friends. You can go leave now and if anything else comes up, I'll give you a shout."

"Thank you, Kate." Melvin stood up and shuffled down the long hallway towards the front door. He intentionally looked away from the office where the body of his friend was laying, leaving a horrible crime scene behind.

Kate looked around the kitchen. She saw two old-fashioned glasses in the sink with soap and water. She wondered if it was a nightcap for the Marchetti's. She poked through the trash. Takeout from a Greek restaurant. That would give the medical examiner an ability to establish a time of death depending how much had been digested.

Kate called communications and asked if they could find Carol Marchetti's next of kin and contact phone number. If they were in town, she would make the notification. If they were out of town, she would call them on the phone. She thought this would be so impersonal, but she knew she would be empathetic and could ask questions that a local officer on a death notification call would not ask.

Chapter Nine

The large bodied Sergeant Alfonso Stewart and the much more diminutive Fiona Quinn walked in. Fiona wore a black UCF ball cap. Kate filled in the supervisor and prosecutor on the relevant facts and then took them on a tour of the murder scene.

Kate escorted the group into the office of Dominic Marchetti. Cody lingered in their shadow. She gave them a few moments to absorb the surroundings and then said, "One would assume that Dominic killed his family and committed suicide. I'm not sold on that theory. As you can see, the weapon is next to his chair as if it fell out of his hand. Two problems with this. In a suicide, with the awkward handling of the weapon at that angle to fire into the temple, when the weapon is discharged, there is a lack of resistance from the trigger hand and typically the recoil of the weapon will kick it out and away from the body. One can probably make the argument that the finger held onto the trigger guard and would've fallen closer to the body, but I still don't believe it would've fallen this close to his side. The second item with the gun is that sometimes in a suicide, because of the lack of resistance in the trigger hand, which is required for the recoil of the pistol to extract the next bullet out of the magazine, the gun will not reload. This pistol has a bullet in the chamber."

Stewart nodded in agreement and said, "Excellent observation, Kate."

She continued, "Most suicide notes, especially as tragic as this in which he has killed his entire family, the notes are typically weepy and much more extensive in their length and confession. This one is to the point and very short on detail."

Stewart asked, "Anything else in here, jump out at you?"

"We will have to see in autopsy, but there doesn't appear to be much misting of blood blow back spatter on his shooting hand."

"Okay. More?"

"No. We can go upstairs and look at the other three victims. They are not particularly gruesome outside of the innocence of the victims. They all three died of what appears to be single gunshot wounds to the chest, and it does not appear that there was any struggle. It merely looks like they went to sleep and never woke up."

The three investigators and prosecutor walked up the stairs, making a noise that echoed through the house. They viewed each one of the three bedrooms and three victims. Alfonzo, the grizzled veteran homicide investigator, always maintained a stoic presence but would purse his lips in displaying his displeasure at the innocence of victims, particularly children.

Quinn's face wore heavy with the expected face of grief and discomfort. Most cops who have had time on the job have been exposed to the bodies of an unnecessary death, either by murder or accident. The deaths of children always gripped cops, no matter how much they'd been exposed to. The flash of light from lightning, followed by a crack of thunder, broke the uneasy silence of the team of investigators.

Cody looked at Kate and said, "Does it ever get easier with time seeing children as victims of violence?" He then glanced at Sergeant Stewart.

Stewart and Kate answered in unison, "No."

Kate said, "Follow me into the master bathroom." As all four walked into the bathroom. Kate asked, "Do you see anything unusual?"

The group scanned a typical bathroom with toiletries scattered about, a used towel on the floor and his and hers sinks with an organization that represented the user's personality. One was organized and one was in a disarray. The two detectives answered together, "No," while shaking their heads.

Fiona spoke up and said, "The toilet seat is up."

Cody chuckled and said, "It would take a woman to recognize that."

Kate continued, "Any female that has had the shock of sitting on the bare bowl in the middle of the night would notice the violation of the sacrilege."

Fiona said, "Amen!"

Alfonso said, "Some men never get trained. Marisol would string me up by my manhood." He gave an uneasy smile.

Kate said, "Could Dominic have used it last? I suppose. You would assume that he would have used it downstairs near his office. If there was an intruder, the killer could have used this toilet."

Cody interjected, "It could have been the son."

Kate answered, "Could have, but one would assume he would have used the hall bath. I think it just doesn't quite fit. Maybe it's nothing, and I am overthinking. We can get it dusted and check for hairs and urine splatter for DNA. Although DNA is difficult to extract from urine." The group nodded in approval and shuffled out of the bath past the body in the bedroom.

Fiona Quinn adjusted her ball cap, opened up her notebook, and clicked a ballpoint pen. She looked at Kate and said, "Okay, what is the game plan?"

Kate liked Fiona's approach to a homicide case. They worked on several cases in the past and Kate always felt it was refreshing to have a prosecutor that did not micromanage the case but deferred to the detective's knowledge, expertise, and intuition. Instead of dictating a strategic plan, Quinn was seeking input. Kate said, "We will have to wait for toxicology results, which could take some time. I don't believe three people could be shot inside the house without someone waking up despite the thunder. If anything, they would've been sleeping lightly because of this thunder. I know I was." Everyone nodded in agreement. "Also, we to have to check DNA sampling and prints on the weapon, computer, keyboard, printer and phone. Cody and I will go over to Hercules Investments and kick over a few rocks and see what happens, and then we have to check with Marchetti's mother and interview her as well. Fiona, we will probably need quite a few subpoenas for financials and cell phone activity. We have to do forensics on all the computers in the house as well. We can check with the neighbors and the relatives of Mrs. Marchetti to see if she was sharing pillow talk or had other concerns. Am I missing anything?"

Fiona said, "As always, it sounds like a comprehensive investigative plan, Kate."

Kate said, "This case is going to have some bad juju. He was well-connected, stole money from a power player, and we've already had somebody from Senator Thorland's office sniffing around. The newsies are swimming around out there like sharks in the water."

Stewart said, "You're right, the media trucks are already out there. The PIO was briefed, and she is on her way. I will call The Caveman and have him call the Captain and Major."

Kate and Cody stayed inside. The two detectives needed to go over the game plan and also stay close while Dee Hanna and the crime scene unit processed the residence. They also needed to be present as the medical examiner, examined and then removed the bodies.

Cody asked, "The Caveman?"

"Our Lieutenant. Jack Willard."

Cody smiled and said, "We used to call him 'The Ghost' when I worked for him in patrol. He was as elusive as a ghost and no one would ever see him unless the news media was on scene. He had more publicity shots than an Instagram influencer. The good side was that he would leave us alone and never bothered us."

"Frank Duffy termed Willard as 'The Caveman' because he never leaves his office and because it's a dark and scary world outside. And maybe he would have left us alone, but Frank was never one to let the lion sleep in their cage, as he called it. So, Frank was always poking him with a stick, and I think he found out that one who provokes the lion can end up being bitten."

"You must pick your battles because if you don't, you can lose the war."

"That is sage advice."

Chapter Ten

The rain had stopped, and the clouds were breaking up as the first rays of the sunrise highlighted the departing storm clouds. Kate looked up and thought it would be nice if the clouds had taken all this death with them.

Sitting in Kate's unmarked car, Kate looked up the email sent to her by communications. Carol Marchetti's maiden name was Swoboda, and they lived in Bucks County, Pennsylvania, a suburb of Philadelphia.

She punched in the digits and took a deep breath, hoping that someone would answer. So few had a landline any longer and many silenced their cellphones at night. If she did not get an answer, then she would have to ask the local police to make contact and ask them to call Kate.

After the fourth ring, a groggy female voice answered, "Yes?"

"Hello, Mrs. Swoboda?"

A little more clarity responded, "Who is this?"

"I am sorry. This is Detective Alexander with the Tampa Police Department, and I am calling to speak with Mrs. Swoboda."

"What's wrong? Is everything all right with Carol and Dom and the kids?" Panic was setting into her voice, she was now fully alert.

"I am very sorry to have to tell you..." a shrieking voice cut Kate off and she could hear a pleading male voice in the background. Mrs. Swoboda was hysterical and the male voice was trying to be calm and gleam some information.

The male voice came on the line and said, "This is Greg Swoboda. What is going on?"

Kate bit her lip and took a breath. "Mr. Swoboda, I am Detective Alexander with the Tampa Police Department. I am very sorry to tell you we responded to a call this morning at the Marchetti residence and found the entire family, including Carol and the children, deceased."

The exasperation was obvious while his wife was wailing in the background. "Deceased? What do you mean? How?"

"Carol, Megan and Ethan appear to have been shot. Dominic also died because of a gunshot."

"What? No, this can be."

"I am terribly sorry. This is horrible news to receive over the phone, but I wanted to call before the news media reached out to you."

The bewildered Mr. Swoboda asked, "The media?"

"Yes, sir. They are outside the house. It won't be long before they will call you for your response."

"Oh, my gosh."

"Can you tell me when was the last time that you had communication with the family?"

His voice quivered. "Yesterday. It was my birthday. We did a video chat with all of them."

"Did everything seem okay?"

"Yes. Yes. They all sang happy birthday to me." Mr. Swoboda began sobbing.

Kate gave him a minute to regain his composure. "Were you aware of any problems in the marriage or threats against the family?"

"No. This is crazy. They were a loving family. Everyone loved them. Carol and Dom met at U-Penn. They had a very sound marriage."

"Were they experiencing any financial problems?"

"No. They were very comfortable."

"You were approached about providing a loan to them."

"No. Where is the line of questioning coming from?"

"I am sorry, sir. I am trying to get an understanding of what your daughter's family was going through."

"How did this happen?"

"We are still in the early stages of the investigation. All I can say for sure is that they appear to have been killed by gunshot. That is all I know at this time. You have my number. Please call me with any additional questions once you have had time to process this terrible news, and I apologize that you were notified over the phone."

"Yes. Thank you." Kate heard Mrs. Swoboda calm down enough to ask something. Mr. Swoboda said, "They're gone." The wailing resumed, and the phone went dead.

Kate inhaled deeply and held her breath for a moment. Making a death notification was the worst part of the job, she thought. She knew the media would not be far behind her in tracking down the family connection and phone number to the next of kin and call for a comment. She exhaled and thought that she would call the Swoboda's back later after they had some time to process the loss of their child and grandchildren.

She turned to Cody. "It was her dad's birthday yesterday. They sang happy birthday. What a gut punch. And today they are dead."

"That sucks. I don't have kids, but I still understand how earth shattering that news is to receive."

"It is. Life altering." Kate rubbed her wedding band.

Chapter Eleven

The two detectives drove north to a community north of Tampa known as a Land O' Lakes. The community is often overshadowed by the publicity surrounding the location of several nudist camps but true to its name, Land O' Lakes was populated with many small and large lakes surrounded by enticing homes and neighborhoods with awesome views.

Kate drove the black Charger down the long driveway, which appeared to be piercing through the woods like a spear. The driveway emptied into a gravel parking area in front of the blue Victorian style home. It seemed out of place from the stucco inspired Florida homes. Kate wondered if Dom was influenced by his mother's selection of Victorian architecture when it came to select his home. Perched on a hill overlooking King Lake, the home stood proudly. Before Cody and Kate made their way to the front door, a redheaded woman in bare feet stepped outside holding a stone mug in her hands. Kate recognized Valerie McCormick from her profile picture on the books on Dominic Marchetti's bookshelf.

McCormick said, "You must be the two detectives investigating my grandchildren's murders. Please come in." Kate thought it was an unusual response, not to mention her son by name. McCormick turned and walked on the wide planked wood floors and took a seat at the kitchen table. The perch had a panoramic view of the lake. She motioned for Cody and Kate to have a seat.

Kate said, "You don't mind if I record this conversation, do you?" She placed a digital recorder on the wood table.

McCormick said, "Not at all, if you don't mind if I record this as well?" Kate figured her attorney had schooled McCormick, but this was a unique occurrence from a grieving mother and grandmother. She opened up her iPhone record feature.

After the initial introductory questions, McCormick said, "Dominic is my only child, and he was never planned. He was the offspring of my second of six marriages. It took me a while to learn, but I finally gave up on marriage and instead of buying, I merely rent. He was a good kid, mostly, but I was a terrible mother. When I get into my writing, I tend to lock myself in a blackout room for hours. I've never been kind to outside interruptions. I also had to travel a great deal to my publishers in New York, as well as for book tours and speaking engagements. My personality could embrace a dark spirit, which is often reflected in the pages of my books. He held my lack of maternal empathy against me."

"In what way did he hold it against you?"

"He willingly accepted my financial resources to support his educational endeavors and this eccentric lifestyle, but he shut me out of his personal life. I've never been inside his house. He and Carol would bring the children once or twice a year. We would usually meet at a restaurant of his choosing. The children were bright and cheerful, which was contrary to the relationship that Dominic and I shared."

"When was the last time you spoke to him?"

"I think it was the middle of last week. He called, trying to be nice on the phone, asking how my latest book project was progressing. I quickly saw through the veil of his superficial intentions. I asked what he wanted, and he told me he made some unwise business decisions that could cost him a significant sum of money, and that he was now on the verge of financial collapse and possibly prison."

Kate watched as McCormick's hand clenched the stone mug. "Did he provide any further details?"

McCormick took a sip of coffee and held the cup to her chest. "No, nor did I ask. But I did ask, how this impact me? He told me that money I sent him the money for the express purpose of being put away for my grandchildren's future education. He had invested in a high-risk commodities account and that this would reflect poorly upon him and, more specifically, me. I told him that this would have no impact upon me because this account was set up without my knowledge and any mistakes were his own. I told him he made his bed and he would have to live with the consequences." She set the mug back on the table, still not letting go.

"How did he take that?"

McCormick began rubbing the stone mug with both hands as if she was trying to get them warm. Kate recognized as a sign of discomfort and a self-soothing action.

McCormick said, "In his typical narcissistic manner. It is a genetic trait that he inherited from me. Began yelling at me and accusing me of abandoning my grandchildren. I told him I have never been in my grandchildren's lives and that unfortunately, I barely knew them. He called me a coldhearted bitch, and I hung up on him. He called back, and he began ranting about what a horrible mother I was, and I hung up on him again and that was the last time that we spoke."

Kate noticed the first expression of emotions. A tightening of her face and gently biting her lip. Her eyes looked away, and McCormick swallowed hard. The reality was setting in that the last time McCormick would ever speak with her single off-spring, ended in an acrimonious manner. She may have been content, but now her dark spirit, as she described it, would be haunted by that last exchange.

Kate paused for a moment and then resumed, "Did he give you the impression that his life was in danger?'

She let go of the mug and pushed it away. "Just that he was on the verge of financial ruin and going to jail. Look, I will agree with him. I was a terrible mother. As he grew older and more independent, that dreary cloud lingered over our adult relationships like an angry storm."

"Did he seem depressed or on the verge of resorting to violence?"

"He inherited his financial acumen from my second husband, Gino Marchetti, who made a mint on Wall Street in the publishing industry. Gino was killed tragically in an automobile accident when Dominic was six years old. He inherited his darkness from me. He's very moody and perhaps bordered on being bipolar. I don't know enough about his adulthood to know if he ever sought, or was treated for, mental health illness. Was he capable of suicide? I suppose. He never spoke of it. Our last telephone conversation was angry, and I would not say he was suicidal. Killing Carol and his children? I would never have predicted that. They always seem to get along, and he actually appeared to be a good father and husband. I don't know whether this was a show that he put on for my benefit. You would have to check with those that knew him on a more intimate level than his mother." Sarcasm dripped off the last sentence.

"How much money did you give him?"

"I made a mistake. I should have set up an account, a trust account that would've protected my grandchildren. I placed too much trust in Dominic and provided a check for $100,000. I never even got a thank-you card."

"How did you find out about the deaths?"

"I heard it on the news, and I called Melvin Storms to confirm the details." She paused and in a reluctant whisper asked, "Do you have any idea when they will release the bodies for burial?"

"I don't know for sure. Perhaps tomorrow? After they complete the autopsies."

"Okay, thank you, detectives." She turned off her recorder and said, "You know the way out the front door and thank you for coming by."

Kate and Cody walked out unaccompanied through the front door and sought refuge from the foreboding darkness of Valerie McCormick. Kate started the ignition and looked at Cody and said, "Wow."

Cody said, "She has about as much compassion as a rattlesnake on a hungry day. The world may have been better off if they had both died in childbirth."

"Cody Danko!"

"I know I'm sorry. You know we can use our life's experiences as excuses, crutches or platforms to speed up to a higher level."

"Cody the philosopher?"

"No. Just speaking from my experience. She reminds me a bit of my father, who is not the kindest of human beings. Let's just say growing up under his roof was not the easiest, and that's why a month after high school graduation, I was in Army basic training and twelve months later throwing led downrange in Afghanistan. But I refuse to allow that miserable son of a bitch to define who I am, and I used him as motivation as a launching platform to build upon."

"Is he still alive?"

"Somewhere."

"I'm exhausted after these two conversations between you and her." Kate sighed heavily.

"Okay, I'll perk things up like a rodeo clown. Hey, if you like barbecue, there is a great restaurant right here in Land O Lakes. Hungry Harry's." He pointed at the red barn with the American flag painted on the roof.

"Looks good and smells delicious." With the window cracked open, Kate took a deep, contented inhale through her nose. "It's sad that it is too early. We need to get to Hercules Investments."

Chapter Twelve

Driving past the upscale international Plaza shopping center, Cody and Kate parked in a high-rise parking garage nestled on a campus of corporate style buildings overlooking a fountain and the Tampa airport. The sun was breaking through the gray clouds, replacing the mood from the horrible night. They entered one of the nondescript buildings and rode the elevator to Hercules Investments. Kate walked up to the receptionist and waited for her to complete a call. The attractive young lady with a beaming smile greeted Kate. "Welcome to Hercules Investments. How can I help you?"

Kate showed her badge. "I am Detective Alexander with the Tampa Police Department, and this is Detective Danko. We would like to speak with Jennifer Bartsch."

The smile dissipated and she efficiently said, "Please have a seat, and I will call Ms. Bartsch."

Cody and Kate sank into a high-grade brown leather sofa with brass rivets. As she fingered one rivet on the sofa, Kate looked around the ornate lobby, furnished with Italian marble and Greek columns. Perched between the columns was a statue of Hercules, holding a globe above his head. A large freshwater aquarium behind the receptionist provided warmth to the atmosphere. Kate thought that her sergeant would have appreciated what appeared to be high-end occupants of the aquarium, which probably mirrored the clientele that entered the lobby.

A door to the left of the lobby opened and a tall thin businesswoman with brown shoulder length curly hair greeted the visitors with an effusive smile. Her high heels clicked and echoed on the marble. She extended her hand and said, "Detective Alexander and Detective Danko, I am Jennifer Bartsch. Please come in." Kate noticed that Bartsch's gaze lingered on Cody.

The two detectives followed the well-dressed businesswoman as she gracefully glided past the cubicle village. All eyes were focused on the two visitors. The cat was out of the proverbial bag. The detectives entered an office with a panoramic view of the Westshore business district in the background. Bartsch handed each detective her business cards and sat behind the desk of a type A personality.

Bartsch's face became businesslike, and she said, "So, I assume that you're here regarding Dominic Marchetti?"

Kate said, "Yes, we are investigating the tragic death of he and his family last evening. We understand he had come under scrutiny by your office for some improprieties. We would like to hear your insight into this investigation."

Bartsch clasped her hands on top of the desk and leaned forward and said, "Dominic was eccentric and you will be able to see once I take you to his office, which we locked up this morning after hearing the horrible news. He was a brilliant economist, but I think he became overconfident in his abilities. He was handling the house account for the two brothers who own Hercules. Dom's expertise was in commodities. Investments in commodities are very volatile, with rapid swings up and down. It is not meant for the week of heart. It was by accident that we noticed the impropriety. The commodities firm out of Chicago routinely sent us duplicate statements that Marchetti was trading. The account I noticed was on a person named Valerie McCormick. I was not familiar with this account and conducted inquiries only to find out that McCormick is the mother of Dominic Marchetti. There was a lot of activity on the account and there were a lot of assets that moved through it. We requested all documentation on the account from the commodities firm and examined all the transactions. It became apparent that an inordinate number of winning transactions were attributed to the McCormick account at a much higher percentage of losing trades, which were placed on the Hercules house account."

"When did you confront Marchetti?"

"Immediately. As soon as I detected the impropriety, I brought it to the attention of the brothers, and I summoned Dominic to my office. I had our IT people remove his access from all computer systems and key card entry points. I then laid out all the documentation to Dom, and he looked like a little kid who had been caught stealing candy. I still remember vividly the panicked expression on his face. He didn't substantiate the actions. I told him we suspended all of his privileges until further notice, and that we would begin procedures to have his license suspended or revoked."

"What was his reaction to that?"

"Horror. You could see he was completely devastated, and that he was contemplating the results of his actions. He pleaded with me for time so that he can repay the funds. I told him this would not erase the egregious actions and that he would have to look for employment outside of Hercules."

"Did you ask him any of the details concerning his mother's account?"

"Yes. He just shook his head and had a look of bewilderment, and dropped his head into his hands and began weeping. It was sad. I felt for him. I can only imagine what was going through his mind. He had an oversized ego and walked around as a larger-than-life figure. And now it was all tumbling down like Humpty Dumpty."

"But they won't be putting any of the pieces back together."

"No. We were all in shock over the revelation of his embezzlement, but no one expected Dominic taking his life and that of his entire family. We all socialized at various corporate events. Like holiday parties, picnics, and cocktail parties. Through those social gatherings, I met his wife and children. They were a beautiful family. The dynamic of the family was peculiar. Dominic was eccentric, and he always appeared somewhat disheveled and disorganized, but intellectually brilliant. His wife and children dressed neatly, polite and appeared very disciplined in their approach to life, but you can sense the love that they all had for one another."

"How were the negotiations going?"

"I was not directly involved in that aspect. Our house counsel was handling the negotiations with Dominic's attorney, Melvin Storms. It was my sense and understanding that Dominic was having difficulty coming up with a lump sum payment. Apparently, his mother never directly benefited from the proceeds of the account, and he was evasive about where the funds had been moved to. We collectively suspected that perhaps he'd move them offshore and was laundering the money. We had no proof of that. He apparently had sought a loan from his mother and she had declined to assist. He was pleading with more time to examine alternate funding sources to reimburse the firm for the missing funds."

"We would like to have copies of all of his transactions that were called into question and a listing of all the accounts that he handled."

"Absolutely. You don't mind obtaining a subpoena first, do you?"

"No. Not at all. I would have expected nothing less."

"Would you like to look at his office?"

"Yes, we would."

The three walked out of Jennifer Bartsch's office and followed her down the corridor. As they passed the rows of cubicles, various faces looked up from their stations and made eye contact with the trio. All the faces were silent and solemn. The news had traveled like a tsunami through Hercules. Bartsch stopped at a closed-door. She flashed a proximity card in front of the card reader and the red light on a panel flashed to green and she pushed the door open. She gestured with her arm and said, "Welcome to the Marchetti Museum. That is what everyone called it, and you can see why. I think quite often a person's office can reflect their personality. As you can see as I've told you, Dominic was peculiar."

Kate's brown eyes scanned the office. The office looked like a bomb had gone off. Papers were scattered and piled all over the desk on every flat surface of the office. On the bookshelves were various Star Trek action figures and a model of the Star Trek enterprise. There were also several James Bond action figures, as well as several die-cast model cars.

"Why were his investments so bad?"

"There were several factors, and he was not alone in his miscalculation. Silver was a tremendous disappointment. He miscalculated because of the policy of the Fed's and the expected need for silver in an improving economy, but the stock market caused investors to sell silver and jump back into the market or bonds. He suffered from investment hubris and developed tunnel vision. Sometimes he had huge wins. This was not one of them."

"Any other clients of his that went down with him?"

"Yes."

"With that subpoena, we can get the client's transaction history."

"Are you aware of any clients that voiced their concerns about his investment strategy or threatened him?"

"Oh no. Not at all."

"Thank you very much. We appreciate your help. My condolences to your business community."

"Thank you. I will start gathering the information and have it ready to go once I receive your subpoena."

Cody spoke and said, "Thank you, ma'am."

Jennifer's smile lingered on Cody as they walked towards the exit of the office, drawing a field of stares from the offices and cubicles.

Chapter Thirteen

Kate called Fiona and asked Fiona if she could prepare the subpoena for the records from the Hercules Investments that pertained to Marchetti's activities. Kate also updated Fiona on the interviews.

This was the part of the investigative arc that Kate really disliked. Getting subpoenas, serving them and waiting on the response. More often than not, the recipients sounded like check bouncers, always looking for more time. Once the documents were received, she had the laborious task of culling through the documents to find evidence.

There were no magic CSI computers that could allow robots to sift through the information. Kate would rather have a root canal, but like an archeologist sifting through dirt, occasionally uncovering a key artifact would complete the puzzle.

Kate's phone rang with an unknown number from an area code of 215. Recognizing the area code from Pennsylvania, Kate answered. "Hello, this Detective Alexander."

"Yes, this is Greg Swoboda."

"Yes, sir."

The solemn voiced father said, "You were right. The news reporters have been blowing up my phone. One said it was murder-suicide. Is that correct?'

"Sir, is there any reason that you would suspect that?"

"No, absolutely not."

"We really are just in the beginning stages of the investigation. I don't like to speculate and right now, all that I can say with any certainty is that it appears all four died from gunshot wounds."

"Did someone break in?"

"As of right now, it does not appear that way. The rear door was unlocked. We found out that Dominic's attorney, Melvin Storm's received a text alerting him that something happened at the house. He believes it was sent by Dom, but we have not concluded that at this time. Upon his arrival, he discovered Dom deceased in the office and called the police. We found the other family members in their beds and it appears that they died where they slept and did not suffer."

Kate could hear Mr. Swoboda was choking up with emotions.

She continued, "I can only imagine what you are going through. I just want you to know that I do my best to find the answers that must be racing through your mind."

"Thank you for your help. We are at the airport. We are flying down on the next flight."

"All right. After you have had time to think about this, did Carol ever show that she felt her life or the family was in danger?"

"No. Never. We text or chatted every few days. The most unusual thing she said was that Dom was changing jobs. She said that he felt unappreciated at Hercules and had a better opportunity with a bio-tech startup. They sounded excited."

"Okay. Well, have a safe flight."

Kate thought about how this was a horrible for them. The feeling that helplessness that the Swoboda's must feel. To get that phone call and not be able to get in a car and drive across town to get answers. Now, they were a two-and half-hour flight from being there to really starting the grieving process.

Chapter Fourteen

It was mid-morning and Cody and Kate returned to an empty squad room. Everyone was at lunch, court, or outworking cases. Kate turned towards Cody and said, "Welcome to the homicide squad room. Make yourself comfortable. That is your desk over there."

She pointed towards an empty desk that Detective Dietz had previously occupied, who'd been one part of the infamous duo known as Dumb and Dumber. They had run the two detectives off for their less than adequate investigative skills.

Kate called the FDLE Crime Lab and asked to speak with Christina Bentham. Kate had met Christina on a tour of the lab. She was a forensic scientist in the trace evidence section but with a specialty in geological materials analysis.

Christina answered the phone, after the introduction Kate asked, "Christina, I have soil samples from a probable walking path next to a house where a murder occurred. If we locate the shoes and pants of the suspect, how likely are we to going to be able to say they walked down the side of this house?"

"Just like fingerprints and DNA, everything comes down to uniqueness. To keep from being wonky on the phone, I'll keep it in simple terms."

"Thanks, I was far removed from the science department in college other than freshman biology and geology."

"You will have a better understanding than most with a little geology."

"Can you make a definitive comparison?"

"Once we examine the shoes and pants, we should be able to make an affirmative analysis."

"Fascinating."

"We will look into the density, texture, characterization, mineral content, nutrients and microscopic examination. Then there are also detritivores like earthworms, ants and termites, especially in our environment."

"You can extract DNA from worms?"

"Yes, and ants or palmetto bugs. If it lives, it has DNA."

"It just depends on if there was a transfer of material to the shoe."

"I understand."

"Most of our soil in the city is called spodosols, they have a high sand content with dark sandy subsoil layers. Now mix that with topsoil, fertilizer and pesticide treatment by the homeowner and the soil becomes more unique. Depending on the vegetation and organic material from the plants and mulch, and perhaps paint chips from the house, the composition of the roof and associated rain runoff, and leeching from the foundation, and as a result, you now are becoming even more exclusive. If water collects, there could be an increased number of fungi. In addition to the microscopic analysis of organic material, soil has pH that can vary from yard to yard. In Tampa, it tends to be high acid. We will also check the macronutrients of the soil such as nitrogen, phosphorus, manganese and potassium.

"It sound promising."

"Once we examine the shoes and pants, we should be able to tell."

"Thank you, Christina for the lesson."

"You can stop by anytime."

Kate was excited by that conversation. Having walked the property, it was muddy on the side of the house. Hopefully, the killer went out the back door and down the sideyard.

Kate called Dee Hanna and told her about the potential soil evidence. Dee told Kate that she found no identifiable prints on the phone. The keyboard and printer had prints for Dom, but no one else. She had collected DNA swabs and sent them to FDLE.

As Cody sat down in his new chair and began swiveling and rocking, Kate told him about the potential for soil analysis if they could locate the suspect's shoes and pants as long as he had not disposed of them. She also told him about Dee's findings.

Opening up her email, Kate began reading a message from Jennifer Bartsch at Hercules Investment. The message was in response to the subpoena that Fiona Quinn sent and was a list of accounts that Dominic Marchetti managed. The accounts also listed the current balance in the year-to-date change in profits or loss.

Kate noticed Marchetti managed a relatively small but exclusive list of investors. They all had substantial investments with hefty balances. One investor stood out from the rest. Brian Poole had lost $200,000 of $2 million. Others appeared to have had more diversified holdings and had not suffered the same fate as Poole.

Scrolling through the list of names, which totaled twenty-three, their combined investments totaled over twenty million dollars. Most of the investors were out of town. Many in Pennsylvania, where Dom started in the business and a few in New York and California. It was always possible that they had traveled into town or even hired some gunslinger to take out the family. There were three depositors in the Tampa area. Brian Poole, Jim Born and Roberto Clemente.

She prepared a list of investors that had lost a sizeable amount. As Jennifer Bartsch said, she was not aware of any threats against the firm or specifically against Marchetti. In reality, those folks would have been more inclined to voice concerns to Marchetti or to the firm.

It would be unlikely without a previous history of grievances that any of them would just show up and slaughter an entire family. Nevertheless, she needed to exercise due diligence and shake the tree to see if any low hanging fruit fell to the ground.

Kate looked over at Cody, who was still rocking and swiveling like a kid with a new toy. As she thought about her first day as a homicide detective, she smiled. She had served a brief period in the missing persons unit before being moved to homicide. She remembered the feeling of excitement at being in the position of speaking for the dead and putting their killers behind bars. She knew Cody was sitting there absorbing that awesome responsibility and contemplating the exhilaration of future manhunts and chases.

"Hey Cody." He turned and looked at her, "Just as a warning, the predecessor of that chair was a bit of a heavyweight and you should check out its stability. You wouldn't want that chair to collapse from under you and get your brand-new suit all dirty."

"This is not a new suit."

"Sure. I'll bet the pockets are still stitched closed."

Cody fingered one pocket and said, "Okay busted. It's slicker than a Halloween cat and yes, the pockets are still stitched closed. How did you guess?"

"I am an observer of life. You will increase your observation skills the longer you spend in this squad. Slicker than a Halloween cat? Sounds like your part redneck, where are you from?" Kate flipped her hair over her shoulder.

"You won't believe it. I am from Romance, Arkansas, but I never spent much time there. My dad..."

"The one you don't like."

"Yes, was in the Air Force, so I spent most of my time between Tampa and LA. LA as in Lower Alabama up in the Panhandle of Florida."

"Romance?"

"We may have lived there, but there was never much romance in my parents' marriage. It was a single-wide trailer paradise until it wasn't. You don't make a lot as an airman at the Little Rock Air Force Base, which by the way, is nowhere close to Little Rock. Half his pay was spent on beer, and half his time was spent mad at the world."

"Well, I am from North Carolina, so we should get along just fine. With that, I have your first assignment. If you don't mind running over to the analysts and have them do a complete workup on these three to start. Jim Born and Roberto Clemente, along with Brian Poole.

The first two didn't lose as much. Poole lost a boatload of cash investing with Marchetti, and I would like to know a bit about Mr. Poole. When they have time, here is a list of three others that live within an eight-hour drive. Poole was the biggest loser and not in weight."

"Sure. My first unsupervised investigative lead. I am giddy with excitement."

She smiled and said, "I have complete faith and confidence in your ability."

She handed him the paper, and he walked out the door. Kate began checking on Carol Marchetti and local associations. There was always a chance that she was the primary target, although there was zero evidence to show that scenario.

At the early stage of the investigation, she looked at the case like a funnel. Every possible suspect was considered and dumped into the wide opening. Only a few would survive the trip through the small opening at the bottom.

The telephone interrupted her thoughts. "Detective Alexander."

Fiona Quinn said, "Girl, you have kicked over a hornet's nest."

"What are you talking about?"

"Let's just say I've had several inquiries from within this office and outside of this office inquiring why there is any additional investigation occurring in an obvious homicide-suicide. So, I am just giving you fair warning that there is a lot of heat behind this case, and we will have to proceed with the caution going forward. That means you are driving this investigation and not your new puppy dog, Cody. There will be a lot of eyes watching this case and the two of us will have to make sure that everything is locked down tight. Thoughts?"

"I plan to work this just like I do every other case. You've had no trouble with my previous investigations. This is the first one that I am saddled with Cody, so he's riding shotgun completely with me. This is not my first rodeo, so I can take the heat."

"Coming from a girl that rides a horse and takes out an intruder in her house, you have well-earned your nickname of Kick Ass Alexander."

"Thanks for the heads up. I'll monitor the rearview mirror. Kick ass comes from my not putting up the bullshit from the boys, as opposed to physical strength. We have to work smarter."

"Amen sister."

"Oh, just to let you know we spoke with McCormick, and let's just say she's not going to win any mother of the year awards. We just started scratching the surface at Hercules, but I'll be sure to update you with any significant changes. Who is the outsider sniffing around the case?"

"Don't worry about that right now. There were a couple of individuals who I hadn't spoken to in a long time that just happened to call today to see how the sun was shining in my part of the world. They just happened to have brought up the case and started asking questions that gave me the impression that they were questioning the inquiry. It wasn't like anyone was trying to throw roadblocks up, but they seem to have come from the point of view of being the voice of reason, and there were more important cases to work. I'm just giving you fair warning, is all. I have got to be in court, so I'll talk to you later."

"Okay." Kate hung up the telephone and stared in silence. She knew from the beginning that this case would have bad juju attached to it, and she knew it was only a matter of time before outside influences started trying to get their nose under the circus tent.

Chapter Fifteen

The telephone rang again and Kate sighed and answered with a hint of annoyance, "Detective Alexander."

"Kate, it's Ron Markman at the Medical Examiner's Office. I just wanted to let you know I was going to start the autopsies tomorrow morning, but our schedule changed and we are starting in an hour."

Kate looked at her watch and said, "An hour?"

"Yeah, we've had a busy couple of days and we were told to move the Marchetti family to the front of the line. I've assigned Jack Matlock, David Tresswick, and Lucas White to conduct the family members autopsies, and I'll be doing the slice and dice on Dominic. There is some energy behind these autopsies to expedite them and complete them as quickly as possible."

"That doesn't surprise me. Do you know who the request came in from?"

"Nope. I'm just a loyal county employee collecting a paycheck every two weeks. Stating the obvious, they all died from gunshots, but you already knew that. I'll see you in an hour."

"Okay, we'll be there."

Autopsies could be interesting. Kate often brought her lunch and shared some downtime with the medical examiners in the break room. Not this time. This was no whodunit. Well, perhaps who did the shooting, but the cause of death was no mystery. No detective wanted to watch the autopsy of a child. Most had children of their own. Kate contemplated the innocence lost and a future never fulfilled. Today, a protein bar would cover lunch until she arrived home and could wrap her arms around her daughter for a few extra moments.

Chapter Sixteen

Driving past the two-tone green wall of Bush Gardens to the left, Kate considered the animals behind the fence and how some animals or predators were roaming the streets. It was her job to put them behind bars. On the right were cheap hotels and mostly fast-food eateries catering to the tourists.

Kate turned to Cody and said, "You worked D-2, right?"

"No. Mostly D-3, you?"

"Yep. Yeah, D-2 was interesting. It covered a true cross section of society. From hood rats to millionaires and everything in between."

"Do you miss patrol?"

"I do. I loved it. Well, you know the fun and excitement. As they say, you have a front-row seat to the best circus in town. Everyday, you made a difference, and when you called it a night, you could feel a sense of nobility and reward."

"Don't you get that in homicide?" Cody asked.

"Yeah, but it's different. I love the puzzle solving, and speaking for the dead and bringing justice, but like these rollercoasters in here at Bush Gardens, patrol was a thrill ride."

"Lt. Col. Dave Grossman refers to us as the sheepdogs protecting the flock from the wolves."

"He is an awesome speaker. I've read most of his books."

"Good stuff."

She parked in the parking lot of the medical examiner's office. The screaming from a roller coaster momentarily distracted her. Kate had thought about how she had taken for granted her last visit to the park with Britney. She wondered if Ethan and Megan Marchetti had ever felt the exhilaration and fear from the Kumba coaster. Never again.

She pushed through the door and was hit with the smell of cleaning products. Cody trailed behind. She knew that many knew detectives had challenges enduring the sights, sounds and odors at the autopsy. She assumed he had a world of experience from his days in the military. No telling what horrific images he had witnessed and seen. Seeing two children on the stainless tables would be hard on anyone. Kate thought she would rather be dropped into a cave filled with snakes.

The two detectives watched as all four corpses were dissected and examined. There was no dark humor this time. Just dedicated pathologists conducting their job in silence. Jack Matlock, Lucas White and David Tresswick noted their discoveries and observations by dictating into the microphones. The clicks of cameras and the sounds of the saws on bone often drowned their voices out.

At the conclusion, the four pathologists consulted in a group. Their grim faces reflected the reality of what they had just encountered. They contemplated the elimination of an entire family from society.

Ron Markham walked over to Kate and exhaled deeply. "Carol, Megan, and Ethan all died from gunshot wounds to the chest and heart. Dominic died from a gunshot to the right temple into the brain. His right hand displayed concentrated traces of gunshot residue. Did he have longer than usual sleeves?"

"No. Why?"

"He had the misting of blowback blood to the hand, but it stopped at the webbing of the thumb like a painter uses masking tape or a drop cloth to shield from the mist of a paint roller. In most but not all suicides to the temple, they use their thumb to push the trigger and the left hand to steady the gun. From the spray, that was not the case here. He was holding the weapon like he would shoot at a target and his left hand was totally clean."

"That's interesting."

"The other interesting part was in most suicides to the head, the victim makes sure the barrel was pressed against the skin, which leaves an abrasion ring from the barrel and ecchymosis around the wound."

Kate turned to Cody and said, "Bruising."

Cody nodded in acknowledgment.

Markham continued, "It was definitely close to the head, but not pressed to the head. You could see the gunpowder stippling."

"That's what I noticed as well. So, that makes sense. If I am trying to kill myself, I want to make sure that barrel is going to do its intended job. Otherwise, it could be canted upwards and graze my head or miss entirely."

"Exactly. In addition, all the victims had digested their evening meal into their intestines, indicating death occurred four to six hours after eating. It appears to be beef."

"Lamb. I saw the discarded boxes from a Greek restaurant along with the order for Gyros."

"Here is the interesting aspect. They all had the same pink colored liquid in the stomach. It had hints of a strawberry scent. Possibly ice cream? We will have to conduct further analysis. Of course, the tox screen will take longer. I'm sorry that you folks have to work on this."

"That's what we do."

"There is no GSR on the other three victims' hands. They died by homicide. On Dominic, I am going to hold off on ruling his cause of death. What do you think, Kate?"

She nodded in agreement, "There are some anomalies with Dominic. I know everyone is eager to close this case, but there are some indications that it could have been staged."

"You are right that there are interested parties in this investigation. I can hold off the wolves for a time. Please keep me updated."

"We will."

Chapter Seventeen

Cody and Kate drove back to the blue-tiled police headquarters building nicknamed "The Blue Monster." The twenty-minute drive was quiet aside from Carrie Underwood, belting out a tune. Kate's mind raced about while she tried to quash the image of the two children being dissected.

Kate reached over and turned the radio down and said to Cody, "This job sucks sometimes. I hope this is the worst that it gets for you. It is horrible to catch this as your first case, because this is definitely the one that churns my inside the worst."

"I've seen some sick shit between the Army and working the street, but you're right, you never get accustomed to kids. I know that this is my first day, but I agree with your analogy of what happened. It's a tremendous leap for a father to cross that fence and takes out his kids. When I was in Afghanistan, one of my platoon mates, Brent Newsome, a formerly effervescent fellow, killed himself one day. His cherub wife, Melinda, who he doted on and spoiled to ends of the earth, pulled the ground out from under him. She took up with the next-door neighbor and former best friend of poor Brent. Sweet Melinda sent a 'Dear John' email. His effervescence dissipated rather rapidly after that. The blackness consumed him. When we found him, there was a picture of Melinda in his lap and the 9 mm he fired through his mouth had blown a fist worth of skull matter against the sandbag behind him. I wanted to take a picture and send it to her so the image would haunt her forever."

"Did you?"

"No. I'm sure she knew, and it had to weigh on her brain. I heard her new boy toy dumped her sometime later. Karma."

"It serves her right."

"Yep. So anyway, the kicking barrel chipped his teeth and like you said, the gun tumbled outward and the gun had not chambered a bullet from the magazine because of the lack of resistance because he was pushing with his thumb."

"It's terrible the number of suicides in the military. Even in the cop world, we lose twice as many to suicide than to being killed in the line of duty."

"Yeah. The VA and the military are trying to be more proactive and getting treatment, but there is always a stigma of getting help."

Kate nodded approvingly. "I never asked if you liked country music?"

"If it has a beat, I like it."

"The driver selects the music."

"I'm good with that."

"I noted you have a lack of a wedding band?"

"I had one once. 14-karat gold with this nice little Celtic engraving. It was really a pretty ring. I fell victim to a trooper school romance. Happens all the time and I should have known better. She apparently preferred her FTO over me. I guess I underestimated her need for constant adoration, and, well, I guess, sex, too. I knew better than to go fishing in my pond. Nothing but drama. I decided it was best for me to fold up my tent and pitch it elsewhere. That's how I landed up in Tampa. Besides, the pay is significantly better here than at FHP. I guess in some ways, I should thank her FTO. He forced me to come to a hard truth sooner than later. She got the doublewide and an acre of land, and I have my freedom and a larger paycheck."

"You are a glass half full kind of guy, aren't you?"

"I try."

Kate guided the Charger through the parking garage.

Chapter Eighteen

As Kate and Cody walked through the entrance of the homicide office, Kate spotted Alfonso Stewart give her the hook with his long index finger. She and Cody made the right turn into the sergeant's office. Cody began admiring the fish aquarium. The hulking supervisor said, "Don't tap on the glass. I've trained them that when they hear tapping, they expect food. I don't like to disappoint them."

"No sir. I would not tap. I was just admiring. Especially the clown fish. I could never keep one alive when I had an aquarium."

Alfonso nodded with approval and asked, "What happened to it?"

"Ex-wife and her backstabbing FTO."

Kate said, "You have to be wary of backstabbers."

Alfonso frowned and said, "Speaking of backstabbers, come on, we need to go see The Caveman."

Kate rolled her eyes, sighed and, without a word, the three investigators walked to Lieutenant Willard's office. As they entered, he was stopping a rolling golf ball with his putter that had been ejected from the automatic putting cup.

Willard looked up and said, "Danko, you golf?"

"No sir. I'm a gamer in my off time."

Willard pursed his lips in disappointment.

Cody added, "But when I was in Afghanistan, I was at a forward operating base and one guy had a driver, and we hit some golf balls toward the Taliban. Then we ran out of golf balls and changed to rocks until we broke the club."

"I'll bet he was upset when you broke his driver?"

"Nope. He no longer needed it. He was playing with the angels."

After an awkward silence, The Caveman asked the investigators, "This Marchetti case, where are we?"

Kate said, "Dominic, his wife and two children were killed by gunshots. He was caught embezzling money from Hercules Investments. We talked with his mother, who is a fiction writer. She denied his lifeline and did not have a close relationship. Melvin Storms, his attorney, found the family. The M.E. is trying to determine the contents of their stomachs. It appears to be lamb and some kind of strawberry drink. Tox screen will take some time."

Willard nodded and rested the putter against his desk and said, "Sounds like a classic murder-suicide."

"Actually, I'm not far enough along to make that assessment."

His lips pursed and then he said, "Why? Some boogeyman walked into a house and shot and killed four people in different rooms and everyone slept through it? Like an assassin with a silencer, and he dropped the gun at Dominic's feet?"

"At this point, I can't say definitively. Seventy-five percent of those who commit suicide have a previous history of suicide attempts or threatening to commit suicide. So far, there is no sign of that history. I want to avoid cognitive bias."

His head cocked to the side like a puzzled dog, as Kate added clarification, "Cognitive bias towards the expected conclusion can undermine the accuracy and correct outcome of a death investigation."

"Well, that leaves twenty-five percent that are outliers or one in four." Kate detected the condescending tone. He continued, "What about the suicide note?"

"It wasn't signed. We're waiting on latent prints and DNA."

He shook his head in disagreement. "Let's get this wrapped up. We need to close this before all the conspiracy nuts come out. Just to let you know, the mayor called the chief, who called the major, and he called me. Get this off the board with urgency, Detective."

"Yes, sir."

"And while we are at it. I received a complaint about you today, Detective Alexander."

"Me?" as she hiked her thumb to her chest.

"Yes. Senator Thorland's chief of staff, Rodney Upton, said that you were rude."

"Rude? I don't think so. He tried to boggart his way into a crime scene, and I simply told him we had to maintain integrity of the scene and he would not be allowed."

"I see you went to the Frank Duffy charm school. The Senator has been an ally to law enforcement. We can use all the friends that we can get. You might want to keep your fuzzy sweater on and be more like Mr. Rogers."

"I was professional..."

The Caveman held up his hand and said, "Enough. Go do your job."

She could feel the rage burning through her body like a hot coal. How dare that ass wipe, Upton complained on her? She took a deep breath to control her anger.

The three walked out and returned to their office. Kate looked at Cody and Alfonso and said, "Do you believe Upton complained about me? That he admonished me." As she pointed down the hallway. "I went to Duffy's charm school. The nerve of him."

Alfonso opened up his massive hand with a calming gesture. "Don't let him get under your skin. He is not worth it."

"This case has bad juju written all over it, and the Caveman is running scared. He has no concern for a proper investigation or scrutiny down the road. Least of all those dead children."

Alfonso and Cody both nodded.

Cody said with a sly grin, "You should have told him the toilet seat theory."

"He would have lost his mind. I choose to keep it simple with him. I didn't explain the suicide challenges. I think it devastated him over your story of golfing in Afghanistan."

"True story."

"You should have seen his face when I told him that my daughter and I are big fans of golfing. He looked up with absolute joy in his face, which was quickly replaced by contempt when I added that we really enjoyed Putt-Putt Miniature Golf."

They both chuckled. Kate added, "The Caveman is a weak, backstabbing coward."

Cody asked, "How do you really feel?"

"Just my careful observations. He will not fight any battles because he is more concerned with his status on the fifth floor, and the beeping sound you hear is the bus backing up after he has driven over you. If you are a suck-up, he will take a shine to you."

"Not being a golfer or an ass kisser has me destined to a life of mediocrity in the eyes of the Caveman."

"You're probably right, but you just gained my respect."

Cody smiled and said, "By the way, Bad Juju is a weapon system in Destiny 2."

"Destiny 2?"

"One of the online games I play. You?"

"Nope. I have enough playing games with my daughter. Like Putt-Putt. Not a lot of extra time being a single mom.

Cody and Alfonso nodded and said, "Keep me up to date. You know he is going to be like a hemorrhoid. I will try my best to keep him on the perimeter. That will only work for so long."

Kate said, "I know. Thank you."

Cody said, "Well, I'll head over to the analysts and see if they have any additional information."

Chapter Nineteen

The lifeless bodies of Megan and Ethan consumed Kate's head. Thinking of those two children laying lifeless in an eternal slumber. She thought of her own Brittany, who she had kissed goodbye in the middle of the night. Brittany had sought refuge from the storm in her mother's bed. She carried Brittany to her grandmother's bed, where she would be safe. Megan and Ethan were not safe from evil in their own bed inside their home.

She picked up the phone and called her mother. "Hi Mom, how did Brittany survive the storm?"

"I wish I could sleep as well as her. I think it was the flashing from the lightning that woke her. She could sleep through an earthquake. How are you holding up, hon? I heard the news. Terrible."

"I'm vertical. It's always bad when it's an adult. Innocent kids while they slept? You are right, it is terrible. Tell her I love her, and I should see you guys at the stables."

"Okay, be careful."

"Always."

Cody returned from the crime analysts with the information they developed on Brian Poole, Jim Born and Roberto Clemente. All had lost money on their commodity trading accounts. "Wow, they really are a great resource."

"The analysts are my secret weapon. They can do real-time crime tracking and if they can't find someone, that means they are occupying a prison cell or six feet under in a cemetery."

"I can see that. Looks like Jim Born is on a kayaking trip out in Montana according to his social media, and his wife and children reflect the same."

"Sounds like fun. Clemente?"

"He flies his own plane and filed a flight plan to San Juan on Saturday."

"We will have to make sure that he is still there. We can have Felix Arroyo check on his location. They did not lose as much as Poole. Only a few grand each, which I wouldn't think gives an incentive for murder."

"So, Mr. Poole runs in higher social circles than you and me. He sold a business that developed retail software and an app. He comes from money and was a big frat boy. Despite his age, he still wears his Greek life like a badge of honor. Apparently, he is in one of the Gasparilla krewes. He is also on the board of a company called LymRX Technologies, which is developing a vaccine for Lyme Disease and research into M.S. and ALS."

"Lyme? Bad stuff. I had a friend in college that nearly died from it. Sad. She was very athletic and almost became wheelchair bound. They thought she had ALS or Lou Gehrig's disease, but she slowly recovered. It took years for her."

"I wonder if Poole has the financial resources to overcome that kind of loss. Could he have come after Marchetti?" asked Cody.

"The real question is he the type to leave the toilet seat up? Let's go have a chat with Poole." Kate smiled at Cody as she stood up.

Chapter Twenty

While writing some notes on her yellow paged notebook, Cody drove Kate's car. They crossed over the short bridge to Davis Island, passing the massive Tampa General Hospital to the left, and entered the eclectic island neighborhood occupied from small pre-war block homes to modern mansion knockdowns.

The two detectives knocked on the door of a large modern home with straight lines, white stucco and a lot of glass shaded by imposing oak trees. The door was opened by a man with his hair shaved on the sides and what hair was left had been tucked up in a man-bun on top of his head. Wearing only blue gym shorts, his bare chest was covered with an artist's pallet of ink. Kate said, "Brian Poole?"

"Yes?"

"Tampa Police, we would like to ask you a few questions concerning Dominic Marchetti?"

Poole's face tightened. "Yeah, I heard he committed suicide and killed his family."

He motioned them into the tiled foyer and stood in his bare feet.

"How did you hear?"

"We were in the Krewe of Kingsmen for the Gasparilla parade. Tragedy travels fast. How can I help?"

Kate said, "We understand you lost a considerable sum from your account at Hercules that was managed by Dominic?"

Poole shrugged and tugged his athletic shorts up higher on his waist. "Hey, it's like gambling. Yeah, I lost, but over the years, Dom delivered. It's easier than going to the Seminole Casino. From the comfort of my house, I can roll the dice. Dom would provide the financial insight. He wasn't clairvoyant, and I accepted the risk and with that, the losses, as well as the exhilaration of gains, which were absolutely euphoric."

"Are you aware of any financial problems he may have had?"

He shook his head. "No, not that I am aware. He had a nice home, but that can be a façade. It's not like we trade balance sheets or bank statements. We are in a social and charitable fraternity in the krewe. Dom and I were friends. We chatted occasionally on the phone and traded text messages. Sometimes we would get together for lunch or meet up at Palma Ceia for a round of golf. I will say that he wasn't a very good golfer." He smiled. When he looked at the two solemn detectives, he dropped the smile and said, "But he did not show that he was in despair."

"Did he mention any problems at work or any enemies?"

"He was eccentric. A collector of oddities and his appearance was not important to him. He was rarely punctual, but I never knew him to have an acrimonious relationship with anyone."

"I noticed you are on the board of LymRX Technology?"

"Yes, I am. We are conducting research into ALS and developing a vaccine for Lyme Disease. Every year, half a million people are infected with the disease. It's very political in the medical community concerning treatment protocols. Some doctors have lost their license for their treatment approach. Many doctors deny its impact. It can be a ravishing disease, especially if untreated within the early stages. Then it becomes chronic Lyme. I had a step-brother that was misdiagnosed with ALS. By the time they diagnosed him with Lyme, it was too late. Even the CDC denies the existence of chronic Lyme."

"I wish you luck. I'm sorry about your step-brother. I know folks that have had it. If they catch it early, you are good to go."

"Exactly."

"How long ago did you lose your step-brother?"

"Last year. He was a marathoner and a big hiker. It was horrible to see him reduced to a wheelchair."

"I guess medicine is not always as clear cut as we would like to think."

"Certainly not."

Cody pointed at Poole's chest and said, "That is quite the canvass."

Poole looked down and tapped his well-defined abs. "Yeah, I like to wear my art. Let me know if you want the name of my artist."

"Thanks, I'm done. I don't plan to add anymore memorials." Poole nodded.

Cody flashed his sly smile and said, "Thanks for your time."

As a squirrel raced up one of the towering oak trees, Kate asked Cody, "What did you think?"

"He had really nice ink."

"No silly." She tapped his arm. "Not his body art."

"He lives in a different world. A frat boy with a bad hairdo. He sounds legit in that he had no problem with losing an enormous sum in a trade. Do you think we should subpoena his accounts and check his financial stability? Like he said, it could all be a façade."

"Could be. We know he has no mortgage on the house that is worth a few million and sold the company that he kick-started for tens of millions. He can be loose with his money."

"I agree. Where next?"

"Let's go back to Melvin Storms. He lives across the bridge in Hyde Park. Then we can grab a very late lunch or an early dinner at Hattrick's."

"I am your shadow and your driver."

"Speaking of which, let's drive back to the Marchetti home and pickup up your car and drop it at the Blue Monster. Then you can resume your chauffeuring."

"Sounds like a plan."

As Cody drove away from the opulent homes, he turned the radio to a classic rock station. His sly grin creased across the face. Kate reached over and turned to the country station.

She said, "The driver picks the music. Only when he is in his car, is senior to the case detective or alone."

His smile never broke as he nodded. "Copy that, ma'am."

Cody parked against the curb in front of the death home of the Marchetti family. Kate stepped out and admired the home in daylight and without having to dodge the rain. She imagined Megan and Ethan playing tag in the front yard or on Easter egg hunts. She thought of what the house looked like decorated at Christmas. Maybe Carol and Dom sitting in the porch swing sipping on a mojito. Now there was a haunting silence. The tragic images flashed through her mind from inside the home.

Without a word, Cody slid into his Ford Focus and drove away. Kate took a deep breath and exhaled slowly. She shook her head in disgust and walked to her car.

Chapter Twenty-One

After dropping Kate's car, Kate slipped into the passenger seat of Cody's car and took a whiff of the inside of the car that had been closed up and sitting under the sun. Her face revolted and asked, "What is that smell?"

Cody nodded. "Yeah, it smelled like the ass of twelve camels. I've been spraying Febreze, and I have three evergreen air-fresheners. Two under the seat and one here." His muscular hand tickled the tree hanging from the rearview.

"Well, it's not working very well. "Whose car was this?"

"Dietz."

She put her hand up. "Say no more. What a slob. It smells like a crime scene of a decomp. The smell of death lingers and infuses with every piece of fabric."

"I know. It's like driving in a body bag."

Kate tapped out a message on her phone, followed by the whoosh. The two detectives drove from downtown, passing through the short tunnel under the convention center and over the Platt Street bridge. They steered south along Bayshore Drive. As they drove past the row of waterfront mansions on the right, Kate looked at one of the many female runners on the scenic path along the waterfront. Her thoughts wondered as she reflected on her love of the four and half-mile run along the world's most continuous sidewalk, but today would not afford that opportunity. She had a killer to catch, even though the prevailing winds of bureaucracy were steering towards a suicide by Marchetti and the murder of his precious family.

Her mind drifted to what despair would go through the mind of a father who would resort to killing his innocent family? Save them from embarrassment and humiliation. Who makes him the judge of that decision? The ultimate act of selfishness or compassion?

If her theory of where the gun was found and the toilet seat theory provided a gateway to continue investigating for a potential murder, who would kill the innocent sleeping and non-threatening children of your intended victim? A person with no conscience. His or her own desire for survival or revenge was paramount to the existence of human life. Especially children.

Cops get hardened by the corrosive nature of the job. Swimming in a toxic environment will darken your soul and spirit. Any incident involving the death of children has led more than a few cops to seek treatment from a bottle of booze or a handful of pills. Sadly, for some, their spiral down never slows.

As they approached Melvin Storm's home in the beautiful Hyde Park area of narrow streets, upscale homes with ample front porches and shaded by towering oak trees, she thought of her former partner, Frank Duffy. His life too circled the drain.

Cody parked along the curb of Delaware Street in front of the palatial home of Melvin Storms. A three-story red brick with white trim home. Melvin had previously told her that his home was a Queen Anne Revival architecture built in 1910. She envisioned the home at night covered in darkness, as her two friends approached the home and would have their lives forever altered in a shooting. Duffy walked up the driveway to the left towards the portico and Rollins to the right hopping over a red brick knee wall and that's when all hell broke loose. Now a distant memory from a couple of years ago.

As they stepped out of the Ford, Cody looked up at the towering façade and said, "This is where the shooting took place, isn't it?"

Kate nodded silently.

Cody asked, "How are they doing?"

Kate sighed, "Rollins is back. He took stock of his life. Settled down and got married. He should be in the office today or tomorrow. Returning from a delayed honeymoon. Duffy is struggling. The cumulative stress over his career, this shooting and then the death of his beloved Bridget, was more than he could tolerate. He sought sanctuary in a Jameson's bottle. The Caveman was organizing a firing squad, so myself and a couple of others, including Alfonso, had an intervention. He is completing rehab and then he is scheduled for a week of the PTS in-residence program at the Franciscan Center with Sister Annie, and Rick Malivuk, our chaplains. The Chief did the right thing and transferred him to the criminal intelligence bureau and away from The Caveman. I think Frank was ready to kill the lieutenant."

Cody shook his head. "That might have been a career ender for both of them." Cody adjusted his sunglasses. "At least Duffy is getting the help he needs. Addiction is a terrible condition. I hope he can stay on the wagon."

"I talked to him the other day, and he sounded good. His next goal is to sell the house and buy a condo over on Harbor Island. He can walk to the Lightning games and take a short drive to work. I'm sure you had some bad experiences yourself. How did you cope?"

"Mine was different. It was a lifesaving decision. Saving a little girl from a monster. Like we would have liked to have done for Megan and Ethan Marchetti."

"Exactly."

"How about when you were in the Army?"

"I focused on positives and reflect on the joy that folks brought to my life. I choose not to think of the negatives. The funniest jokes and scenarios are what I remember. You ever been in a shooting?"

"Never."

Cody nodded in silence as they walked up the walkway to Storm's house.

Kate's mind wandered to her tough mentor. Frank Duffy was a cop's cop. He had a strong exterior and foundation. His wife, Bridget, was his safe harbor and therapist. No matter how bad of a day he had at the office, he could always count on the serenity of home. This was his counterbalance. All those horrific scenes over the years take a toll. Each scene undermining and loosening another block in the foundation. He had just survived a gun battle, the only person unscathed. When his Bridget succumbed to cancer, his foundation collapsed.

It was tough watching his descent into despair. His morning cocktails of sports drink mixed with caffeine drinks. Despite his mint gum, her nose could pick up the scent of the Jameson's whiskey. His astute mind aimlessly drifted off into oblivion for long periods. The ringing of the phone would cause an unnatural startle. When she called him in the evening, there were times he was hammered, and other times he would not recall the conversation the next day.

She had heard from a reliable source that The Caveman was on a hunting expedition to gather enough evidence to fire torpedoes into Frank, and get him canned before his eligibility for retirement. Kate knew the only way to save Frank would be to get him to wave the white flag and ask for help. He could be insolent, and trying to get an alcoholic to admit that he needed help was always a challenge. Before her death, Kate had assured Bridget that she would look after him.

Kate invited his two daughters, who were worried about their dad, along with his cousin, a priest, Alfonso, and herself. It was like a surprise birthday party without the cake and balloons. The surprise party was not well received. Eventually, they chipped away at the veneers, ending in tears and sobs by everyone.

The next morning, his cousin drove him to a rehab center to get him help. Alfonso went into the Caveman's office and told him that Frank would be on sick leave for three weeks tending to personal matters. He also told Caveman that the Chief had authorized Frank's admission to the Franciscan Center's Operation Restore PTS program, as well as his transfer to the Criminal Intelligence Bureau, thus giving notice to the Caveman that Frank was untouchable and had the Chief's blessing.

Fortunately, this happened prior to the Chief announcing his retirement. A difference of a couple of days and Frank would have been lined up on the wall awaiting The Caveman's firing squad. Now the department was being guided by an acting chief until the mayor decided on a permanent replacement.

A couple of mockingbirds chirped a song to each other in the tree, as a few leaves drifted towards the ground. The grass still appeared damp from the night rainfall.

"Sounds optimistic. Frank is looking forward and leaning away from despair."

Kate swallowed hard. "Yep. Come on, let's talk to Melvin again."

"You don't suspect Storms, do you?"

"He found the murder scene. I'm doubtful, but I will keep our options open."

Chapter Twenty-Two

They walked up the steps to the wraparound porch. Kate admired the white mosaic tiled porch and swing. She thought about how fun it would be to swing with Brittany and talk about life's lessons and dreams. The flickering gas lamps were an ornate embellishment to the glass-paneled door. After ringing the doorbell, they could see the image of a person walking towards the frosted glass.

Melvin opened the door. His normally meticulously styled long white hair was in a disarray. That will happen when you find your pal and his family dead in the middle of the night. He escorted them into the entryway in view of the grand staircase and motioned to them to proceed into the small receiving room, with a dormant fireplace at one end and a crystal chandelier hanging from the ceiling. Cody and Kate sat on a plush couch and Melvin collapsed into a Queen Anne styled chair. He looked haggard.

Kate hooked her hair behind her ear and opened the conversation. "Melvin, I'm sorry to impose. I know this has been a dreadful night, but I wanted to follow up with you on a few things."

Melvin nodded and sighed, "I understand."

"When you arrived, you entered through the rear door. Did you try the front door?"

"It's a blur now. I went to the front door. Rang the doorbell and knocked. When there was no answer, I walked down the side of the house. I again knocked on the back door and tried opening. It opened. I called out to Dom and continued down the hallway to where I found him. I ran out the back door and called you folks from my car."

"Was it raining?"

"A frog strangler. Almost lost my umbrella. My shoes got soaked."

"Did you notice any other wet footprints in the house?"

"No."

"Did you notice if the front door was locked?"

"Ahh... I don't know. Like a squirrel running for safety, I ran back the way I came. It was definitely locked when I tried from outside."

"Did you go upstairs?"

He leaned back in his seat. "God no. I am thankful for that decision."

"Speaking of God, was Dom religious?"

"Not that I believe. I never heard him say anything. Now that you mention it, he wanted a civil ceremony for his wedding. In fact, he and Carol had an argument over it, and he dug his heels in said absolutely no church. His funeral plans make no mention of last rites or priest."

Kate thought of the suicide note. He wrote, "I ask God to have mercy on their souls and to please forgive me." Not concrete evidence, but a non-religious person would not be asking God for forgiveness. Ask his family for forgiveness? Yes. Perhaps facing his maker, he was now willing to acknowledge His existence.

Kate continued, "Would you call him an atheist?"

"Honestly, being a twice a year Episcopalian, we just never discussed religion."

"We just spoke with Brian Poole. Despite losing money during Dominic's embezzlement, he did not seem to harbor any ill will. Are you aware of anyone that lost money that was threatening him?"

"No. Not that I am aware. I would think that Dom would have said something."

"Poole mentioned the krewe. Any problems there?"

"I am in the same Krewe of Kingsmen. It's a fraternal and charitable organization. Someone might disagree with the starting time of the golf tournament or how many beads to buy for the parade float, but we were all friends."

Kate clasped her hands together. "We would like a list of the members, so that we can check with them to see if anyone else was aware of any acrimony."

Melvin adjusted in the seat and ran his fingers through his unkempt hair and fidgeted in the chair. "I thought this was a suicide? You are asking questions that give me pause that perhaps the entire Marchetti family was murdered? Am I a suspect?"

Kate leaned forward. "Melvin, this is not your first kiss at the prom. We have to be thorough in solving the misadventure. Since you brought it up, and you were sadly the first person to find him, can you explain where you were earlier that evening?"

"Kate, you are right that this is not my first dance with you. You are a highly skilled and meticulous investigator, and I respect you."

Kate nodded in understanding of his platitudes. She wondered if he was blowing smoke up her skirt and trying to charm a female. Would he have told

Cody that he was athletic? Probably not. He was trying to soften her up, or maybe he was being sincere. After all, she caught the man who was planning to kill Storms in this very house. She said, "Well thank you, Melvin."

"I won't waste your time calling my partner to represent me. You can geolocate my cellphone and see that it was stationary from 7:00 pm. I'll gladly give you access to my alarm and camera system. What time I set my alarm, which was closer to my bedtime and my cameras will show I did not leave prior to the text message. I was binging Seinfeld on Netflix. I needed a laugh. You can see my internet activity to confirm that I turned it off near midnight. My wife, Nancy, is out of town. I realize that if I was creative, I could easily fabricate this alibi and that it is not rock-solid, but that is all I can give you. If only I had a mistress, and you may think of me as a legal lizard, but my wife of 35 years will tell you I am hopelessly in love with a fabulous bride."

Kate smiled, rubbed her wedding band on the right hand and felt a pang of loneliness being almost as old as Melvin and Nancy Storms had been married, and Kate was already a widow. "Melvin, thank you for your help. Seeing a friend suffering a violent end is a terrible sight. My condolences."

Melvin stood, "You're still not calling it a suicide."

"Time will tell, as it does for all things."

Chapter Twenty-Three

As they slid back into Cody's car, Kate's face crinkled and she said, "We need to leave the windows open."

"I'll work on it. If you're not too nauseous, could we put some groceries into my empty stomach?"

"Hattricks?"

"Anything but a 7-11 chili dog."

"Drive. Unless you are too weak."

"I'll make it."

Cody found a parking space on the street in front of Hattricks. The historic red brick building highlighted the green and gold façade. As Frank Duffy would say, you can't decorate character. Hattricks had plenty of character with lots of wood and red brick and an open ceiling exposing the ductwork and piping. They sat at an open table long after the lunch crowd had vacated and looked over the menu. The vibrant brunette server touched Cody's shoulder and asked if they were ready to order. Kate ordered the Greek salad and Cody ordered the mojo pork sandwich. They both stayed with water.

Kate asked Cody if he had questions concerning the investigation and how they were proceeding. It was a mini lecture on death investigations, the importance of keeping an open mind and to follow the evidence. When their meals arrived, they mostly ate in silence as they devoured their food. The first meal of the day for Kate aside from a protein bar in the middle of the night and one before the autopsy.

When they returned to the homicide office, they greeted Cody with a surprise at his desk. They covered his desk with decomp respirators, bottles of Febreze and small bottles of Vicks vapor rub, cherry lip balm sticks, and PPE suits piled in his chair. Detective Lester Rollins stood up and pulled on his suspenders and said, "Goodnight, Danko. We all chipped in. We all heard your city car smells like a rolling death chamber."

Cody's permanent grin widened to flash his snow-white teeth. "I am humbled by all of your kindness and concern."

Alfonso stood in his doorway and said, "If you need to put a bullet into Dumber's former car and put it out of its misery, let me know. If not, we can spot you a full interior detail."

Cody chuckled and said, "Thank you, sir. It reminded me of some of the Humvees I rode in. Minus the sand."

Kate pulled her hair back into a ponytail and threaded it through a scrunchie. She said, "Take note. The Vicks goes under the nose. You already know how to use Febreze and with the cherry lip balm, it will minimize the smell of decomp. It's an odor that no cop will ever forget."

"Or a soldier."

"Yes."

Kate asked Rollins if he had developed any leads from the neighborhood canvas. Some of the curious neighbors had answered their doors. With the storm the night before, no one, despite being awakened by the storm, heard anything other than thunder. No screaming aside from their own children or their barking dogs. Most people who had cameras, had their field of vision impaired from the rain and darkness. The consensus was the family was well liked and viewed as good neighbors.

Cody and Kate spent the rest of the day preparing and organizing the murder book. The spiral binder filled like a high school notebook. Tabbed by sections. The investigative chronology, notes, witness interviews, judicial aspects, including affidavits for search warrants, subpoenas, evidence, crime scene log and photos, victims, and suspects.

Having a reputation for composing the best murder books, Kate took pride in her work. If the murder went cold, the following investigators could get a good grasp of the case. She knew it would be inevitable that a cold case detective would judge the actions of the previous detectives. She heard of a cold case detective from another city that never wrote a single document in several years before handing the now freezing cold case to another detective. Kate wondered how that was possible. The disrespect for the victim and family. Then she thought, how did a supervisor not detect that incompetence?

Kate also tutored Cody on how to write the requests for subpoenas for the various financial and cellphone records for the case. She sent the requests to Fiona for the subpoenas. Kate knew that because of the heat behind this case, Fiona would do a quick turnaround so that they could immediately send them out to the recipients.

With the investigative arc slowing for the day, Kate wrote out a plan for the next day. First was to check on any updates from the crime scene unit and the medical examiner's office. Besides reviewing all financial and cellphone records, Kate wanted to interview relatives and friends of Carol Marchetti to determine if there were problems in the marriage or any suspected infidelity from either partner. She would also check with the teachers to identify the children's closest school chums. Perhaps one of the poor kids had confided with a friend some insight into the inner sanctum of the Marchetti home.

The best laid plans often went array. Inevitably, all plans could be tossed to the side with a hot lead or an unexpected curveball. Here, she was expecting more camels circling the outside of the investigation, wanting to know what was going on inside the tent. The genuine concern was some of those camels getting their nose under the tent and interfering or causing a detour.

As she was walking out of the office for the day, Kate saw the Caveman venturing out of his office. This was as rare of a sighting as seeing an albino alligator. But unlike an agile gator, she was trapped.

"Hello, sir."

The feckless boss said, "Are we close to wrapping up the Marchetti murder-suicide?"

"We're working on it."

"Keep me updated."

"No problem."

As she continued walking with barely a pause to respond to his inquiry, she felt like turning and giving him the double barrel finger salute. She knew she would be the one caught and her flagrant dislike of The Caveman would destine her to a reassignment to the property section or midnight patrol. An alternative that she thought might not be so bad.

Chapter Twenty-Four

As Kate drove out east out of Tampa on the Leroy Selmon Expressway, her mind drifted back to the images from the previous dark morning. The children. They looked like they were still sleeping, if not for the bullet hole through their innocent heart.

To her, it was unfathomable how someone would execute a sleeping child posing no threat. Especially a father. Yes, she was aware of family annihilators. They were rare events, but everyone was quick to call this one and close the case. She would not disagree with the concept that he was circling the drain professionally and wanted to save their suffering and humiliation. It would take a very desperate person consumed with darkness to kill their own kids.

The toilet seat was perhaps an innocent distraction. Maybe he came up to check on the family or kiss Carol one last time. Maybe he was never trained to put the seat down or was defiantly noncompliant. As Cody said, perhaps Ethan had used the toilet. Scared of the storm, like Brittany, he came in to see his mother.

The suicide note showed a cold distance to his family. For a very nonreligious person, it would be odd to ask for the forgiveness by God. He didn't sign it either. Most people didn't leave notes. A few left audio or video messages. She knew statistics said that only about a third left a note.

The autopsy showing that the gun barrel was not in contact with the skin didn't make her feel comfortable about the suicide. Why take the chance that you would miss? Although many shot themselves in the mouth by essentially sucking the barrel, the eyes processed the sight of the gun. This image would reaffirm what the ultimate outcome would be. The temple shot provided some separation from the final shot, but was more difficult to execute. Especially if the gun was not aligned properly. More than a few missed the mark and lived with a scar or a disability.

It was the gun that bothered her the most. Anyone who has ever fired a gun knows there is a recoil. That kick, if not resisted, will cause the weapon to come out of the hand. It's one thing to aim at a target in front of you, another to hold a gun at an awkward angle like towards your temple. Kate pantomimed the action. The canting of the wrist places you in an awkward and challenging position to maintain the grip as the weapon recoils. Especially that after the autopsy showed he held the gun with one hand. Resistance charges the next bullet into the firing chamber. A non-supported wrist will fail to provide the resistance.

If he had used the thumb grip method of grasping the gun and pushing the trigger with his thumb, the recoil would have driven the pistol up and away. The blood misting indicated that he awkwardly gripped the gun like most people shooting at a range would grip the handgun.

What would cause the masking of the blood misting on his hand, and why the mist only covered part of the hand and not the entirety? Kate thought the only plausible explanation would be if someone had gripped Dom's hand on the gun and thus covering a large part of his hand.

She called an old friend, Bret Bartlett. Known as an expert barrel sucker, he had retired as a captain from the police department. He was a passionate firearms instructor and an expert marksman. In his retirement life, he was making a profitable living, embracing his true love of guns, along with his wonderful wife. Bret explained limp wristing was a real occurrence and in numerous brands, not just the lighter weight weapons like the Glock and in a 9mm. He added that not only could you have a fail to feed but also a stovepipe when the spent casing jams the cycling of the weapon. He added that although it could happen, but was not that prevalent. It wasn't a guarantee and certainly not enough to prove beyond a reasonable doubt.

Bret wrapped up the conversation. "I remember you on the range, and you never had that problem with a limp wrist or recoil management, as we like to call it."

"Lots of practice and great instructors like you and Julie Dickey. It was nice to have a female mentor that could shoot the center out of target."

"There are few males and females with her skills. That's why she was on the TPD shooting team."

"Thanks again for the trip down memory lane and your expertise."

"Always a pleasure Kate."

As Kate considered meeting her mom and Britney, her mind flashed to Trent Sellers, her romantic interest. Friend or something more serious? They were more serious, but she threw cold water on the fast-burning fuse. He was too good, too fast, and she felt out of control. Maybe that was her real problem. She always needed to be in control. It was up to her to look out for the family nest. She was afraid of sharing time away from Britney and with a new love interest. Perhaps her friend Patti was right. After today, and all the other days in homicide, she had seen proof that life could be short and an unexpected ending could come at any time. Embrace it while you can.

Chapter Twenty-Five

Instead of driving to the house, Kate drove to the Over the Moon Stables. She parked next to her jeep, which her mom was driving with Brittney. Kate walked up to the fence and gave a hug to her mom. The embrace felt good, like a blanket on a frosty night. Kate lingered in the embrace longer than she normally did.

Her mom pulled back and looked into Kate's brown eyes. "Tough day?"

Kate nodded and said, "Yep." She swallowed hard and gave a meek smile. She turned back to look with pride as she watched Britney parading around on top of the all-black stallion, Knight. Her ponytail bounced with triumph as she guided Knight around the coral. She came to a stop and dismounted the horse with eagerness to run into the welcoming arms of her mom. Kate's embrace was more like a vice grip squeeze. "I love you sweety."

"I love you too, mommy."

After the release, Kate helped Brittney back into the saddle and watched her trot off. The pony tail protruding from the helmet once again bounced with joy that matched her smile. Kate wiped a tear from her eye as she thought how fortunate she was to have her daughter while tending to the murders of Megan and Ethan Marchetti. The kids who will never experience the milestones in life. High school proms, graduation, careers and what impact their lives may have had on society.

Kate walked into the office and plopped down on a well-worn and comfy couch. She released the ponytail and threaded her hands through her auburn hair. Patti Moon, the owner, stood up from her desk behind the counter and walked around and sat down as well. Patti hooked her short hair behind her ear.

She looked at Kate and patted her knee. "Girl, you look like you have been on an all-night trail ride."

Kate looked over at her friend and said, "I wish." Kate sighed and said, "Today, I had my toughest scene that I have worked."

"That murder-suicide that was on the news?" Patti patted Kate's knee.

"Yeah. I can tolerate when scumbag one kills scumbag two. I can even handle domestic murder-suicide. But to see two children still in middle school and about the same age as your own child murdered in their sleep in their own bedroom. It's the worst of the worst."

"I wish there is something that I could say to ease your pain. Life sucks sometimes. There are no guarantees and you, of all people, know that. You have buried your dad and your husband. You were almost a victim yourself. In fact, you have cheated death more than a cat using up all nine lives."

They both chuckled and Kate said, "I'm not convinced it's a suicide."

"I know you can't give a lot of details, but know that the Marchetti family is extremely lucky to have Detective Kate Kick Ass Alexander on the case. As tenacious as you are in life, as a survivor and as an investigator, you are a kick ass girl."

"They tagged me with that because I wouldn't take any shit off the boys at work. I may not be as physically as strong as the guys, but I think we ladies have to work smarter. Back to the caveman days, we had to protect the nest while the men were hunting. We are the protectors and defenders of the family. It's in our DNA to kick ass and survive. Those men could never survive child birth!"

They both had a backslapping laugh. Kate pulled out her scrunchie and flipped her head back to unleash her shoulder length hair.

Patti said, "When I was still a woman of the law, I had a chief who talked about new hires. He asked, is this a person you would go through the door with or if you were the victim of a murder, would you want this person to be the investigator of your homicide? You embody either scenario."

"Well, thank you." Kate smiled and patted Patti on the knee.

Kate said, "You are like the character in the Peanuts cartoon Lucy, the psychiatrist. I owe you five cents."

"Over the years of me listening to your belly-aching and whining misery, you owe me a lot more than a nickel!"

"You are right. What would I do without a good friend like you?"

"Well, you could start with having your own in-house therapist like Trent again."

"We are still friends."

"You have friends. You need someone that will ride you like a real cowboy!"

"Oh my gosh, I can't believe you said that." Kate's face burned with crimson warmth.

"It's true. Trent was a keeper. The fact that he is a psychiatrist helps with the therapy session. Girl, you have more baggage than a caboose."

"I know, but I've got it sorted. At least I hope."

"You're in a good place now. You are a thriver!"

"You're damn right, girl!"

"If you're not going to ask Trent, then get a puppy."

"A puppy?" Kate let out a howling laugh. "A puppy? Just what I need."

"A faithful companion. Something to cuddle up with and pet in the middle of the night."

"I love dogs. We had a golden retriever before Brittany. He was our first child. As good as that sounds, I also remember the separation anxiety the dog suffered when we were gone and the potty training. The wake-ups in the middle of the night. I have a phone that does that often enough. And the hair! It always seemed like I was vacuuming."

"Golden doodles. Problem solved. No shedding."

"One problem solved. Add the cost of dog food and the vet bills." Kate started twirling a few strands of hair with her hand.

"Okay, then you need to re-invite Trent back into your life. At least he doesn't shed."

"Thank you, Charlie Brown's Lucy. I'll reconsider. I'll throw a nickel in the jar. I need to gather by my child and get home to cook dinner and fall asleep. Thanks for listening, Patti."

"Everyone needs a little cowgirl therapy because..."

Kate and Patti sang in unison, "Cowgirls are tougher than shit!"

Chapter Twenty-Six

The next morning, Kate walked into the homicide office and Cody was at his desk. Kate stopped and put her hands on her hips and asked, "Where is my coffee?"

"Kava Culture Bar is a block up the street that way." As he pointed out the window with his sly grin.

"After taking you under my wing, and this is the appreciation that I get? You brought me coffee yesterday. With that treat anticipated, I denied myself coffee."

"Yeah, that's a shame, Kate. No wonder you are a little cranky."

"Cranky?"

"Full transparency. Yes. Here I will share my energy drink."

"Your lips have been on it."

"Better than attached to your ass and sucking up by bringing coffee to you."

They both laughed. Kate said, "Good one. Did you get much rest?"

"Yep. Got a workout in, made dinner for my mom, and a little gaming, and then off to bed."

"Do you live with your mom?"

"Actually, she lives with me. A subtle difference."

"A couple of years ago, she stumbled, fell, broke her arm and bruised her face. After being abandoned by her asshole husband, she was alone. She also has M.S. which causes flare-ups now and then."

"M.S.? That's similar to Lyme."

"Very similar and often confused and conflated with each other."

"So, this LymRX would also interest patients with M.S.?"

"It could."

"So, your father left her?"

"I don't consider him my father. She was having a hard time. I bought a townhouse off Soho and had her move in. There are more activities for her, and she has made friends that she walks with in the mornings."

"And you cook for her. Like frozen pizza, MRE's out of the pouch?"

"Nope. I took a cooking class that Publix offered. I'm not a chef, but I can cook hotdogs with the best." He smiled.

"I'll keep that in mind. Does she ever hear from your dad?"

"Nope. He would be as welcome as a cactus at one of those nudist camps in Land-o-Lakes." They both had a good laugh at the image.

He said, "So, I looked at Carol Marchetti's social circle. She played tennis at Palma de Mallorca in the mornings. I thought we could stop in and have a chat with her friends."

"The real housewives of South Tampa would love you to stop by. They would look at you as a piece of eye candy. I would love to be a hidden microphone listening to those ladies when they see you."

"I'm not looking for any relationships."

"Oh, better yet. A boy-toy."

"That could be construed as sexual harassment, ma'am."

"Just making an observation and providing a warning as you enter the lush green landscaping of the country club."

"Thanks for the warning."

"I'm going over the records while you are gone. Let me know if you need any backup. One more thing, could you swing by the kid's posh school and talk with their teachers? See if there are any rumors after the fact from students and if they had any sense of despair."

Kate handed a sheet of paper with the school address. Cody looked over the page and nodded. As Cody walked towards the exits, Kate couldn't help but admire his 'V' physique. She could see his well-defined but not overstated traps and deltoids. She smiled to think of the first impression he would make with the ladies.

Felix Arroyo, one of the newer homicide detectives, walked into the squad room with a very attractive female on his arm. She looked like a smiling model on the runaway. Everyone was eager to meet Mrs. Silvia Arroyo. Kate couldn't help but noticed the smile dropped faster than a free-falling elevator when she walked up to introduce herself to Silvia. Kate could almost feel the chill in the handshake of a person who she had never met before.

After the Arroyos vacated the room, Kate turned to Rollins and mouthed, "What was that about?"

Rollins looked around and said, "What are you talking about it?"

"The death stare and the chill of a witch's curse by Silvia."

"Jealousy."

"Jealousy? Look at her. She could be a Victoria Secret's model. Killer body and complexion."

"You have to understand that Felix was quite the swordsman in the day. She may have put a leash on him, but hell, she can't watch him all the time."

"It's bad enough fighting for playing time on the field with you guys, but now I have to worry about the wives as well?"

"Have I not always bowed in reverence to you?"

"Yes. All of you welcomed me to this squad despite all the murmurings on the street."

"Murmurings?"

"You know. She only got homicide because she is a girl."

"You don't believe that."

"No. Actually I don't. It's because I'm a damn good cop."

"Yes, you are. You've earned your place. Keep in mind the WAGs Club can be brutal, Kate."

"The wives and girlfriends club?"

"Oh yeah. Man, they are always talking shit among themselves. Lots of gossip. Who's being promoted, who's getting divorced, who's knocking boots? Someone probably penciled you in that you were sleeping with someone, and Silvia heard you may be on the prowl."

"That's B.S. I have never slept with anyone down here. But you are right, I've heard the rumors. Maybe I should join the WAGs club."

"Invitation only. They claim to be a support group. It's not a girlfriend's club. They can cause a lot of drama and for that reason, my lovely bride has no interest."

"Sounds more like a knife fight, and keep your back against the wall."

"Indeed, my sister."

Chapter Twenty-Seven

After Cody left, the first order of business was to call the medical examiner's office. They had already decided that most of the lamb they had consumed for dinner had emptied into the intestines. The mystery pink substance that was found in the stomach was a much later addition.

"Hi Ron, it's Kate. Any updates?"

"Well, I received an inquiry from the State Attorney's office."

"Fiona Quinn?"

"Nope. The State Attorney, Brian McClung. He wanted to know when I was going to have a ruling."

"You didn't provide an answer, did you?"

"I told him the appearances showed murder-suicide, but I was not prepared to render a decision until further evaluation. Mr. McClung was not pleased. He said that he needed to close it so that Fiona could work on more relevant open cases. I told him that his staffing assignments were not my concern, and that I would not be making an unsubstantiated opinion without further forensic investigation."

"Wow. Good for you, Ron. Mr. McClung can be very persuasive."

"Just a few minutes ago, I received back a preliminary on the pink substance. A fruit smoothie, topped off with what would be known as zolpidem tartrate, which is the generic version also known as Ambien, a sleep aid."

"The entire family took sleeping pills?"

"The children should not have, but I know mothers that sneak a little bourbon in the evening formula. Perhaps with the storm coming, they doped the kids. Some people do it for their animals. I have to wait to see how much was in the bloodstream."

"Would they have slept through the gunshots?"

"Depending on the amount. Also, Dominic had some bourbon in his stomach contents. I have not received his blood alcohol content yet."

"Hang on a minute." Kate opened up the file of crime scene photos taken by Dee Hanna. She opened them up in a thumbnail pattern and looked at the ones with prescription bottles. There were no bottles of zolpidem tartrate in the house, nor any smoothie containers. She had complete confidence in Dee's thoroughness to know that if there had been a prescription bottle of anything to include over-the-counter medication, Dee would have photographed it. There were two glasses in the sink filled with water. Perhaps Carol and Dom shared a nightcap.

"Ron, I just went through the crime scene photos. There is no zolpidem tartrate in the house. I'll have to call their doctor to make sure and there are no smoothie containers. Unless they made it in the blender and put it away. There were two old-fashioned sized glasses in the sink but none in his office."

"Carol, have any bourbon?"

"Not in the stomach. Could be in the bloodstream. But why him and not her?"

"This case gets stranger."

"It certainly does."

"But why would Dominic have taken a sleeping pill and bourbon if he was planning to kill himself?"

"It would be odd. That's why in consideration of inconsistencies in his suicide, I am leaning towards homicide. I have to wait for the blood levels to return to be feel confident in my decision."

Kate considered what she had just learned from the preliminary autopsy about the sleeping pills. She had only used them once. That was after Jake was killed. Although she slept well, it wracked her with wild dreams that were bothersome when she awakened. She decided that a sleepless night was better than a haunting sleep. She researched the side effects and found that was reported widely by users.

There was no evidence of them drinking smoothies. Perhaps they went out and consumed them elsewhere. Now, there were two drink glasses that were filled with soapy water in the sink. If Carol did not have any alcohol in her system, who was the second glass and why was it not in his office?

Her phone rang, and she smiled. "Chuckles, how are you?"

"My lovely, I'm fine. How about you? I read about that horrible case of the dead family."

"Yes, that is sadly my case."

"Oh, that is horrible. I couldn't imagine. I won't keep you. I was checking on Frank. How is he doing in rehab?"

"He is over halfway through. He is good. Thanks for checking."

"I may have been just an informant, but I considered him a friend."

"I think he thought of you the same. How is Jerome?"

"Ugh. We've been together for so long that we bicker like an old married couple. Today, I wanted to go out to lunch, but he said that he needed to Keto and hit the gym. So, I'll eat by myself or you could join me?"

"I would love to, but not during this case."

"I understand. Ta-ta and stay safe, my darling."

"Always."

Kate fingered her wedding band. She never considered herself and Jake the bickering couple. They were almost always enthusiastic partners in their endeavors. She knew most people would consider that as rare as unicorns and rainbows.

She reflected on Chuckles calling to check on Frank. The tough cop had a soft underbelly, and that he had forged a tight connection with the informant was indicative as to the real person he was. They bonded over their love of cooking and trading recipes. Chuckles was also a rarity. He was money as an informant. Not in it for the money. More for the companionship of Frank. All Frank had to endure was refereeing the drama between his prized informant and his partner Jerome.

Chapter Twenty-Eight

Kate started the laborious and boring job of reviewing records. Some records would provide leads, but in judicial proceedings, you better have collected, sorted, and reviewed them. You didn't want to be the one left exposed by a defense attorney who asked the question that you did not know or were not expecting.

She perused the voluminous information forwarded from the analysts. It was all hands-on deck, and Kate sat in awe of their accomplishments. They had a link analysis chart with all the victims and their contacts, either through business, social, and family circles. They hyperlinked each person into a comprehensive background report.

One thing that jumped out was that several of Dom's connections in the Krewe of Kingsmen were also associated with LymRX Technology. Besides Dom, Brian Poole, and Kash McCool, all three shared the same mutual connection. Who has a name like Kash McCool?

Kate opened the file on Kash. He was born Aakash McCool in Texas, to Ankita Pasrija and Thomas McCool. He lived just outside Houston in the Woodlands. His parents both worked at the same company that sold piping to the oil industry. He also dropped out of college after one semester at a community college. He found employment with a biotech firm and then with a financial services company. She clicked on the link to Black Pool Investors.

There were many problems at Black Pool. According to news articles and a federal indictment, the owner was running a boiler room cold-calling customers to invest in a huge lithium discovery in Texas that was nonexistent. The U.S. only produced one percent of the world's supply of the critical element necessary for the green energy initiative. The only previous deposit in the U.S. is in Nevada. The callers alleged geologists said it could be the biggest find of the decade and was necessary for electric vehicle batteries and as proof, a lithium hydroxide refinery was being built near the find. This would cut transportation costs and speed up processing. Once the lithium deposit becomes known, this stock could increase over a hundred percent. Time is running out.

Don't wait or you will miss out on this once in a lifetime opportunity. Oops. Nothing but a big con.

Aakash dropped the AA and simply became Kash. Kate read where Aakash legally changed his name to Kash after the collapse of Black Pool.

Kate called Roxanne Snelling from the FBI, who she worked with in the past, "Hey Roxy." Kate snickered over the phone. "I know you hated Frank calling you that."

"Among many other things. How is Frank? I haven't seen him since his wife's funeral."

"It's been tough on him. He is adapting." Kate knew this was an exaggeration. "Have you ditched those high heels yet?"

"Not a chance. I'm sporting a pair as we speak."

"Feds! You folks will never learn."

"We should go shoe shopping sometime."

"I'd rather go for a gyno checkup. I handpicked my flats and athletic shoes online. Thank you very much. If you are up for lunch, I can do that."

"You're on. I'll even buy."

"I'll buy if you can do me a favor?"

"Perhaps."

"Need to know and top secret, I get it. Okay, so I am working a family homicide."

"I read about that. Horrible."

"You have no idea. Anyway, one guy that is associated with the patriarch was employed in Houston for a company named Black Pool Investments, which the FBI shut down and arrested the owner. My guy, Kash McCool, worked there. I wanted to know what his involvement in the scam was and if they had any charges on him."

"Great name. Kash. Yeah, I'll check into that and get back to you."

"Thank you, Roxanne."

After hanging up with Roxanne, Kate opened up the website for LymRX Technology. A sleek and impressive looking website. The company was advocating the development of a breakthrough treatment for Lyme Disease. Caused by the saliva of a deer tick the size of a poppy seed, the disease, if not initially diagnosed and treated, can cause irreparable harm to the body affecting multiple organs, including the brain and the nervous system. Referred to as the "Great Imitator" and is often misdiagnosed with many other diseases such as M.S., ALS or chronic fatigue syndrome. As a result, the company was also conducting research on ALS and M.S.

According to the CDC, nearly half a million people are diagnosed every year with Lyme and many more are not diagnosed. Within the medical community, there is widespread disagreement on treatment protocols for those that develop chronic Lyme disease. Many patients are subjected to long-term disability and intravenous antibiotic treatment with many side effects. LymRX Technology, while working with a consortium of researchers and bioengineering experts, has developed a breakthrough one dose intravenous form of the drug that has shown remarkable success on lab specimens and mice.

Kate recalled hearing of a doctor in North Carolina that had lost his medical license for treating long-term Lyme patients with antibiotics. They essentially labeled him a heretic and lost his practice. His patients had to seek alternative medical professionals, leaving many distraught.

Kate knew of ALS, also known as Lou Gehrig's Disease was a debilitating and ravaging neuromuscular disease. One of the Tampa officers had succumbed to ALS, several years earlier. Kate watched the sad demise of a once fit and energetic police officer reduced to being bound to a wheelchair and eventual death. She had also read of a new hemorrhagic disease originating from the Congo that was also passed by the tick. That was in addition to the half a dozen diseases passed in the U.S. from various ticks. The devastation by such a small bug was stunning.

Chapter Twenty-Nine

Kate's phone buzzed, and she read the caller ID as Roxanne Snelling from the FBI. Kate answered, "Who says the FBI is slower than a moonshiner on tax-day?"

"I have to say, I've not heard that one before. I had to process that one for a hot minute. You do realize that the FBI has entered the computer age and we have at least 64K RAM!"

They both chuckled and Kate said, "I'm hoping that you have some info for me."

"Yep. I talked with the case agent. He said that Kash was a top producer in sales or Aakash as he was known. He quickly realized that fire surrounded him and cut a deal to cooperate and testify against the owner of Black Pool, David Gingham.

The case agent said that Kash McCool was an impressive witness and had the jury on the edge of their seats. His only penalty was to give up his Series 7 securities license and entered a deferred prosecution agreement. Gingham was found guilty and sentenced to 48 months."

"So now, I have to deal with Kash in my backyard."

"Let me know if you start sniffing any improprieties that might interest me."

"I will. Thanks, Roxanne."

As she ended the call, she looked up as Cody walked into the squad room after returning from interviewing the wives of South Tampa, wearing a cute smile on his face. Kate had looked up from her records and nodded. "I was right. How many slipped their phone numbers to you?"

"None." He stroked his dark blond hair with his hand resting on the back of his neck.

"Just wait. They will call and leave you voicemails. Detective, my husband is out of town. I think I heard something outside. Could you come and check the outside for signs of a possible intruder?"

"Not like that. They are appreciative of our investigation."

"I'm sure they are. Anything good?"

"No, not really. The consensus was that the Marchetti's were a lovely family. Everyone thought the world of them. Carol was great at planning for various charities and the kids were always polite and contributors as well. They said that despite their polar personalities that Carol and Dom were as connected as two links in a chain."

"No infidelity or threats against the family?"

"Nope. They were all shocked. They said they played tennis with her each week and were involved with the planning of the festivities surrounding the Gasparilla Parade."

"What about the school?"

"When you said posh, you were not joking. K through 12. Thirty-eight thousand per year for each student. "

Kate whistled. "That is almost our annual salaries for two kids to go to school."

"I know steep. The teachers had not picked up any rumors of misdeeds from other students. Ethan and Megan were good students, well behaved and well liked."

"That makes it even worse. Nice family killed as they slept. The only consolation is that it was quick, and they never knew what happened. Okay, thank you for doing that." Kate opened an email that had just arrived. "I just received a notice that the mother is planning a memorial for the family this evening."

"She didn't waste any time."

"No, she did not. I wonder how she gets along with the Swoboda's?" asked Kate.

"I sense they are quite different."

"Indeed."

Kate said to Cody, "Let's take a drive to LymRX Technology out by the airport. I want to see what they have to say and to talk with Kash McCool, the CEO."

"Kash? That's a cool name. Get it? Cool as in McCool."

Kate scrunched her face. "Yes, I get it. Don't give up your day job, detective. A comedian, you are not."

"Who is Kash?"

"He was involved in a big fraud out in Houston. Changes his name and shows up on our doorstep. He is the listed CEO of LymRX, which was also linked to Marchetti and Brian Poole."

"Interesting."

Kate continued, "McCool may not have been involved in violence in the past, but he is a criminal. Maybe it's nothing and a waste of time, but maybe he is a low hanging fruit that fell out of the tree. I just want to check under the hood. Someone that has a previous criminal history and is now associated with a murdered family, deserves a shake. When you consider Kash was involved in a large fraud and then you also have Dom involved in the fraud of Hercules, my curious meter gets activated. Even if Kash is not involved, and we arrested someone else, that person's attorney is going to ask if we checked all possible suspects."

"We don't want that to happen."

"No. I've not been called out like that, but I heard it happen elsewhere. That's like showing up in court in your pajamas. Fully exposed."

Chapter Thirty

Kate and Cody drove to the address listed on the website for LymRX Technology. The office was in a corporate office park, mostly populated by square, low-rise buildings of cement and glass tucked back into the nicely manicured, landscaped campus. As they stepped out of the car, the two detectives looked up toward the sky to the sound of an airliner that seemed to barely clear the trees on its final descent into the Tampa International Airport.

There were few cars in the mostly vacant parking lot. As they entered the sun-drenched atrium of the building, Kate noticed as their heels echoed in the building that there was no other activity. She noticed only one suite where there was a movement from a receptionist.

The suite listed for LymRX Technology was dark. The two detectives leaned up to the glass door and peered through. Like two kids peeking out their window on Christmas Eve. Santa was not coming. There was no activity inside the office. The sign on the door said LymRX Technology, Focused on Today's Science for a Better Tomorrow.

Kate said, "Well, this is interesting. I would hate to be in commercial real estate right now. It could take a long time to survive the telework phase. I wish we could telework."

"No, thank you. I enjoy getting outside."

"I was saying it tongue in cheek. I too would go nuts staying at home all day. Let's check with the leasing agent. I saw the sign out front."

Dialing the number for Phyllis Smallwood, Kate learned she was in the area and had just completed a walk through with a client. Smallwood said that she would be over shortly. Kate wondered if she was showing property to a perspective client or doing a final vacancy walk-through with another departing client.

Walking to the lone office with a receptionist, Kate introduced herself and asked if she had seen anyone coming or going from LymRX. The pretty brunette with her hair braided said no, but then added that several months earlier, several people came into her office and said they were reporting to the casting call for Kash McCool. The receptionist reported a high volume of activity and then nothing over the past two months.

As they stepped out into the atrium, Kate was about to speak when they turned to the front entrance. A blonde with a full face walked towards them. Phyllis Smallwood extended her hand to shake and Kate noticed a small tattoo on her wrist in script. After the introductions, Kate said, "Looks like you have plenty of vacancies."

"You have no idea. This market is in a freefall. I feel like strapping on a parachute to soften the landing. Most of us have hung our shingle out in the residential market, which is on fire, but it's like starting over. Who knows how long that will last with the economy?"

Kate added, "Like being on the Titanic."

"And no lifeboats left."

"Sadly, we are here about LymRX Technologies."

"Ugh. I met the owner. Kash McCool. Anyone with a name like that should have raised a red flag. He was good. Very flamboyant and charming. I'm in sales and I bought into this guy's vision. He sold me. I almost wanted to buy what he was selling. He could have sold Palm Trees in Michigan. He was that good. He signed a three-year lease with a two-year extension option. They paid a security deposit after he asked for the first two months to be free. Supposedly, the business was moving from Texas. Everything was wonderful until the two months were up and we came over to check when the rent was overdue. We found the space appeared vacant, aside from a bunch of medical equipment inside."

"Medical equipment?"

"Like microscopes and stuff like that. I can show you."

"I would love that."

Phyllis unlocked the door, and the three walked into the darkened room. Microscopes, beakers, test tubes, shakers, glass enclosures, refrigerators filled with samples, and other technical looking equipment sat abandoned.

Long rows of lab benches appeared like they were ready for their occupants to return. Lab coats were slung over the chairs with the LymRX Technology logo embroidered on the left chest. Each station had a goggle sitting in the chair.

Kate thought it looked like a legit laboratory. Except it was too sterile. No personalization of the space. There were no family pictures. No litter. In fact, there were no waste baskets. The appearance of the lab would have impressed anyone who had taken biology in school.

Picking up a microscope, Kate read a sticker affixed to the bottom that read Pyramid Lab Rentals. Kate turned towards Phyllis. "Next door, the receptionist said there were several people that came in and asked about a casting call. Do you know anything about that?"

Looking puzzled, Phyllis said with some hesitation, "No."

Kate said, "This looks like one big scam, like he was running in Texas. This was merely an illusion. Probably to entice investors. Nice office space, all the equipment is a rental. The casting call leads me to believe that he hired actors to legitimize the illusion. I don't think that LymRX Technology has plans to fulfill their lease. They have packed up their circus tent and hit the road."

Phyllis covered her mouth briefly and lowered it to her throat. "Well, I am not surprised. This is not good news."

Chapter Thirty-One

After returning to the Blue Monster, Kate and Cody began calling casting agents in the Tampa area. As she went down the list with a succession of negative responses, she hit pay dirt on the sixth inquiry.

The Ybor City Talent Agency provides models and actors for local productions and commercials. Kate spoke with the owner Erika Allen, who said that she briefly spoke with Kash, who said that he was filming a promotional video and presentation in relation to a biotech firm. He paid the agency fee, and Erika put the posting up on the Ybor City Talent Agency website. Kash hired thirty actors and models for the day. Kate asked for the names and contact numbers of the models or actors that were hired. Erika promised to email the list of those that were hired.

Once Kate received the list of cast members, she went into Alfonso's office. His enormously thick fingers were checking the dampness of the root system for his orchids. He had always said that between his orchids and fish aquarium; they provided balance to the violence that he encountered daily. Kate plopped into a chair with a sigh.

He looked with downcast eyes, "Troubles?"

"This entire case. This is your fault." As she pointed to him.

He leaned back in his chair. "Me?"

"That wake-up call in the middle of the night."

"The Caveman called a little while ago and wanted an update."

"He is like sand in my bathing suit. A constant irritation."

"He is nervous and scared. With an acting chief, the front office is in a disarray. No one wants to make waves, and they are worried about the mayor. Is the Mayor going to appoint the acting chief or go outside and select a professional chief? It's anyone's guess." Alfonso said.

"A professional chief?" Kate asked.

"You know, like mercenaries. Every couple of years, they move to a higher paying and larger profile position. They have no loyalty to the employees or the community. Their only loyalty is to themselves and the mayor."

"Or the next job."

"You're right. So, The Caveman is more disoriented than a kid blindfolded, playing pin the tail on the donkey. He has no idea who to suck up to, so he is kissing everyone's ass."

"And this case has a lot of heat."

Alfonso said, "Like the flames are licking at our asses. I would encourage you, with all speed and efficiency, to wrap this up. This Krewe of Kingsmen has a lot of political juice. It's coming from forces outside the city, through the mayor's office and downhill from there. Let me know what you need."

"I need to divide this list of actors to track down."

"You got it. I want you to hear this from me. I just submitted my retirement notice."

"No!"

"I can cover for you on one last case."

"Getting tired?"

"It's time. I want to enjoy life while I can. This business has become very perilous over the last few years."

"It has. It's a political knife fight daily, and we are one bullet from being killed and one mistake from being indicted." Kate said with downcast eyes.

"You are right. There is no other profession that is as scrutinized as ours. Not doctors, not lawyers, not the newsies and not politicians. For me, it's more about enjoying my retirement while I still have good health and a fabulous wife to enjoy the sunsets and a cocktail."

"I'll miss you and so will everyone else, but I will applaud your safe arrival to the finish line."

"I'm not there yet."

"You're coasting now."

Kate felt a pang of sadness as she considered the loss of a devoted supervisor who always had her back, as well as someone that she considered a friend. She had lost two of her closest allies. Frank Duffy and now Alfonso. She felt a pit in her stomach. She felt like she was aboard a ship, rolling in a turbulent storm without a helmsman.

Despite the storm, she would have to guide the ship into a safe harbor and fight for what she believed in. Justice and the victims. In this case, the Marchetti family. This family would not be a convenient end to an inconvenient conspiracy.

What conspiracy? She knew trying to advocate with The Caveman that this case was about a conspiracy would not be well received. He would have a nervous breakdown. If she could locate Kash McCool, he could be the link to the missing piece of a jigsaw puzzle. Or was it just a coincidence that Marchetti was connected to McCool and his family died by a depressed and depraved Dominic? She had to find McCool and interview him.

Kate and Cody drove to a mid-rise condominium complex on Harbor Island, connected by two bridges to downtown Tampa. The island was mostly inhabited by mid-rise and high-rise condominiums and apartments. Cody drove across the bridge, passing the Amalie Arena home of the Tampa Bay Lightning and NHL champs.

She looked down at the winding Riverwalk following the shoreline of the Hillsborough River. How she wanted to lace up her running shoes and take an exhilarating run along the 2.6-mile path one-way. A good five-mile run round-trip with enough space to cool down. She could free herself of all her anxiety. This case and now the sad notice that one of her mentors was retiring was a dark cloud hovering over her mood. Maybe tomorrow she could complete a run.

"Cody, you ever run along the Riverwalk?"

"No. I have taken my bike for a ride down there. They did a spectacular job on it. I've been to various festivals in Hixon Park next to the Straz Center."

"Downtown has really changed over the last ten years."

"If I was single and no family, this is where I would want to be. Why did you pick South Howard?" Kate asked.

"SoHo has more conveniences for me and my mom. Doctors' offices, grocery, drug stores and lots of food choices."

"And nightlife."

"There is that as well." He smiled back at her.

Chapter Thirty-Two

The detectives arrived at the apartment building and parked on the street. They entered through the main entrance of an elegant lobby with leather seating and a grand piano. Kate and Cody passed the leasing agent's office and tailgated a resident into the elevator. The bushy headed college age resident gave a glance at the two detectives. He continued yapping on his Facetime call with a squeaky voiced female about some drama with her boss, not allowing her to work from home anymore.

Kate and Cody stepped off at 6th floor and left the elevator traveler to continue his journey alone. They walked down the well-lit and bright hallway to Kash's apartment. Kate knocked on 606. After three failed attempts, they headed back towards the elevators.

They arrived at the leasing manager's office. A tall black woman, who exuded an air of confidence and a bright smile, stepped out to meet them. She impressed Kate with the handshake of strength. "I'm Alicia Howard. How can I help you?"

After Kate introduced themselves, she said, "You have a tenant named Kash McCool, who is living in apartment 606. We were conducting a welfare check on him. No one has seen him lately, and no one has seen him at the company he owns, LymRX Technologies. We found one of his close friends murdered and we wanted to make sure that he was okay. We just knocked on his door and no one answered. Could you let us in to check and make sure that he is not hurt?"

Alicia's hand covered her throat and said, "Oh my gosh. Absolutely. Hold on. Let me see the last time that he used his access card for the garage or the building." She stood over her desk and typed into the keypad. "It looks like he has not used his access since Sunday evening at 8:00 pm in two days. Of course, he could have left his car in the garage and tailgated another resident onto the elevator like you two just did."

Kate smiled with a caught me smile. "Thank you."

"Let's have a look. Hopefully, he is on a business trip and not home."

Alicia rang the doorbell. She then knocked. With no response, she inserted the key and opened the door and called out, "Mr. McCool. Leasing agent. Anyone home?"

Kate and Cody pushed past Alicia and looked through the apartment. The furnishings and furniture were modern and high-end. No Kash McCool.

Kate noticed the bed rumpled and not made. There were a lot of empty hangers, leaving a few suits and dress shirts. She ran her fingers across the hanging clothes and then opened the inside of the jackets to examine the labels. All high end. The same for the dress shirts as she fingered the material. They pulled the dresser drawers open.

Kate said, "No underwear, no socks and no suitcases."

Cody considered her statement and then nodded in agreement.

They walked back into the living area. Cody rifled through some papers on the kitchen counter and held up a delivery form from a furniture staging rental company. Two pages that accounted for almost everything in the apartment.

Cody perused the wine rack and said, "This isn't grocery store wine."

"I wouldn't know. But most of this is all an illusion, like LymRX Technology and everything in this guy's life. He left in a hurry." She pointed to the kitchen table. "Almost a full cup of coffee and a bowl of cereal."

"He probably caught the news about Dom and it was time to exfil." Cody said.

"Yes indeed. Well, Alicia, we don't see any blood or signs of a struggle. I have my doubts that you will see him again."

Alicia responded, "His rent is up to date. We won't be able to do anything until he falls delinquent."

Kate twisted her mouth. "He has skipped on us. Thank you for your help, Alicia. Here is my card, if you see him again or have any inquiries from him, please call."

"I will."

Chapter Thirty-Three

In the State of Florida, everyone has a SunPass transponder, especially in Tampa. Most of the major arteries aside from I-4 and I-75 were toll roads. Checking Kash McCool's SunPass toll transponder account, Kate saw no activity on Sunday or around the time of the murders. Late Monday morning, his car triggered the system at the airport entering the economy parking garage and according to the transponder, his Range Rover was still parked somewhere in the twin multi-level parking garage.

Kate opened the file for his cellphone. There was a lot of activity on the phone until Monday. The last call made pinged the cell tower at the airport. Since then, all was quiet.

Kate called the Tampa Airport Police Department and spoke to Detective Ruth Young. Kate worked with Ruth on the same shift before she retired. Like so many cops, Ruth couldn't afford the out-of-pocket insurance and had to take a retirement job just to avoid paying over a thousand dollars a month for health insurance coverage.

"Hi Ruth, it's Kate Alexander."

"Hey Kate, I was just talking about you the other day."

"I could only imagine."

"Remember, we had a crime scene that was on Bush?"

"Memories!"

"Yep. A guy returned with his sweet thing of girlfriend to his motel room and we had the area closed off. He told us he had taken Viagra and his clock was running and desperately needed to get to his room. You told him to stay a-*head* of the game, he might be better running back up closer to I-275 and getting another motel room for a couple of hours to alleviate the pressure!" Ruth erupted in her trademark laugh that was contagious to everyone around.

Kate chuckled along and said, "Speaking of which, do you remember the time at the outboard motor shop when the owner was getting frisky with his office manager and he got his legs tangled in his underwear? Then he lost his balance and fell, hitting his head on a workbench?"

"Knocked himself clean out. All his manhood was being exposed. Tales of D-2. Glorious memories. So, honey, I'm sure you didn't call to revisit old memories."

"You're right. I am trying to locate a silver Range Rover that entered the economy parking garage on Tuesday afternoon at 11:11 am. He is a person of interest in the family of four homicide."

"Oh no. Here we are laughing it up."

"Ruth, you know life can be short. We have to laugh when we can."

"You are right, hon. Give me the plate number and I'll call you back."

"Thank you, Ruth."

Chapter Thirty-Four

Kate began going through the credit card records of Kash McCool. You can usually tell a lot about a person from their credit card purchases. With Kash, he was living the good life. Expensive tastes in food, liquor, entertainment and clothes. His spending on the credit card ceased on Sunday evening before the murders. His spending spree came to a freezing halt, leaving a balance of twenty-three thousand dollars.

As she continued going through his transactions, she observed large purchases for under ten thousand dollars. Payments from his bank account quickly followed all the transactions. Kate recognized he was keeping the transactions below the ten-thousand-dollar threshold limit to stay under the radar of alerting the Treasury Department. The process was often called structuring and most banks would report this activity, but by the time a federal agency glommed onto the report, months would have passed.

He split the purchases between two crypto exchanges. Having worked in the banking industry prior to joining the police department, Kate was familiar with the world of high finance, but most of her time was spent in human resources hiring and firing employees. She called an old colleague, classmate at Duke and a member of the men's cross-country team. Sometimes they trained together. She had not spoken to him in several years, so she text his number and asked him to call her.

A minute later, the incoming call showed Robert Lusk. "Bob, how are you?"

After several minutes of trading life stories, Kate asked, "Bob, as much as it is great to catch up, I really need to pick your genius brain for a tutorial on crypto and going off the grid. I have a guy that appears to be shoveling dirt on his tracks and he is structuring purchases using his credit card on two crypto exchanges. Any words of wisdom?"

"Each of those two crypto exchanges has a public ledger that you can locate amounts and times. With the timestamp of the credit card, you can synchronize the purchase date, time, and amount with the public ledgers to identify the crypto wallet, which is a numbered account. No names are published."

"Then I can identify the wallet and I can identify him?"

"Maybe. So, we just had a case with the FBI. They did just that and seized the Bitcoin. They could only recover a portion."

"Why is that?"

"The bad guys converted most of the Bitcoin to another crypto currency called Monero, which is virtually untraceable. Monero uses what's called ring signatures to conceal user's identity. The ring signature includes the signer and a group of non-signers to form a ring. Kind of like a shell game. Once it's converted to Monero, they have their digital wallet similar to an encrypted thumb drive, and they can access Monero from any phone or any computer at a hotel, library or a friend. Once it's in the wallet, no one can monitor it unless they have the password."

"It's not like you can walk into McDonalds and buy a quarter pounder and fries with crypto." Kate said.

"No, but they can use it for gift card processing companies. So, they can get gift cards for any big box merchant, grocery store, restaurant, hotels or Amazon. He could even exchange it again for Bitcoin and withdraw cash from a Bitcoin ATM. They are all over the place."

"Well, aren't you as joyful as a slice of hot apple pie?"

"You know, we both enjoy a slice of hot apple pie. Sounds like if this guy is making every attempt to run deep off the grid, you will need the muscle of the FBI or the Marshals to track this guy down. With the volatility of crypto, it's hard to say if he made money, lost or maintained."

"Anything is more than what he had when he arrived in town. It's enough to take the money and run. Bob, thank you so much for the intro class. You were always the high flyer destined for greatness at the bank."

"I wouldn't say that." He chuckled softly and said, "Take care Kate, it was great catching up."

"It was. Bye, Bob."

⛓ ⛓ ⛓

Kate considered the bad news from Bob Lusk concerning the crypto hole. She had been hoping to find airline tickets, food purchases or ride share charges at the airport. Not even an ATM withdrawal. Kate was feeling disappointed when her phone rang.

"Hi Ruth. Did you find it?"

"Sure did. Level three. Nothing appeared out of order and nothing in plain sight raised suspicion. We put a clamp on it so he has to call us. It also buys you time to get a search warrant. We can't consider it abandoned and technically, his SunPass is still valid. We don't have any reason to tow it."

"No, you're right."

"I found something interesting. We had a report on Monday of someone riding a bicycle through the garage. Sometimes we get kids looking to break into cars, and sometimes we get fitness buffs trying to simulate climbing mountains. We had the recording, and I looked at it. It appears to be Kash McCool from his DL photo pedaling out of the garage. I can send the video and photo of him to your email. I also checked passenger manifests and the hotel on the property. There is no record for Kash or Aakash McCool."

"That's great Ruth. That would lead me to believe he is still in town. He has just dropped off the grid. Thank you, Ruth!"

"Not so fast. He could have flown out through one of the FBO's."

"FBO?"

"Fixed base operator. We have two within a bicycle ride of the parking garage. If he flew out on a private charter, there would be no record outside of the purchase. He might have to flash a driver's license, and they wouldn't even screen his baggage. No TSA, no record. Just a puff of smoke."

"You are a bundle of good news. Thank you, Ruth."

"Anytime hon."

Chapter Thirty-Five

After drafting an affidavit to search the silver Range Rover at the airport economy parking garage, Kate and Cody headed to the county court building. Once the judge signed the actual warrant, they headed out to the airport. Kate had arranged to meet Detective Ruth Young at the entrance to the parking garage.

Ruth, with her vibrant smile and blonde hair, was eager to meet an old friend, "Hi Kate. You haven't changed. You can still outrun the cheetah and the antelope."

"Not as fast as I once was."

Ruth looked over at Cody. "I'll bet she has single-handedly chased down more feeling felons than anyone else. She may have been a cross-country runner, but she should have been a sprinter. Even the guys called her a human K-9, until someone called her Kick Ass. That stuck."

Cody said, "I haven't had that opportunity yet."

"Just stand to the side and watch. Pure joy."

Kate interrupted, "Well, Ruth, you look great."

"I feel good. I notice the gun-belt is a little tighter, and I have to visit Miss Clairol a little more often. C'mon, let's look at your suspect car."

Ruth escorted them to the car parked on the third level. Kate listened to the sounds of airplanes taking off and landing, along with cars echoing through the expansive garage. Despite the noise, Ruth's voice bellowed over the racket, "Once you told me the warrant was signed, I had our locksmith do his magic. One of our guys is standing by along with a tow truck. I assume you want to take it for a full workup?"

"It's always nice to work with someone who is solid like you that knows the drill."

Ruth laughed, "That comes with experience and a few gray hairs."

Kate touched her hair and said, "Do I have any gray hair?"

"Stop! Let's have a look inside."

Ruth stood at the back as Kate read the search warrant to the vacant SUV as if it were alive. Once completing the mandatory verbal reading, Kate and Cody began their search from each side. As they opened the car door, the freshness of a clean car hit them. Kate sniffed the air. They examined every cubby, every compartment, and under the seats. They found nothing but the owner's manual, the leasing papers and abandoned cellphone that was powered off.

Kate looked over and said, "Clean. Not even dust. He probably had it detailed. About the only thing left is for the lab rats is to check for blood traces. Thank you, Ruth. It was great to see you again. We need to do lunch."

"Absolutely."

Kate looked at Cody and said, "I'll tell you. She was a hoot to work with."

"I can tell."

Chapter Thirty-Six

They drove to Signature Air terminal adjoining the airport. The towering white double peaked tent awning was a unique architectural enhancement. Kate found an empty spot to slide into and she and Cody walked towards the terminal building.

Kate pointed up towards the double tent awning and said, "Frank Duffy said it reminded him of Dolly Parton's bra."

They both laughed and walked through the automatic doors. A group of businessmen in golf attire stood in the waiting area, sipping coffee, waiting to be called to the Lear jet parked outside on the tarmac.

Kate and Cody walked up to the counter next to the doors leading to the apron and access to the airplanes. It appeared the golf clubs were being loaded into the cargo hold of the sleek jet.

Kate identified herself to the young girl with flowing and radiant raven hair. Her name tag read Samantha. The girl's vivacious smile tightened to a more serious look as she listened to Kate ask if she had seen Kash while showing a picture of him. Samantha shook her head, but offered the detectives an opportunity to examine the video recording from inside and outside the private terminal. She instructed them to go up the stairs and meet the operations manager, Donnie Miller.

At the top of the stairs, an exuberant smile from Donnie Miller, the operations manager met them. "Sam told me you folks are hunting a fugitive."

Kate answered, "I wouldn't say a fugitive. A person of interest, perhaps."

"Well, if you have a big enough wallet, this is one way to get out of town and put time and distance between yourself and the law."

Kate grimaced. "Do you keep records of the passengers?"

Donnie's smile silenced. "No, afraid not. Only the planes and pilots. They generate the revenue for us, not the passengers. There are no regulations to track them either. The crew usually looks for identification. If they are flying across the border, then passports are required and they will be inspected on the other end. It's like renting a car with a driver. I'll let you look at the video and see if your man came through. We can see if he flew out and then we can find out where he went."

"Thank you, sir. That would be great."

Donnie set them up in an unoccupied office and gave them a tutorial on how to operate and search the video system. The first camera view Cody and Kate viewed was looking out across the parking lot. Kate looked at the time stamp from when Kash pedaled out of the parking garage.

Cody and Kate huddled around the computer screen. Cody moved the cursor to play, and they sat there watching. Eight minutes later, Kash coasted into the parking lot and glided up to the terminal. They switched to another view, which captured Kash stroll into the waiting lounge. He took a seat in the lounge area and watched the television. Kate figured he was catching the latest breaking news on the Marchetti killings. While Kate and Cody were up the street at Hercules Investments, Kash had pedaled within a hundred yards of them and now was potentially making his escape.

Kate felt frustration realizing that he had the funds to pay for a private escape and could have conceivably left the country because he was not on the radar. She knew that Bolivia, Ecuador, Nicaragua and Venezuela were not friendly to extradition to the U.S. She crossed Venezuela off the list. With the political and economic upheaval, she didn't think Kash would enjoy that chaos.

Kate thought if she were on the run and had to choose, she would pick Ecuador. Great diving, hiking and rafting. What's not to love about the Galapagos? Throw in, they use the U.S. Dollar as currency and awesome chocolate, what was there not to like in Ecuador. With a passport, access to crypto, and a pocketful of gift cards, Kash could live the highlife. Her mind drifted to a memory of her and Jake diving and snorkeling in Belize. She smiled at the memory of the crystal clear aqua waters, and the barrier reef with beautiful coral and brightly colored fish.

After about fifteen minutes, Kash strolled up to the counter. The same counter that Sam was working. They could see on the screen, a blonde with a short bob style cut was at the counter. He talked for three minutes and walked away.

They switched views and watched the parking lot view again. They watched Kash spin out of the parking lot on his bicycle and turn south on Westshore Boulevard. There was another FBO to the left, but Kash turned right and rode away.

Kate stuck her head into Donnie Miller's office. "Excuse me, Mr. Miller. Do you know when a person working the counter with a blonde bob cut will be at work?"

"Yep. Marci. She is down there now."

"Oh, that's great. I appreciate your help."

"Anytime, detectives."

Cody and Kate walked downstairs and returned to the counter. Marci smiled and her eyes locked on Cody like the radar of an approaching airplane. Kate nudged to Cody to take the lead.

Cody said to Marci, "Hi Marci, we are with the police department. Mr. Miller said that you were the one on duty when this individual came in here on Monday morning."

She was oblivious to Kate but enthralled with Cody like a fangirl at a rock concert. "Yes, he was. I noticed him walk in and look around and then he sat in the lounge watching television. I assumed he was waiting on a crew."

Cody pointed at Kate, causing Marci to break eye contact with Cody for just a moment. "We noticed you had a conversation with him."

"Yeah, he asked how you would book a flight out of Signature. I let him know we are not like an airline. We merely facilitate and host private flights. I told him he would have to contact an individual charter service to hire. Like using Uber or Lyft."

"That is a good analogy. Anything else?"

"Yes, He asked how much a flight cost. I told him he would have to get cost estimates from the charters. He asked about how much they cost and I told him they start around six grand, depending on the size of the aircraft and the destination. I told him that there were multiple FBO's and small airports that accommodate charter flights. He also asked what identification was necessary. I told him that most crews asked for a driver's license unless he was flying out of the country. He would need a passport to be accepted in the receiving country."

"Were there any flights leaving during that time?"

"I believe there was one. One of our regulars, a group of insurance folks."

"What was his demeanor?"

"To be honest, he seemed to be a little desperate. Like the person trying to catch the last train of the day. He was also kind of sweaty, like he had just run from the parking lot. He had a few minutes to cool down sitting here." She gave a half shrug.

"Marci, you have been helpful. Here is my card. If you see him again, please call me." He flashed his smile, exposing his white teeth.

"I certainly will, Detective Danko. That is a strong name. I like it." Her cheeks lifted and her smile filled in the opening.

Kate and Cody walked towards the exit, and Kate turned towards Cody. "That is such a strong name. I'll bet Marci is weak in the knees and has to take a seat. You all but took her breath away."

"Oh stop. She was just being nice."

"She was insightful. Sounds like Kash is considering an escape. We know he left here and turned right away from the other FBOs. He could fly out of Peter O. Knight on Davis Island, Tampa Executive, or there are several small airports in Pinellas."

"He certainly has the funds to pay for it."

"We can have the analysts make up a flyer and have them send it out to all the FBO's and airports in the area. Pinellas Sheriff covers the airports across the bay and Hillsborough Sheriffs have their air operations at the executive airport."

Chapter Thirty-Seven

When they returned to the office, Cody split off. He had to attend a meeting at the State Attorney's Office concerning an arrest that he was involved in while he was still assigned to patrol.

Kate knew that most people who said they were going off the grid never really could. There was a rare exception, like Boston mobster, Whitey Bulger, who stayed off the grid for sixteen years. Kash was definitely running. He was attempting to go underground. Like Whitey Bulger, Kate thought if she ever made a run for it, she would leave town where no one would know her. It always surprised her how often fugitives never ventured far from home and their support system.

She knew Kash was running a scam. LymRX was a complete theater production, including actors, stagehands, and props. He left his apartment, which was furnished with rental furniture. He abandoned his car at the airport, hoping to give a red herring that he flew out. But instead, he rides out on a bicycle. But he has no suitcase or even a backpack. So, where is he staying? Someone in his support system?

Kate called the law offices of Melvin Storms and scheduled an appointment and was relieved to find that he could meet right away.

She walked over to Melvin Storm's office in downtown a few blocks from the Blue Monster building of the police department. His office occupied one floor of the forty-two story Regions Bank building capped with a green gothic style roof.

The conference room provided a splendid panoramic view of the Tampa skyline. Melvin looked like his old self and more like the cross-examining legal assassin from which his reputation had been earned.

Kate asked, "You look like you have been able to get some rest."

"Some. That night and the images in my mind will haunt me a for a long time. Especially realizing his family had suffered the same fate. I met them and knew them. I wonder if there was something that I could have done and realized how depressed he was."

"I recently read a book on mass killers and family annihilators where the individual is sucked into a negative emotional vortex. Everything in their life is collapsing. You might have predicted their suicide but not murdering their entire family. In this book, the author also said that depression is the most easily concealed mental health illness. Look at Robin Williams. One of the funniest men, and yet he was consumed with darkness."

Melvin sighed and combed his fingers through his white hair, "I suppose there is some truth to that."

"From statements of folks that knew him and Carol, they all said that they appeared to have had a splendid marriage."

Melvin nodded, "I would agree with that."

"The family annihilators that I have studied all had some dysfunctionality at home. Here, there is no evidence of that. They loved each other for who they were."

"I saw nothing or heard nothing from him that would give that sign. Dom was eccentric and crazy, but he adored his family."

Kate nodded in agreement.

Melvin stared at Kate. "Wait, are you still not saying this was not a homicide-suicide?"

"I'm saying that it is still under investigation, and there are some things that are not adding up."

"Like?"

"I really want your honest opinion of Dom's mood with the embezzlement."

"Dom was very concerned. For argument's sake, let's just say he had backed into a porcupine and it was going to sting. He may have been a brilliant economist, but he was not a criminal. He knew Hercules was going to fire him, and he would lose his trading license. But another company had already approached him to oversee their finances, so he was upbeat. Carol came from money. They had a chain of video stores that Blockbuster bought to increase their market share. They sold at the height of video stores before it all came crashing down. She was the only child. Her parents had her late in life."

"Her parents were unaware of money troubles."

"Well, he wouldn't be the first client to give me a false impression. He told me they could ask for an early inheritance."

"Why the embezzlement?"

"He was mad at the Stimson brothers for not treating him with his perceived value."

"Said every corporate crook. Okay, let me ask about this company. Did Kash McCool have anything to do with it?

"Why yes? How did you know?"

"His name came up as we were kicking over rocks. What do you know about him?"

"Not much. It was a biotech startup with some sizeable investors and government support. I know the law, but there is a reason that I didn't go into the sciences. Dom looked at the company and was excited about their future. I know that Brian Poole, who knows a little something about tech startups, was onboard as well."

"Do you know anything about Kash?"

"I met him a few times at a couple of social gatherings. Very outgoing. Seemed like a pleasant fellow."

"Do you know anything about his friends?" Kate asked.

"He had a girlfriend with him. Stunning girl. Jazz was her name. I believe she was in real estate. Olive skin and long black hair." He illustrated long hair with his hands.

"What would you say if I told you that Kash was a fraud?"

His eyes widened. "In my line of work, I am usually not surprised, but in this instance, I would be."

"Let's just say that he projected a slick façade."

"Does he have anything to do with the demise of the Marchetti family?"

"I don't know yet."

"Melvin, thank you for your time."

Chapter Thirty-Eight

Walking behind the Regions Building towards the riverfront, Kate reached the Riverwalk. She felt the cool breeze from the Hillsborough River blowing across her face. This was a great time of the year before the heat and humidity of the summer overpowered life outside. She paused just a moment and closed her eyes and tilted her face towards the sun. For a moment, she smiled and thought how wonderful this felt. She had escaped the world and all the problems. No death.

The sound of running shoes striking the brick pathway interrupted her thoughts. A millennial female with a fast pace past Kate. She continued to watch the tall girl with long strides move further away. Kate felt like a racehorse being restrained by a horse halter. She wanted to slip into her running shoes and just keep running until she collapsed.

Her phone rang, and she frowned. "Detective Alexander."

"Yes, Detective, this is Rodney Upton, Senator Thorland's Chief of Staff."

Kate rolled her eyes. "Oh, yes, I remember. I also remember you tried to crash a violent crime scene and then complained to my superiors when I refused your entre." She emphasized the accent on entre.

He cleared his throat, "Well yes, ahh, I was not impressed with your tone. We have a certain expectation of our public servants."

"Whatever, Rodney. I'm very busy. How can I be of service to you?" Her face tightened with contempt.

"Yes, ahh well, you told me to call if I thought of anything. It occurred to me that Dom expressed some concerns about his involvement with a fellow named Billy Savage and the company he had started."

"What concerns?" She felt like she was a largemouth bass being baited by a withdrawing fishing line. She knew Rodney was hoping to get some nibbles on the line.

"He wasn't exactly clear. He was reticent to provide much information. He just said that Billy was a shady character, and he was sorry that he ever became involved with him or his business."

"When did this conversation take place?"

"I don't recall exactly. Maybe a week ago."

"Do you know this, Billy?"

"Oh no. I prefer to associate with people improving our community."

Kate shook her head in disgust. "And he didn't mention the name of the business or the type of the business?"

"No. In hindsight..."

Kate cut him off, "That's odd, Okay, thanks for calling."

"Oh, detective, are there any updates? I thought this was a homicide and suicide?"

"We don't comment on active investigations. Have a nice day, Rodney." She ended the call and muttered, "What an ass clown."

It ruined her peaceful stroll down the Riverwalk like a stormy day. She thought that Rodney Upton was trying to get information from her. He had probably already talked to Melvin Storms and learned about the Kash McCool line of inquiry. Was he throwing some additional meat into the cage as a red herring, or was he just getting his ear to the door to find out how the case was going? If he believed it was a suicide, why throw Billy's name out there as a wild goose chase? Perhaps that was intentional. She would have to use her investigative skills to determine Upton's motive.

As she entered the green grass of Curtis Hixon Waterfront Park, she could no longer resist the temptation. She increased her stride and broke into a full gallop. Mothers with strollers looked concerned, as they could no doubt see her badge and gun as her jacket flew open. She didn't care. It felt good as she slowed to a fast walk and enjoyed her lungs filling with fresh air.

Chapter Thirty-Nine

Jazz! Who was Jazz and where was she? Perhaps that was her given name or was it short for something? Worked in real estate? Like was she an agent, or an assistant, residential, commercial or maybe an affiliate business like mortgages? Every time that you shot a rubber band, you were hitting someone in the real estate business in the fast-growing Tampa market.

Lester Rollins looked at Kate. "Kate, my friend, you look lost."

"Not lost. Just thinking of finding a stunning beauty with olive skin, long dark hair and has a name of Jazz."

"Well, aside from the name, you are describing yourself."

She flipped her hair. "My hair is brown and shoulder length. My skin tone is not olive. I am far from being stunning. The only thing you got right was my name is not Jazz. You need to adjust your observation skills or have your eyes checked."

"The WAGS think you're pretty."

"Are they still talking about me?"

"Baby, they are always talking about someone. If they are not saying that you are an imbecile or ugly, then it's a win."

"I guess being in a male-dominated field, there is always going to be some shouts from the mezzanine section."

"It's life."

Alfonso stepped out of his office and said, "Kate, we are being summoned again to the cave."

Kate looked over to Lester Rollins and rolled her eyes. "Lester, wish me luck."

"Anyone venturing into the fool's cave should be armed and wearing body armor. He is a backstabbing son of a bitch, for sure. Good luck."

She and Alfonso walked down the hall. She felt like the teacher escorting her to the principal's office, as she followed the lumbering figure of Alfonso. If they were in sunshine, his shadow would have engulfed and comforted her on the journey into the sun. They walked into The Cave.

Lt. Willard the Caveman stood from behind his desk with his hands on his hips. "I thought I told you to close this case."

"Which case?" answered Kate.

"Don't be coy with me." As he rubbed the sheen on his scalp.

"You don't want me to prematurely close a case and then to find out weeks, months, or years later that we are exposed for having done a shoddy job."

"You don't have to be Sherlock Holmes to see this case for what it is. Close it."

"I can't do it."

His eyes furrowed, and his lips tightened in anger. "You are out."

"Out?"

"This case. I would also start looking for a new home outside of homicide. Maybe as a district detective."

Before Kate ruined her career, Alfonso stood. "You are not doing this. She is the best homicide detective that we have. I agree one hundred percent with Kate that there are more leads to investigate."

"Sergeant, I know you are a short timer, and I don't think you want to slide into retirement on suspension for defying a lawful order. Consider what I just said. Your record ruined and tarnished for any future employment. The three musketeers. Frank Duffy infected both of you with his insolence."

Alfonso closed the distance with his superior and lowered his voice. "You spineless backstabber. I know you are jockeying for a promotion. You couldn't investigate yourself out of a wet paper bag with both ends open."

The Caveman retreated behind his desk. "Be careful, sergeant. Reassign it to Arroyo."

Alfonso continued, "Your little puppet Arroyo can close it, but your name will be the approving signature. When this IED goes off down the road, your stink will be all over it. Let's go Kate, I need a shower."

"I don't like your attitude."

"Me either."

The two detectives walked down the hallway like they had just left a funeral. In some ways, it was perhaps their own. Alfonso retiring on a sour note and Kate being reassigned.

When they returned to the sergeant's office, Kate closed the door and said, "This is all politics."

"Yes, it is. Someone wants this case shut down. You have walked into a swarm of mosquitos. This case involves a lot of the power brokers in the city. Not just politics, but power, money and social standing. That is what a lot of these people thrive on. Your inquiries have made larger waves than a surfer's paradise. The Caveman is spreading his jam around the entire slice of bread, so that all corners are covered regardless of who becomes chief."

"Except for us."

"Please, He doesn't care about anyone but himself. Period."

"Am I really shutting this down?"

"Hell no. You will make a copy of the murder book and give it to Arroyo. You have 24 hours to kick over as many rocks as possible and see how many lizards run out. After that, become more discrete. I have thirty days to cover for you as you investigate this Kash McCool. After that, the party is over for both of us."

"I'm going to miss you. I have to warn you, I just planted an IED."

"What?"

"The M.E. discovered sleeping pills in all family members, including Dominic."

"If that is the case, why would Dominic take sleeping pills if he was going to use a gun? What were the levels?"

"That's what they are waiting for. Enough to overdose or enough to sedate or enough to take the edge off. There were no pills in the house. The M.E. is prepared to declare Dominic a victim of homicide. When that happens."

"Boom!" They both broke in laughter at The Caveman being caught in a terrible situation.

Alfonso continued, "I'll tell Arroyo that you are writing up a few things for the murder book and he'll have the book tomorrow for him to write up the final report to close it out. He will report back to the Caveman that we have died on the hill and raised the white flag of surrender."

"Arroyo, the puppet and the boss's bitch."

"We have to hope the M.E. holds off for a couple of days on the ruling. You are wasting time. Go brief the gunslinger, and the two of you can saddle up and cause mayhem for the next day. Bring this home." He pointed toward the Cave, "I want the joy of shoving this so far up his ass that he will need a proctologist to find it."

"Roger that."

Chapter Forty

Walking back to her desk, Kate was greeted by Rollins and Cody, who had returned. Rollins, stood up as he pulled the toothpick from his mouth and said, "You survived The Cave."

"Barely."

"Well, I spoke to one of the cast members of the LymRX charade. He said they gave everyone a script and told they were filming a commercial and a promotional video. He said that Kash McCool instructed them to stay in the role the entire time and embrace their part, even if someone questioned them. They provided each person an index card with their screen name, job title and role."

"Really?"

"Yep, and they had one day of screen rehearsals followed by one day of the video. Then they there was a cocktail soiree with booze, food and politicians along with investors. They yelled, cut and everyone left. He said that he had no further contact with anyone."

"Thank you. That provides a little more background." Kate motioned for Cody to follow her. She walked him outside the front entrance of the Blue Monster, past the silhouette memorial for fallen officers.

"She said, "I want to talk away from listening ears."

"I'm all ears."

They walked across the brick paved road of Franklin and entered under the oak canopy of Lykes Park. She heard a car beep their horn as a car dipped into a vacant parking space. She updated Cody on the situation with the case and their timeline.

Cody shook his head in disbelief as he kicked some oak leaves off the walkway. "That asshole. We are going to frag him."

"You mean like they did in Vietnam and roll hand grenades into platoon leaders' tent."

He had a cunning smile. "Exactly, but it's a virtual hand grenade. Everyone is a vulnerable to a mistress."

She grabbed his arm. "Wait, Willard has a mistress? Who is he banging? Someone inside the department?"

Cody extended his open palms. "Calm down. Not that I know of. Everyone has a mistress. Mine is gaming, and yours are horses and your daughter. His is golf."

"Okay, I'm listening? How do we change the trajectory of him closing this case because of his mistress or love affair with golf?"

"That's his vulnerability. Let me think of how to deploy this virtual hand grenade. This will actually be fun. Even if it blows back on us, you are no worse off than going to a district detective, and me? They reassign me to a corporal in D-3 on midnights? He really can't hurt me."

"Maybe I'll join you. Go back to uniform. It was always fun in patrol."

"That's the mindset we have to have."

"Thank you for making the glass half full."

"My pay remains the same. I sleep in a comfy bed without the fear of RPGs or nighttime raids from the Taliban."

"Thanks for having my 6."

"I have your 360!"

Chapter Forty-One

Looking down on her phone, Kate read a new email that arrived from the bank investigator. Kash McCool had just used his debit card to withdraw $300 from an ATM at the Dallas Ft. Worth Airport.

Panic hit Kate. If he had made it to DFW, he could fly to anywhere in the world. There were no charges pending against Kash. As long as he had his passport, he and his crypto currency could set up shop anywhere. His only concern would be after charges were filed and if the country he had settled, had an extradition treaty with the U.S.

Maybe he had flown out on a private charter under the radar of the police. But why stop in Dallas? He should have landed at a more innocuous airport in the vicinity without the concern of being spotted by the law. There had to be a dozen small airports in the area without the scrutiny that DFW would maintain.

Homicide was her focus, but she knew Kash had been more involved in a financial fraud. Kash McCool's life was nothing but a façade. He had a fake business with fake employees and equipment. Even where he lived was fake, including his staged furniture and furnishings. Investigating the fraud would take months to get all the supporting documents.

Had Kash's fraud been uncovered by Dominic Marchetti and resulted in the death of the entire family? The love of money is the root of all evil. Many fraudsters' addiction to money had resulted in murder to cover their crimes. Kate did not know if Kash had resorted to killing, but it would explain his sudden departure and going off the grid.

When she had been out at the FBI visiting Roxanne Snelling in the past, she passed the squad devoted to white collar fraud. They filled every cubicle with banker boxes of documents. Everyone was trying to go digital, but on a wide-ranging financial scheme, you had to have paper to sort. She had heard one agent complaining about the lack of toner cartridges for the printer. She could only imagine how much ink and paper filled those boxes. She was not enthused about working a complex fraud case. She knew she would need help from the FBI to open that can of slinkys.

As soon as any part of the fraud was started through the internet, he could be charged with Florida Communications Fraud Act. That statute applied to anyone using a communications technology in a scheme to defraud.

She had not even accessed his business records and analyze what his financial statements purported, but she suspected he was lying worse than the carnival palm reader. Nor did she know who the victims were and where they were located. She knew that Brian Poole was an investor. How much did Poole invest and what was he promised in return for the infusion of capital?

This was going to take time and go outside the boundary of 24 hours. Kate penciled out a list of what they could do before she handed the case over to Arroyo. Her mind drifted to Arroyo bragging to his pretty wife that he had this big case that he had to close because Kick Ass Alexander had no game. The pretty wife would post in the Facebook group of the WAGS and brag about her husband's exploits. Kate realized she could not listen to boo birds and had to focus on the immediate investigative leads.

She called the bank investigator and asked if they could pull the ATM camera recording from DFW airport and forward the recording. Unlike the old days when film had to be developed, or onsite recordings were used, in today's market, everything was digital and stored on the cloud for easy retrieval.

Chapter Forty-Two

After the phone call from Rodney Upton that disturbed her Zen moment along the riverfront, she now had to look into the unsavory character, Billy Savage, that supposedly Dominic Marchetti feared. She sat back at her desk and started running the name. She also asked the analysts for help to make any connections between the two.

The analysts called back and had no established links between Marchetti and Savage. They sent over everything that they could dig up on Savage. He had a business called Savage's Landscaping. What does a lawn guy have anything to do with a finance guy?

He had a previous arrest several years earlier for a DUI, but no other arrests. His business and residence address were one and the same in Riverview, Florida. Kate looked at her watch and decided that maybe she could text Savage while he was still at work and ask for an appointment for an estimate. If he didn't respond, then she could stop in Riverview, which was southwest of Tampa on the way home.

The text worked. Kate corresponded via text and told Billy that she would meet him at an address that was next to the Marchetti's. She grabbed Cody and drove to Hyde Park to meet Savage. Right on cue, a beefy black pickup with a crew cab towing a sliver trailer with a name stenciled on the side, "Savage's Landscaping" parked on the curb. The image of colorful butterflies and grass offset the harshness of the name. Three males sat in the passenger seats eating food from wrappers.

A burly man wearing a straw cowboy hat jumped down from the truck. He tipped his hat and smiled at Kate.

"Howdy, I'm Billy Savage. As you probably know, I take care of your neighbor's house."

She could tell he had a pinch of chew in his mouth. "I know." She pointed at his belt buckle. "Do you still rodeo?"

He smiled and looked down while kicking with the point of his boots at the ground like he was kicking at old memories. He looked back up, "No ma'am.

My bones aren't as flexible as they were once a time ago. I made the circuit throughout the state."

"Having bones not flexible goes for most of us."

"How can I help you today?"

"Billy, we're actually police detectives and I wanted to ask about the Marchetti residence." As she pointed to the murder house.

"Yes, ma'am. How can I help?"

"Did you hear what happened to them?"

He tilted his head slightly like an inquisitive dog. "No, ma'am."

Kate thought that was odd. It was a big story. "What was your relationship with Dominic Marchetti?"

"If that's the fella's name, I only exchange pleasantries with him if we crossed paths. But I ain't seen him too often. It was Miss Carol that I did business with. Are they okay?"

"So, you never had any problems with him?"

"He shook his head. No, ma'am."

"Do you know where you were Monday morning, starting at midnight?"

He rubbed his chin. "Yes, ma'am in bed. I get up at 6:00 am and hitch up the trailer at 6:30. I pickup the guys a mile away, we stop for breakfast at Wawa and drive to Hyde Park. We usually get to the first customer about 8:00 am and start to work."

"Do you drive the Selmon Expressway?" Kate asked, knowing his SunPass toll transponder would back up that story as well as transactions at Wawa.

"Yes, ma'am."

"What time do you go to bed?"

"I usually get home and eat at 6:00 pm. Watch a little TV, have a few beers and climb into bed with the Mrs. around 10:00 pm.

"When was the last time that you communicated with either Mr. or Mrs. Marchetti?"

"A month or so ago? I just cut their lawn and many others here." As he swept his hand in an arcing gesture.

"Are you aware that they are dead?"

His eyebrows arched with surprise. "No ma'am. Both of them?"

"Yes, and the children."

He removed his hat and lowered his head. "I am truly sorry for that, ma'am. I didn't know anything about that. I don't keep up with the news much."

"Thank you for your time."

"Yes, ma'am." He sauntered off to the pickup truck and drove off.

Kate looked over at Cody. "What did you think?"

"Call me crazy, but I'd say he dint know squat."

"I agree. He's just an old cowboy busting his ass. I believe we were dispatched on a wild goose chase by Upton. I think that is so we tie ourselves up chasing our shadows, while pressure is mounting to close down the investigation."

Chapter Forty-Three

Once in the car, Cody pulled out his digital recorder and a cellphone. "So here is the deal. I am going to use my burner phone."

"Wait, you have a burner phone?" She put her hand on his elbow and tugged a bit.

His face exposed the slyness. "It comes in handy with some Tinder date that gets a little too clingy. It's only after a couple of dates that they get past the burner."

"So, you use Tinder?"

"It cuts out the pressure of fix-ups or fishing at the bourbon well. This way, you can find people through the app and find similar interests. You make initial contact through the app. It's like a virtual meat market. You arrange to meet for a coffee and go from there. You should try?"

She put her hand to her chest. "Me? Ahh no."

"You said that so judgmental."

"Telling me you have a burner phone tells me what I need to know. How many get past the burner phone?"

"Not many. Okay, let's get back on target. I'm going to call The Caveman."

"Aren't you worried he will recognize your voice?"

"Nope. I have a voice changing app, so that I can alter the pitch of my voice."

"Who are you? You have a burner phone and a voice changing app to alter the delivery of your voice. Who does that?" Surprise erupted across her face.

"I do." As he grinned.

"You are, as they say, a box of chocolates. Full of surprises."

Cody started the recording with the date, and time and each detective identified themselves as witnesses. Cody dialed the phone number for the cellphone of The Caveman and engaged the voice changer with a higher pitch voice.

"Hello, Lieutenant Willard?"

"Who's calling?"

"Yes, this is Sherman Hawthorne. I am on the board at the Palma de Mallorca Golf Club." Cody was serious.

"Oh yes, Mr. Hawthorne, how can I be of assistance?"

Cody nodded and mouthed, got him, "You can call me Sherm. May I call you Jack?"

"Yes, Sherm."

"Well, Jack, the reason that I am calling is the club is very thankful to you for your handling of this tragic case involving the Marchetti family. From my understanding of this case, it was pretty straightforward homicide and suicide. Poor Dom had made some terrible life decisions that ended tragically. There was no point dragging this out for its obvious conclusion. That detective was acting like Columbo and wouldn't let it go. She really made quite an annoyance at the club and disrupted the harmony in the club and the neighborhood."

"Well, the case has been reassigned and will be concluded tomorrow afternoon."

"That is why I'm calling Jack. We had heard through your chain of command that you made that decisive decision to clear the logjam so to speak and bring this to a conclusion, so that we can have the memorial service and move on. We here at Palma de Mallorca would like to thank you. Do you play golf?"

"Yes, I love golf. I consistently shoot in the 80s."

"Why, that's quite impressive, not to mention being the supervisor over the homicide unit. The upper echelon must think a great deal of you. I am sure that you will continue to move up the ranks. I can tell you we will pass along our satisfaction to the mayor and the next chief."

"Why thank you, Sherm. I certainly appreciate your endorsement."

"You have certainly earned it, Jack. I want to offer you a complimentary foursome at the club. Just pull up to the valet stand and ask for me. If I'm not there, I'll leave an envelope. When you decide to use that foursome, let me know so that I can put your expenses on my tab at the club. Drink and eat as much as you and your friends want. Let's say we meet at nine tomorrow?"

"Yes, that's great, Sherm. I'll see you then. Thank you so very much. This is wonderful."

"The thanks are all mine for removing that detective."

"Sometimes, we have to make hard decisions. I look forward to meeting you."

"Likewise. Goodbye."

Cody ended the call and spoke into the recorder with the ending time. He and Kate fist bumped each other. They both laughed with exhilaration.

Cody said, "The fragging has begun. We have rolled the grenade into the tent. It won't detonate until tomorrow."

"Sherman Hawthorne?"

"An officer in the army that no one liked. It was easy to get into the personality."

"This reminded me of *Ferris Bueller's Day Off* with the recordings."

"A classic."

Chapter Forty-Four

The email dinged on Kate's phone. She opened the attachment from the bank investigator containing the photo of the ATM surveillance photo at DFW. Kate and Cody leaned in as Kate enlarged the image. They looked at a male with a black ball cap, a black COVID mask, and wearing sunglasses.

Cody said, "Yep, let's put his wanted photo out. A man wearing sunglasses and a mask is all set to rob a bank. What do you think, is it, Kash?"

"I don't think so. It looks like the ears are paler than his face. I think this person put makeup on to darken their skin. The forehead looks different as well as the length of the earlobes. Eyebrows are definitely different. Kash has dark, full brows. Not the same. Now, I couldn't testify in court on that, but I believe he sent his credit card to a buddy to use in an effort to throw a red herring our way and distract us."

"I agree now that you point this out. Besides, if he is using crypto, why go to an ATM using your own card to draw attention that perhaps you're flying elsewhere? In theory, he could purchase a plane ticket with cash as long as he used his driver's license as an identification. It would take time to go through the airlines for passenger manifests."

"Where is Kash? He is good. I am impressed."

She snapped her fingers, "Tinder or is it Match? We can subpoena his account."

"If he had one. Match is more for folks looking for serious relationships. Tinder is more Kash's style of casual dating. You should join Match."

"Oh, so you think I am a Match type person? No, thank you."

"I'm just saying that you appear to be more the type of wanting a meaningful romance than a casual hookup. It would give you options outside the Blue Monster."

She snapped her head back. "What have you heard?"

He put up his hands in surrender. "Nothing actually. Well, I heard that you don't play inside the sandbox. You are one of the few. Take my ex-wife. She married me because there were few other options outside of the law enforcement field. Then she exchanged me for another cop. It's tough to meet and establish relationships outside the department. If it makes you feel any better, most people find you desirous."

"Desirous?"

"Attractive, pretty..."

"Like they want to get into my pants?"

"Nope, not going there. I did not say that."

"Hmmm, okay. Let's see what Tinder has to say. I also want to get a search warrant for his apartment."

"We've already been there?" as he raised an eyebrow.

"That was a safety check. He left in a hurry. Maybe he left something behind."

Kate called Fiona Quinn at the State Attorney's Office and explained that she needed more subpoenas and a search warrant.

Fiona said, "Girl, I just want you to know this case is seismic. I have to report directly to the boss, but Mr. McClung came in earlier and said you were closing the case and not to speak to you until I received the final report."

"We're talking now."

"No. You called me and I answered the phone."

"Okay, I have until tomorrow to run a few things out. Then Felix Arroyo will have the case reassigned to him and he will close it as a homicide-suicide."

"Okay, so the race is on. Why don't we have your new sidekick, Cody, request and write the affidavit and the subpoena request so that I can say with a straight face that I did not facilitate your investigation."

"I like that idea."

"You have pissed people off."

"I have disrupted the status quo of the elite class and no one likes to be embarrassed. I think when this is over, we will have caused a great deal of humiliation."

"Okay, send Cody. The on-call judge is Perkins. He won't be a problem."

"Thank you."

Chapter Forty-Five

Tapping away at the keyboard, Kate completed the affidavit for the search warrant to search for articles of a crime, namely plans for murder, fraudulent documents relating to LymRX Technology and any documents in furtherance of said crimes and related to plans to flee the jurisdiction. She spelled out the linkage between the Marchetti's and Kash McCool, as well as the fraudulent business operations. To stay under the radar at the State Attorney's Office, everything was written with Cody being the affiant.

Judge Cyrus Perkins was the presiding judge. Kate had become concerned about the level of interference from forces outside the department. Everyone was keeping an arm's reach, but their impact was real. All she wanted was the truth. They only wanted to protect their power. It was a backstabber's club with no loyalty to anything or anyone but themselves.

Fortunately, Judge Perkins appeared to swim in a different pond and would be less likely to be looking out for the power brokers. Fiercely independent, he always stood up for the common people. At least, she hoped.

Kate drove the few blocks to the Hillsborough State Attorney's Office and dropped Cody curbside. She knew this would take a little while for Cody to meet Fiona, have her read over the affidavit, and walk across the street to the judge's office, explain the case to him, and hopefully watch him scribble his signature approving the search.

While she sat in the car listening to some Chris Stapleton music and humming along, she looked at her phone and pulled up her favorites. She took a breath, lowered the volume and called Trent Sellers.

The comforting voice answered, "Hello stranger. How is my favorite police detective doing?"

"Lonely, tired, sad, angry, and frustrated."

"Oh my. It sounds like you need therapy."

She smiled, "Most definitely. You wouldn't know a good therapist?"

"Well, let me think. I do, but from the seriousness of these symptoms, it may take more than one session."

"More than one? Hmm. Patti Moon from the Over the Moon Stables said I need a puppy."

"Oh, like a service dog. Patti is very insightful. She taught me how to ride a horse."

"I remember when you rode in like Rip Wheeler from Yellowstone to save the day."

"I could be your service animal until you get a puppy."

"You could? Tonight?"

"Sure."

"Do you still have some Papa's Pilar Rum?"

"Blonde or dark?"

"Definitely dark. I'll call when I'm on the way."

"Me and Papa will be waiting."

She thought about her vacation with Trent to Key West and their discovery of Papa's Pilar Rum on their tour of the Hemingway Rum Distillery. That introduction of rum allowed her to ease her anxiety about the trip. She had previously ridden motorcycles with Jake before his death and they fished and dived off the Key's. Those memories were softened and replaced with recent memories of sightseeing, riding mopeds, good food, rum and soft sheets.

Patti was right. She needed that someone to be in her life to provide balance. She had a two-dimensional existence between Brittany and work. Even a stool has three legs for support and Trent was a good man, despite being placed on hold by her fears of involvement. She was relieved that he was so willing for her to make an after-hours visit.

She watched Cody walking briskly towards the car, wearing a smile of satisfaction and waving the paper like the winning lottery ticket. He jumped into the passenger seat with an enormous sigh of relief.

"I got it."

"I see that. Any problems?"

"I explained the case to the judge. He read over it, signed it and said good luck."

"Yep. You got your cherry popped. Congratulations on the first of what will be many in the future."

"We will see after my fragging party tomorrow. Thank you for your help. You essentially wrote this, but now, because of an excellent teacher, I know the process."

"Let's go see Kash's apartment."

Chapter Forty-Six

The leasing agent, Alicia Howard, opened the door to Kash McCool's apartment. The two detectives called out his name and announced themselves in case he had returned. They knew that was doubtful. All indications were that he was on the run. By law, Cody read the search warrant out loud despite Kash not being there. A quirky requirement of the Florida law. They told Alicia that they would lock the door and notify her when they were leaving.

Kate said, "The first time I saw a search warrant executed was by Greg Stout before he became the PBA President and retired. Funny guy, who always had a joke to tell. So he had a search warrant for an abandoned suitcase at a hotel on Bruce B Downs. He had to read the search warrant to a suitcase. It was just the two of us and a Samsonite."

"I hope the suitcase didn't talk back."

"Nope. It was holding too many secrets." They both chuckled.

Cody took the second bedroom and bath, while Kate began her search in the master bedroom bath. Toothbrush was gone. Medicine cabinet empty aside from a bottle of ibuprofen. For a single male's bath, it was orderly and clean. Perhaps he had a cleaner. She looked under the sink. Nope, there was the cleaning chemicals and rubber gloves.

She moved into the bedroom. She had previously noted he did not make the bed, but at the same time, he was not a restless sleeper. It was almost like a turndown service with the blanket folded over and divot from his head in the pillow instead of a chocolate. He wasn't too restless. Unless he used zolpidem tartrate to knock himself out like the Marchetti's. She could see the indentations from the missing suitcase and nothing else appeared out of place or disturbed since their last visit. She ran her hand between the mattress and box spring and looked under the bed. Nothing.

She pulled out all the drawers out of the nightstand and dresser. Aside from the few contents, there was nothing concealed. He lived like a temporary resident of a hotel.

They both converged at the same time in the living room and echoed to each other, "Nothing."

Kate began pulling the cushions out of the sofa and the chairs. Cody looked under the dining room table and each chair. Kate opened a drawer to the end table. Inside the drawer were some papers pertaining to the lease and a slick-looking brochure to LymRX Technology. She flipped through what is known as a presentation pitch deck, meant to be shown to interested parties for investments or affiliated marketing, clients and the sort.

She sat down and began reading. The first page about was about Kash. She knew he was a college dropout from the FBI. This description alluded to his striving towards his Ph.D. in bio-engineering. He may have strived for it, but one semester in college falls short of his doctoral thesis. The description continued that he left the fertile fields of Silicon Valley to return to Texas, where he focused on starting a technology company focused on developing rare mineral extraction methods that would create a future generational paradigm shift in technological advancements in green energy. After developing the success of the company, he sold the company to investors. She laughed at whoever writes these descriptions. He worked in a boiler room selling fabricated lithium deposits in Texas and the company was closed by the FBI.

Dr. Woodruff Spencer was listed as the co-founder. He had an impressive resume of educational and professional achievements as a neurologist. He had conducted vast research into neurological disorders and had witnessed many patients suffer irreparable harm from the ravages of Lyme and ALS and gave up his thriving practice to focus on research and development of life altering therapeutics to combat the advancement of the diseases.

She looked up the doctor online. It wasn't long before she found Alan Woodruff Spencer. He dropped his first name. He also voluntarily dropped his Texas medical board license because of a painkiller addiction. He was also convicted by the Feds for Medicare and Medicaid fraud. Kate wondered if he was still wearing an ankle bracelet and figured he was the man at the ATM wearing a little darker skin foundation makeup.

On the next page were three paragraphs. One for Lyme, one for ALS, one for M.S. and the impact on patients. There was a timeline that was one big lie on the founding of the company and the research and development of the therapeutics.

The next page was a vague description of the product they were developing. Sponges locally harvested in Tarpon Springs, known as the sponge capital of the world, have found to be a treasure trove of biochemical compounds used in their highly evolved defenses. The tectitethya crypta sponge has previously been used to develop compounds used in anti-viral, anti-cancer, the HIV drug AZT and Remdesivir used to treat Covid-19.

Bioactive compounds harvested in the Amazon Rainforest and combined with synthetically produced compounds using technology advanced by Covid-19 research and antibodies harvested from survivors have shown tremendous potential and progress on inhibiting the advancement of these wretched diseases with stunning results. Wow, that was a mouthful of nonsense.

There was a picture of Kash pointing to a tree in the jungle and a closeup of a flowering plant growing on a tree. Kate wondered if they photoshopped Kash into the picture. There was also a picture of Kash holding a sponge in front of the sponge docks of Tarpon Springs. Kate figured that was an actual photo, since Tarpon Springs was only thirty miles north.

She knew the sponge angle was another ploy to convince investors that LymRX Technology would benefit the local community and Florida. She looked up the tectitethya crypta sponge and found that it was primarily found in the Caribbean and the brackish waters of Florida. It is also a crumbly sponge found along reefs. Probably not so much in Tarpon Springs. Certainly not enough to harvest, and definitely not like the sponge he was holding.

There were pictures of laboratory settings which were probably picked off the internet images along with a mound of sponges. Kate looked at the financial page of assets, fixed assets, liabilities, and stockholder equity. Reflecting back to her class in accounting, she knew they had zero fixed assets because the company didn't own a single microscope or test-tube. It was a fraud.

She handed the brochure to Cody and stood up from the sofa.

"Here, have a look. This is nice furniture. I'll say that he had good taste."

"Like the wine. It's the type that is used to impress aficionados and those who shop and eat at Bern's. I don't think that you will find anything under $50 and most going north of a hundred."

"Let's call it a night. One lousy brochure, but it again shows the con he was spinning. We can take photos as we are leaving to go with our arrival photos to prove that we didn't damage anything. On the receipt, document the one business presentation pitch deck. Let's go to the memorial service. I would like to see who is coming and to meet Carol's family. Then it is the end of the night."

Chapter Forty-Seven

They drove separate cars to the funeral home outside the northern territory of Tampa. Alongside a busy road with retail and commercial development, they found the few remaining spaces in a busy parking lot.

Visiting funeral homes was like a knife in the gut of Kate. Every funeral home seemed like the same architect designed them, furnished by the same interior decorator, and every funeral director attended the same school of solemnity. Not to mention the awful background music. The consistency also brought back the same terrible memories.

As she walked towards the final resting place for the Marchetti family, like all the other funeral homes, there was a small group gathering just outside the building, smoking and vaping. Once she pushed through the door, there was a throng of grieving friends and relatives. Aged from school chums through the elderly. Some looked lost, while others were engaged in willful banter.

As she entered the viewing room, Kate gave a head bob to Cody to follow her. They walked to the front, where a table provided a platform for the four urns in front of a framed photo of the individual and another group of family photos of happier times. None included Valerie McCormick.

The two detectives said a silent prayer and moved to the receiving line to offer their condolences. Someone that McCormick introduced as her agent was sitting next to her. Carol's parents sat giving mostly fake smiles to the visitors. Mr. and Mrs. Swoboda looked numb. Kate knew exactly how they felt. These were overwhelming events.

They receded to the back of the room and found two vacant upholstered chairs to occupy. Kate noted the celebrity level status of the visitors. Even the Stimpson brothers appeared. Kate wondered if they would write off the debt owed by Dom or sue the estate. Flip a coin.

The Krewe of Kingsmen sauntered in, wearing sad faces. Funerals will do that. They would not be throwing beads. One of their friends was dead. Leading the way was Brian Poole, and his caboose was Rodney Upton. Melvin Storms trailed the group as he gave a head nod to the detectives.

A clergyman started the service with a prayer for the departed and one for those left behind. A few folks stood up and shared their memories. Thankfully, Kate was relieved at the brevity of the service.

As she stood to make her escape, she noticed one visitor that appeared to be more emotional than anyone else. His unkempt, bushy hair matched his slouchy clothing. Whoever he was, he stuck out like a zebra in a coral of horses.

Kate tried to make her way through the crowd. She felt like she was exiting a Disney ride of tightly packed thrill seekers. She could see the man of her interest at the front of the crowd moving further away.

As she reached the parking lot, she saw the man enter an older, faded maroon Saturn. She closed the distance once she broke free of the crowd. The tail lights shined bright and then followed by the white reverse lights. Kate picked up her pace as the car backed up. The reverse lights turned off and the brake lights dimmed. Kate held up her cellphone and snapped a picture of the rear of the car as it headed out the parking lot.

Cody called out to Kate and said, "Who was that?"

"I don't know. But we are going to find out. In this tidy crowd, he stood out like a pimple on my face. He was in an almost sobbing fit as he skedaddled. We will work on him tomorrow after the fragging party."

Cody flashed a mischievous smile and said, "I look forward to that. See you tomorrow."

She text Trent that she was on the way. Her mood lightened.

Chapter Forty-Eight

Jamming to the Brothers Osborne, Kate pulled up into the driveway of Trent Sellers. Kate called her mother.

"Hi Mom. If you don't mind, I have an early start in the morning and I'm going to spend the night with a friend if you don't mind watching Brittney for the night."

"Not at all, honey. Tell Trent, I mean your friend, hello."

Kate smiled. Mom always seemed to know, "Thanks Mom, I will."

She opened the trunk and reached into a duffle bag of extra clothes. She always carried extra clothes, never knowing when a crime scene would contaminate her clothes or she had an unexpected invitation to spend the night with someone special. She shoved a few items into her backpack and slammed the trunk closed.

She rang the doorbell, and the smiling face of comfort opened the door. They embraced like old friends and Kate clutched tighter enjoying the moment a bit longer. Less like friends and more like lovers consoling each other. A quick peck on the lips and they separated.

Trent said, "I was just finishing up. I have a surprise."

Kate looked at the kitchen counter, and there were two plates. Each had a hot pretzel and a jar of Nutella in between and set next to the canteen style bottle of Papa's Pilar rum.

"Just like at Taps after the play at the Straz Center."

She sat down at the bar and unleashed her ponytail. She fluffed her hair with her fingers. Reaching into the jar of hazelnut chocolate, scooping a spoonful and plopped it on the plate next to the warm pretzel. She heard Trent depress the icemaker and tumble a few cubes into an old-fashioned size glass, which he set down in front of her. He spun the cap of the rum still attached by a chain and splashed the dark rum over the cubes.

Trent swirled the glass and said, "To our friendship."

She smiled and clinked her glass to his. "To friends."

Kate took a small inhale of the sweet, robust scent and tasted the balanced, flavored rum. "Mmmm. My gosh, I've missed this."

"The rum? It's available in most stores now."

"No. This. All of this. You."

She stood and came around the counter to meet Trent. She looked into his almond-colored eyes and moved her lips towards his. The warmth and softness of his lips sent shivers through her body. She could smell his cologne, which was like a comforting old sweater. They kissed passionately as Trent framed her face in his hands.

They separated and Kate said, "Mmm. That too was good."

"Yes, it certainly was."

They returned to either side of the counter, breaking pieces of the pretzel and dipping each into the chocolate. They sipped on the dark rum and caught up on events in each other's life. For the first time in a long time, Kate escaped from life and work. It enthralled her with that feeling of freedom and no worries for the moment.

"I do have one work related question. A Trent 101 inquiry on the mindset of conman."

"They come from all kinds of background. Good families, dysfunctional families and everything in between. They have an obsessive pursuit of power, money, status and relevancy. Nothing will stop them from achieving their goals. They suffer from a delusional belief in their abilities. Obviously narcissistic and some suffer from psychopathy. They believe they are special people and have low empathy. If they are suffering psychopathy, they would be devoid of a conscience."

"Thank you, Professor. Capable of killing?"

"They are generally not violent. To conceal or eliminate a barrier to their ability to succeed? In some cases, yes. One case that comes to mind is Christian Gerhartsreiter, who claimed he was part of the Rockefeller's. He killed a couple in California who may have been on to him to for defrauding one of the victim's elderly mother. In one of his false identities that he assumed, he had the gall to use the social security number of David Berkowitz, the Son of Sam. He is not the only killer conman."

"How about the entire family, including children?"

"Killing children while they slept? They would probably be psychopaths or sociopaths. Were they born with wickedness or was wickedness cast upon them?"

"Wicked the play!"

"Exactly. That was a good time."

"Yes."

Trent poured more rum, and they continued talking and dipping a pretzel into the gob of chocolate. The conversation changed to wonderful memories of their time together and the acceptance that Kate had realized that perhaps she needed a more meaningful relationship in her life to offer more balance.

Trent walked around and slid his hand behind her neck and drew her in for a long, passionate kiss. When they separated for a moment, they held each other's gaze and smiled. He took her hand and guided her towards the bedroom.

Chapter Forty-Nine

The next morning, Kate was tapping the steering wheel like a drummer for Brad Paisley. She knew she wore a glow that could not be concealed. She realized she had been depriving herself of joy for far too long. Yes, she had baggage, but Trent understood the additional luggage and was accepting of the extra parcels in the trunk that were attached to Kate. He was a keeper.

Kate steered past downtown and weaved her way south towards the golf course to meet up with Cody. She drove down MacDill Avenue through the old money neighborhood and turned into the parking lot of the Palma de Mallorca Country Club.

She met Cody, and they walked up to the valet, whose hair was a shade lighter than strawberry. Cody handed the valet an envelope with the name Jack Willard from Sherman Hawthorne written on the outside. "Hey, if I give you a twenty, when this bald guy pulls up in a gray Ford explorer that looks like a cop car asking for this guy Sherman Hawthorne, could you give this envelope to him, please?" The redheaded valet looked at the envelope, the twenty and the two detectives and said, "Sure."

"Just tell him that Mr. Hawthorne couldn't make it and said to give him this envelope."

The valet nodded and said, "No problem. What if he doesn't come?"

"Oh, he will. Trust me. If not, you just made an easy twenty. Thank you."

The two detectives walked back to Cody's car. When Kate opened the door, the pine scent from the air fresheners wafted upward.

"I smell the pine trees are working."

"That and a good cleaning." He looked over at Kate. "If you don't mind me saying, you look happy. You must have had a good sleep last night. Or you're so excited to attend your first frag party."

She smiled, "I've come to conclusions about my life and come to terms with a few things. I am set to open the door to new experiences. One being this fragging party. By the way, speaking of fragging, I planted an IED on Willard."

"IED? How so?"

"The M.E. found sleeping pills in the bloodstream. Depending on the volume and add in the inconsistencies of the suicide theory, he is inclined to rule it a homicide."

"So if The Caveman closes this case as a homicide-suicide and the M.E. rules it straight up homicide, Willard will have some explaining and a face full of egg."

"Exactly. I said this case had bad juju."

"Okay. Here we go. Showtime."

They watched as Lieutenant Jack "The Caveman" Willard drove his city issued Ford Explorer to the valet. Cody took some snaps with his camera and then started a video. Once the valet handed the envelope through the window to Willard, Cody jumped out of the car and walked out to flag down the supervisor. When the SUV came to a stop, Cody walked around with a cheerful face.

"Hi Boss. What are you doing here?"

"I came to meet someone, but they weren't here."

"Ahhh. Have you ever heard the term being manscaped?"

Willard's face looked puzzled. "No. I don't think so."

"It means that your balls just got shaved. Not that you had much, anyway. That envelope that you received from Sherman Hawthorne with a foursome is valued in excess of five hundred dollars if sold at a charity auction. That gift was in direct relationship for your efforts in closing down an investigation. A homicide investigation and reassigning a detective, a female detective. Have you not heard of the hashtag MeToo? I'm not the one that enjoys backstabbing my own, but for you, I will make an exception. I could go to internal affairs and the press, but I would rather that you reassign Alexander and me back to the Marchetti case. I will also expect you to run interference for us and grow a spine."

Before he could answer, Cody held up his phone and showed the pictures and then played a small snippet of the recording from the conversation with Sherman. The furious anger flashed through The Caveman's face and then you could almost read his mind as he considered his options. Fear became more pervasive and then desperation.

He finally spoke, "Listen to me, you little asshole. I am going to make your life miserable. You and your sidekick are done. I can make counter charges you attempted to extort me."

"Yes, you could. It would be mutually assured destruction. We would all go up in a mushroom cloud of smoke. Only ashes of our existence. But you see, me, I don't care. I would go back to patrol, the Army or whatever. When you've slept on a cot in a dirty hooch in Afghanistan and lost a lot of friends along the way, do you really think you have anything of value so great to me? Do you think that I would forego justice for this case and to not right a wrong? What have you to lose?"

"Goodbye."

The Caveman dropped the car into gear as he rolled the window up and drove away. Kate walked up to Cody. "What did he say?"

"Not sure. I have his attention, and he will consider his options. None are good."

"What was in the envelope?"

"Two brochures. One for golf lessons and one for manscaping?"

"You did not."

"Yep, sure did."

They both burst out laughing as Kate slapped Cody's arm.

Chapter Fifty

After leaving in a celebratory feeling, Cody and Kate drove the short distance from the golf course to Davis Island and to Brian Poole's home. Pool answered the door, this time wearing a loose-fitting blue linen shirt covering his tattooed body and with his manbun still balanced on his head. He waved them in and they followed him to a very modern living room overlooking a pool and Tampa Bay. Lots of straight lines, white and some gray tones for accent matched the exterior.

The two detectives dropped into a gray microfiber sofa with chrome accents.

Poole lounged on a sofa across from them with his arms stretched across the top. "How can I help you folks again?"

Kate leaned forward, her hands clasped together. "It was an awfully sad event last night."

He nodded in agreement, "Tragic."

Kate leaned forward and asked, "How well do you know Kash McCool?"

He smiled and said, "Very well. I consider him a business partner as well as a close friend."

"How long have you known him?"

"About four months. Ever since he arrived here from Texas."

"And where did you meet?"

"Under the thatched roof of Four Green Fields."

"The original or in Hixon Park?"

"The original on Platt Street. He was a regular. Sometimes he was there before I arrived and sometimes would come in after. After a while, we struck up a conversation. We had similar interests, and we hit it off."

"What interests?'

"We liked the same beer, shared an interest in business, the tech world, hockey, pretty girls and his business model was dear to my heart, since I lost my step-brother to Lyme Disease that had been misdiagnosed as ALS. Why all this interest in Kash?"

"We don't think he is what he represents. When was the last time that you spoke to him?"

"We traded messages after Dom and his family's tragedy. He has kind of gone dark since. What do you mean, he is not what he represents?"

"You were an investor in his company? How many others?"

"Yes, I was, and several other folks that understood the potential benefit."

"How about his girlfriend? Did you ever meet her?"

"Beautiful girl. Jazz was her name. I think she was a model."

"Do you know where she lives?"

"I think she lived in Ybor. Okay, so I've patiently answered your questions. What is going on?"

"We believe he is running a fraud. Have you been to the LymRX Technology office?"

He laughed, "Sure. Top-notch research facility. I was there for the grand opening. They had already been open for a period of time, but this was the open house blow it off the hinge's celebration."

"Who was at the open house?"

"The Primo Caterers. The best in town. Some of the other investors and typical politicians were there to gloat and suck up free food and liquor. They had a string quartet too. It was a nice presentation."

"We were there yesterday. No employees. It was dark. All the equipment was a façade. Rented. All of it. The same for his apartment. All rental furniture. Kash left in a hurry after the murders. He drove to the airport and abandoned his car, and he left his cell phone behind. He converted a lot of his cash to crypto."

"You're shitting me?" as he leaned forward.

"Nope."

He sat back and exhaled heavily, while looking up at the ceiling. His right hand rubbed the back of his neck. "I saw the financials before I invested."

"It was never an audited accounting. He made the numbers up and put them into a spreadsheet. He really didn't have a pot to piss in."

You could see the denial working through his brain and the result was panic as the realization that he had been played. Then denial again, "No, I met with Dr. Spencer, who had synthesized the drug. Kash was working on his PhD. In bioengineering. Dr. Spencer and Kash had met with a shaman in the Peruvian Amazon and found the Matico plant leaves used as an anti-inflammatory in the body. Suma to enhance the immune system and Lapacho to treat infections along with antibodies from recovered patients and drugs the laboratory produced and compounded together with miraculous results. Not to mention the locally sourced sponges from Tarpon Springs that they extracted from proven compounds used in many other applications. I met two patients that had been healed. I saw the before pictures when they were both wheelchair bound. I also saw the pictures from the Amazon. They had to paddle in a canoe to meet this shaman."

"I don't know about canoe and the jungle cruise. He hired actors from a local casting company. Did you know that Dr. Spencer, who dropped using his first name Alan, surrendered his medical license because of his addiction to opioids and was arrested for Medicaid and Medicare fraud? Kash didn't make it past his first year of college. He dropped out."

Poole asked, "He had entered into a contract with Christos Georgeakopoulos, who owns a sponge harvesting company in Tarpon. You know that Tarpon Springs is the sponge capitol of the world?"

"So, I've heard."

Cody jumped in. "Kash McCool was involved in a company called Black Water Investments that sold stakes in nonexistent lithium deposits for electric vehicles. He was the top salesman and the prosecution's star witness."

They let that dangle for Poole to process. Kate broke the silence, "Do you have any reason to believe he would have been involved in the Marchetti deaths?"

Poole flexed his hands behind his neck and rubbed the back of his head and let out with another puff of air, "I don't know anything anymore. We were all in the krewe together. Dom was planning to come over to LymRX Technology to become their CFO. He said he was tired of working at Hercules. They seemed to get along, and I saw no animosity between them."

"Where were you the night of the murders?"

"Here. I had a small group for dinner. Kash and Jazz were here. There were six of us. Kash seemed to be a little off. Kind of distracted, like he had something on his mind or bothering him. I even asked him if everything was all right and said he was just tired. Everyone left around eight before the storm blew in."

"How about you? What did you do the rest of the night?"

"I went to bed with Krystal Lincoln. She left after breakfast." He winked at Cody. "You can confirm with her. She works at a doctor's office. I can give you the number. Have you checked his boat?"

"Boat?"

"Yeah. Port 32 on Gandy. It was a beauty. A thirty-six-foot Baja Outlaw. It had a small cabin. They sell for north of three hundred thousand. That thing would scoot. I think it was called the…" There was a hesitant pause. "The Robber was the name of the boat."

Kate nodded and said, "Okay, thanks, we will check it out."

He hung his head in disgust. The detectives stood up and thanked him for his help. With a great deal of effort, Poole pushed himself out of the chair and walked them to the door.

Chapter Fifty-One

As they stood outside under the ancient oak trees, Kate looked at Cody and asked, "What did you think?"

"I think he got duped into a professional con. He may have made millions when he sold his company, but he is a flash in the pan like a lot of app developers. They strike gold like a one hit wonder boy band. They sell out to some hedge fund for a bazillion dollars, but it does not mean he was adept at business."

"Kash does his homework and identifies Poole as vulnerable because of his step-brother dying. He finds his interest and schedule and then starts blowing smoke up his ass. I did almost laugh when he was talking about the boat scooting and..."

"The Robber is the boat's name. You can't make this up." Cody interjected.

"Okay, new lead. Let's head out to the Gandy Marina and find this boat. Maybe Kash is hiding out on it. There was no boat registered to him. Maybe he is leasing it. That would be a place to hide out."

As they were stepping into their car, Kate received an email from the analysts. As she read through it, she looked at Cody and said, "Remember that odd guy from last night?"

"Mr. Saturn? The guy that I didn't see?"

"Yes, him. So, his name is Arthur Goldsmith. He lives South of Gandy in SOG. Has a few arrests for disorderly, marijuana, but nothing major. He was really broken up and crying at the service last night."

"We'll let's pay him a visit."

They drove back across the short bridge to the mainland and drove south on the Bayshore Drive. They didn't speak as they became sightseers, taking in the sights of the bay, the walkers, the runners along the sidewalk and the mansions on the other side of the Boulevard of Dreams, as it was also known. Kate hit the re-circ button on the A/C as they picked up a foul odor that periodically emanated from the bay at certain times.

Kate said, "I don't know what smells worse, the bay or the inside of your car?"

"I thought the cotton candy air freshener and pine trees did the trick."

"Now it smells like sweet pine forest. Better than morgue decomp eau de perfume."

They took the Selmon expressway to Gandy Boulevard and drove past shopping centers and fast-food restaurants as they headed towards Westshore Boulevard. Turning left into the working-class neighborhood of simple and small homes.

Some were well cared for and some not so much. Investors were buying up many of the properties and flipping for a profit. Arthur Goldsmith's house had been bypassed by investors.

They pulled up in front of a small house with an overgrown yard and a wobbly chain-link fence. Under a carport was the maroon Saturn Ion.

Kate said, "They called this neighborhood Rattlesnake. It was first settled by a guy who opened a rattlesnake cannery here. It's long gone."

"Huh, that's interesting."

They knocked on a door that was peeling. The tousled man that was wearing the same frumpy clothes from the night before answered the door.

"Hi Arthur Goldsmith?"

"Yes?"

"We are with the Tampa Police. Could we step inside?'

"I wasn't expecting company. We can just stay outside."

Kate was relieved that if the inside looked anything like the outside, it was probably a good idea. "I saw you at the Marchetti memorial service last night."

He squinted towards the sun and said, "What's this all about?"

"It's a long way to drive from Rattlesnake to that funeral home. It's not like you were in the neighborhood and dropped in. I noticed you appeared close to family?"

"I saw it on the news and wanted to pay my respects."

She lightly touched his bicep. "I could see that the service moved you. I just wanted to ask informally what your relationship was with the family?"

Goldsmith pulled a vape pipe out of shabby jeans pocket and took a deep draw off the pipe. He paused just a moment and exhaled a cloud loudly. Kate could see that he was considering his options and buying time. She also noticed the green t-shirt with a breast pocket may have been one of those comfy shirts that you hang onto for a decade or more.

His eyes watered and he bit his lip, as his voice cracked, "Not the family, Dominic."

"How did you know Dom?"

"We met at Westshore Pizza. We both liked their beer and cheesesteaks. I was from Philadelphia, and he went to school up there. We were Star Trek fans became friends. He gave me a job."

"A job?"

"A friend of his, Damien Williams, killed himself last year and Damien's wife, Marcy, was pretty distraught. Dominic asked me to look in on her and do odd jobs, take her to appointments and basically be a companion."

"How did Dominic feel about the suicide?"

"He said that it was a selfish act and Damien had left his widow all alone to find her own footing again. To be honest, Damien's suicide pissed Dom off. Especially, that he killed himself inside the family home."

"We are still conducting our investigation, but some people say that Dominic committed suicide after killing his family because of the Damien Williams suicide, and he wanted to save them from the struggles that Marcy endured. Would you agree with that statement?"

Before she could finish her statement, Arthur was shaking his head, "No. No. No. Never. He loved them dearly. He detested the act of suicide. We had many conversations over drinks about Damien. He one time said that he would never tap out and would go down swinging with his last breath."

"You appeared to be very close."

"Yes. We were." He sobbed as he tried to control his outburst. His whole body shook with emotion.

After he regained control of his emotions, Kate asked, "Did he tell you he felt threatened?"

"No. He said that he was working on an exit plan from Hercules. He went to his mother, but the bitch turned him down." Kate could sense the vile. "He was thinking of suing them for not abiding by their contract with him. He was pissed at the way they threw him out. He said that he was going to join a biotech startup but according to him, the company had beautiful wrapping paper on the outside but was an empty box inside. Like criminal hijinks going on."

"Criminal in what way?"

"Fraud. That's all he said. He never said he was worried, and he said that he was considering going to the FBI. He also felt if he did, that he could keep himself from being prosecuted on the Hercules affair."

"Did he ever mention the name Kash McCool?"

"I knew of him. He thought he was a conman." Arthur chuckled.

"How about infidelity?"

"What? What do you mean?"

Kate looked at him and said, "Arthur, if you don't mind me asking. Were you more than friends?"

He bit his lip and rubbed his stubbled beard. He shook his head and through teary eyes, he said, "Yes." And exhaled deeply. He pulled the vape pipe again and took another hit.

"I only ask in case he was perhaps being blackmailed or were you perhaps jealous?"

"No. He loved his family. He adored those children. There is no way that he would have hurt any of them. We had our friendship. I understood he had no plans of ever leaving his family."

"Do you think that Carol knew, or anyone else?" Kate asked.

"No, absolutely not."

"Where were you on Sunday night into Monday?"

"Right here. I was supposed to tend to Marcy Williams' pool that morning. Once I heard the news reports, I was a basket case. I went to Marcy's in the afternoon and we consoled each other. I know I don't have much, and you may think that I was a parasite to him. He showed me kindness that I have not felt in a very long time. He respected me for who I am."

"How much was he paying you?"

"Two thousand a month. Cash. I would have done it for gas money, but he insisted on paying me. He offered to buy me a newer car. I refused. He said that he did not want to take advantage of our friendship."

Arthur once again became choked up with emotion. Kate patted his arm again and bid the sad man farewell.

Once in the car, Cody said, "I didn't see that coming. How did you know?"

"I wasn't for sure. As emotional as he was, and the intimate details he knew of Dom and the family, yet still being an outsider. If anyone questioned him about Arthur, he was the companion for Marcy that he could use as cover. I just suspected. My only concern is if he could have been motivated by jealousy or perhaps someone blackmailing Dom and chose to kill him after he refused to cooperate. Kind of a longshot. We will leave that part out of the interview. No reason giving the tabloids some salacious headlines that are irrelevant to the case."

"They appeared to come from different worlds."

"I'm not so sure. If it wasn't for Carol, Dominic would have lived a hoarder's existence. I think they were closer than you would think. His parentage, education and intellect dovetailed him into the premium class. I believe his preference was closer to living like Arthur. Frumpy clothes, dive bars and cheesesteaks."

"You are very observant."

Kate scoffed, "Of course. Females have to be. We are the protectors of the nest. It's why we have a longer life span." She winked.

"And here I thought it was because females always belittled and nagged men."

"Careful!" As she held up her pointing finger.

Laughing, Cody said, "Well, in my humble observation, I believe that Arthur lost a lot from the death of Dominic. Companionship and money."

"Yes, we can cross him off the list."

"Let's keep rolling. Onto the boat."

Chapter Fifty-Two

Turning into the parking lot of Port 32, they could smell the salt air mixed with the scent of grilled food from the Hula Bay Club Restaurant.

They entered the office and waited for the attendant behind the desk to finish a telephone call. He had stringy long hair and motioned that he would be done in a minute.

Cody whispered, "The Robber?"

The attendant hiked his thumb behind him toward the slips. There were stacks of boats in dry storage inside the cavernous facility. A forklift's engine rumbled and the beeping of the machine backing up echoed through the building.

They walked out to the slips, looking for The Robber. They passed all kinds and sizes of boats. Seagulls screeched overhead, as one landed on a pier. A preppy looking boater with pink shorts strolled down the pier as his flip-flops clapped on the deck. After passing a few boats, they spotted the blue and white boat with a cartoon face wearing a mask and the script wording The Rob-Her.

A middle age man and women were eating salads and sipping what appeared to be mimosas. Kate and Cody identified themselves. There was a fork dropping response. They dabbed their mouths with napkins and stood abandoning their fluted glasses.

Kate said, "Do you know Kash McCool?"

Their faces brightened as the slightly rounded woman said, "Oh sure. A dear friend. Is he alright?"

"Yes, I believe so. We just wanted to ask him some questions and heard he might stay on your boat."

A passing boat filled with excited boaters playing hip-hop caused a slapping of the water against the boats.

"No. I'm Robin Campbell and this is my husband, Dick." Dick's face was shielded by a large-brimmed hat, but he had missed his last application of sunscreen. "We met him at Dukes." She pointed at Duke's Retired Surfer's Club.

"He bought us a few drinks, and we got to talking. He used to be in the Coast Guard."

"The Coast Guard?" asked Kate.

"Yes. He went to the Academy and commanded a cutter in Alaska. He started up a biotech firm here in Tampa."

"Alaska?" Kate rolled her eyes and looked at Cody. They both shook their heads.

"It was like listening to a Nat Geo documentary on the hunting, fishing, hiking and wildlife expeditions." Robin was getting wound up, and Dick just nodded.

Kate cut off Robin. "Excuse me, Robin. Did he use your boat?"

"Sure did. We were going to Europe for a month and we let him use it. When we came back, the boat was like Mr. Clean had come through and a full tank of gas." The red-faced Dickie continued to nod like a bobble head.

"Did you, by any chance, invest in LymRX Technology?"

Suzy looked over at Dick and they both nodded. "Sure did."

"I notice a bit of an accent. Midwest?"

"Ohio. We sold our manufacturing firm and got tired of shoveling snow."

Dick stood up and tilted his straw hat. "Now we shovel sunshine and saltwater."

Robin cackled. "Kash is a very nice young man."

"When was the last time that you saw him?" Kate asked.

"A month ago?" She looked at Dick, and he nodded. "He was here with his girlfriend, Jazz. Beautiful girl. Just before we left for Europe. We just returned on Monday morning. Finally, back in the sun and warmth."

Dick nodded approvingly and pointed to his red face.

"One last question. Do you know where Jazz lives?"

Robin's mouth twisted upward from the corner. "Sorry, no, I'm not sure. Somewhere in Tampa."

"Thank you for your time. The name of the boat is cute. A play on your name?"

Dick spoke, "That, and she has been robbing my wallet since we were kids in high school." They laughed together as Kate and Cody waved goodbye.

As they walked out past the row of boats bobbing up and down in their slips, the screeching of a seagull overhead caused both of them to look towards the cloudless blue sky and the gray and white soaring bird overhead.

Kate said, "Wait until Robin and Dick check their wallets after Kash gets done with them."

Cody said, "I'm looking forward to meeting Kash. Coast Guard, outdoorsman, adventurer and biotech startup entrepreneur."

"And full of shit. I'll bet you would really like to meet Jazz. Everyone seems smitten with her. Well, after lunch here at the Hula Bay Club, let's go find her."

"Looks like another couple that were snookered by Kash. He used their boat to impress everyone else."

"There is no telling how many victims are out there."

Chapter Fifty-Three

Grabbing a table overlooking the marina at the Hula Bay Club, Cody and Kate felt a cool breeze blow across the table. They watched ships and wave runners gliding through the marina, looking to tie up or to dock at a slip. They browsed the menu as the server, a cute Asian girl with an energetic smile and personality, took their order. Her name tag read Kim on her white polo shirt. Cody ordered the mahi-mahi tacos and Kate ordered the tuna sushi roll.

Kate pulled her blowing hair into a scrunchie, forming a ponytail. While they waited for their orders, Kate's phone rang. "Hi Sarge."

"The husky voice said, "I don't know what the two of you did, and I probably don't want to know, but The Caveman rescinded the reassignment of the case with no further explanation. He said he had time to reflect on his decision. You are back on the court. I would suggest that you try to wrap this up as quickly as possible before he changes his mind or someone does it for him."

She smiled, "Fully understood. Thank you for the good news. After you retire, I'll let you know what we did to change his mind."

"There is probably a statute of limitations. Frank Duffy's legacy partner continues to haunt The Caveman. Be careful."

"Cheers."

Kim placed two ice teas on coasters and left the two diners.

Kate ended the call and looked over at Cody with a smile creasing from ear to ear. She reached across the table and they shared a fist bump.

"The fragging party was a success. We are back on the horse. As the Sarge said, we better giddy-up because there is no time to waste in case he changes his mind or someone pressures him more than we could."

"I only wish we could salute with proper drinks instead of ice tea." She picked up her glass, leaving a ring on the coaster and clinked glasses with Cody.

He said, "I'm glad it worked out. It could have backfired. Let's take the win."

"Yes!" Kate looked down and saw an email. "Maybe some more good news. An email from Tinder."

"Oh, do share. I am giddy with excitement."

"Her name is Jasmine Norris. I'll send her information to the analysts and after we eat, we can head over to her address once they track her down."

"I can hardly wait. Do you think she could be involved?"

"Possible. Unwittingly or willingly. She could be a victim as well. We will have to be careful and see how it goes. Cody, you could be there to pickup the emotional pieces of a broken-hearted woman, when she realizes he is a big fat fraud. You could provide comfort in a time of need."

He dabbed his mouth with and napkin as he chuckled, "We will see how this unfolds."

Chapter Fifty-Four

As they slid back into the hot car, Cody turned the A/C to high. Kate looked over to Cody and asked, "Have you ever been to Tarpon Springs?"

"Nope."

"Nice town and great Greek food."

"Like Greek salads?"

"C'mon man. I'm talking baklava, gyro, souvlaki, stuffed grape leaves. It's so good."

"I'll stick with the salad."

"I want to call the sponge man. I would love to drive up there, but I want to see what he has to say before wasting an hour and half round trip."

She put her phone on speaker and dialed the number. On the third ring, a young female answered. "Georgeakopoulos Sponges."

"Yes, this is Detective Alexander with the Tampa Police Department. May I speak with Mr. Georgeakopoulos?"

"Please hold."

After a brief delay, a husky voice answered. "Hello. This is Christos."

"Yes sir, I wanted to ask you if the name Kash McCool rings a bell?"

"Oh, that guy."

"What do you mean?" Kate tilted her head.

"He ordered a thousand dollars' worth of sponges. First, he wanted me to loan them to him. He said he was filming a promotional add and would feature the sponges and list us in the credits. He tried to tell me he needed them for a biotech company. These sponges he wanted are called wool sponges because they look like the wool on sheep. Great for bathing, but not for medical research. I could tell he was a bag of wind."

"Did you fulfill the order?"

"Only after I ran his credit card, and he cut down the order to two hundred bucks."

"Did you ever meet him?"

"Nah."

"Are you aware that he said that he was planning to use your company as a local source of sponges?"

"Listen, this guy smelled like the fish rotting on the docks. If he was using my good company's name, me and my sons are going to find him and kick his ass. Then I'm going to sue him. I never met him or agreed to enter into any business relationship with him. I hope that I have made that clear. My grandfather started this business sixty years ago. My family name is on the building. I'm not risking our reputation for some flim-flam man."

"Mr. Georgeakopoulos, thank you for your time."

"No problem."

Kate looked over to Cody and crinkled her nose. "Well, I don't see a need to take a field trip to Tarpon Springs. Let's go find Jazz."

Chapter Fifty-Five

After the conversation with the sponge man, they drove across town to the east of downtown Tampa into Ybor City. Kate rolled down her window and inhaled the prevalent aroma of cigars.

The historic neighborhood surrounded 7th Avenue, which was the heart and spine of the district. Established in the 1880's, Ybor City became the working, shopping and residential area for Cuban, Spanish and Italian immigrants that worked in the cigar factories. Many of the historic Spanish inspired buildings remain. The street was bustling with tourists, restaurants, bars and after dark nightclubs. And yes, cigar shops.

They found Jazz's townhouse a few blocks off of 7th. The townhouse was part of the building of townhomes that appeared to be newly built but with historic accents in the design. Kate thought this would be a nice place for a young person. Historic vibe and within staggering distance of the Ybor clubs and nightlife. They parked on the street. Cody rang the doorbell and after no response, he knocked on the door. They meandered back to the car.

"Hey Cody, why not live here?"

"No way. You are always looking for me to move. What's wrong with where I live? Ybor is too busy for me."

"And South Howard isn't?'

"Point taken, but it's more accommodating. I have the convenience of grocery store, drug stores and more residential. I'm close to the gym, the Bayshore running path, and my mom feels more comfortable there than she would here. That's the icing on the cake. If mom is happy, I'm happy."

Kate pulled her email from the analysts on the workup on Jazz. She had a lively presence on social media. She apparently had worked for a modeling agency in Ybor and was now a real estate agent for Right Now Realty.

Kate looked up Right Now. They listed Jazz as one of their top producers. Kate immediately became mad at her own thought that this girl was successful in sales because she was good looking. She had a become victim of the same bias used against her. She knew some officers believed the only reason she was promoted to detective was because she was good looking. Her thoughts prejudged Jazz. Why cast aspersions on an accomplished girl and belittle her because she was pretty?

Kate looked at the last townhouse in the complex and noticed a lockbox on the door. She searched the address and sure enough, the unit was for sale. Kate called the real estate company and left a message for Jasmine.

"Hi Jazz. My father is friends with Brian Poole and Brian recommended you for real estate. I was driving around Ybor and I just noticed this townhouse for sale. I hoped you could help take a look. It appears to have a lockbox. I'm only in town until this evening, so I would love to see it today, if possible." She ended the call.

Cody said, "Wow. Good call. I'm impressed."

The phone buzzed and Kate almost dropped it. "Hello, this is Kate."

"Hi, you just called me. This is Jasmine, but everyone calls me Jazz. I am familiar with the listing and spoke to the listing agent. It is still on the market. They entered it into the MLS yesterday. So, you would be the first to see it. I can meet you there in 15 minutes?"

"That would be great." Kate gave a thumbs up to Cody as she listened to Jazz go over the current market and particular listing and the financial forecast on purchasing. Kate was impressed with Jazz's intellect and knowledge. Now she really felt bad about judging her earlier.

Kate said to Cody, "She is on her way. She might be pissed that we called her here on false pretense, but I don't want her to have a false narrative about Kash rehearsed. Look at her picture. You and her would make beautiful babies together. You could be like a Hallmark love story."

"You are crazy. Who needs Tinder? I have Kate trying to arrange dates for me."

Cody looked over her shoulder as Kate scrolled through Jazz's social media posts. The night before, she was at Coyote Ugly and a few nights prior, she was at the Bad Monkey. As they scrolled through the voluminous images, there were countless selfies taken with Kash. It looked like they enjoyed each other's company. She had not tagged him in any of the posts and therefore, he had no social media profile.

A red Mercedes SUV pulled to the curb behind them. They could see Jazz wave to them from behind the windshield with a contagious smile. Kate felt a pang of guilt knowing that Jazz was hopeful for a quick sale that rolled right into her lap and instead was about to have her world rocked.

The slender and graceful model walked with confidence to Cody and Kate. She could have been walking down the runway displaying the latest fashions.

Instead, walking into a buzz-saw. She extended her hand and her handshake was firm.

"Hi Jazz. I apologize for using false pretenses to meet us here." They held out their badges and said, "We wanted to talk to you about your boyfriend, Kash McCool."

Jazz's hand grasped her neck, "Oh my gosh, no. What happened to him?"

"Nothing that we are aware of. We wanted to know if you have seen him lately?"

"So, you don't want to see this listing?" Her hands went to her hips.

"No, we apologize again. I know it was a crappy thing to do. Just in case he was with you, we didn't want to alert him."

"What has Kash done?"

"Is there someplace that we could go, so your neighbors are not becoming too curious that two cops are out here talking with you?"

"C'mon inside."

She unlocked the front door of her unit and escorted them up the stairs to a sunbathed, bright living room. Kate looked around and determined the gray-colored mid-century furnishings looked to be straight out of the West Elm catalogue. Kate and Cody walked across the light wood flooring and sat across from Jazz, who sat in a matching chair.

"When was the last time that you had contact with Kash?"

Her hand was stroking the fabric while her foot was tapping the floor. "On Monday, morning. He stopped in before my first appointment. He looked a bit out of sorts?"

"Like how?"

"Out of breath, a little panicky, and you could see panic in his face."

"What has happened to him? I am worried."

"We don't know. His name came up in an investigation and we wanted to ask him a few questions. When he came to see you, what happened?"

"He asked to use my computer. So, I booted up my laptop. When I brought him a glass of water, I saw he was on Craigslist looking at places to rent. Later on, I checked, and he had wiped the history."

"Did he give any explanation?"

"I told him that his actions were worrying me. He said that he was worried that he had gotten in over his head and had done something idiotic. He said that what he did may have cost him his relationship with me, but to keep me safe, he needed to go off the grid for a while and he would explain to me someday."

"Did you ask him what he did?"

By now, Jazz's arms appeared to be giving herself a consoling hug. "Yes. By this time, I was scared and crying. I asked him what happened, and he said the less that I knew, the better off that I was. He kissed me, and said I was the best thing that happened to him, but that I had to forget about him." She sniffed her nose.

"Have you had any contact with him after?"

"No. I sent him emails, texts and voicemails. Nothing since. Then I read about the Marchetti family and I really became worried."

"Why would the Marchetti family concern you?"

"So, Kash owned a biotech company developing a treatment for Lyme, M.S. and ALS. You mentioned Brian Poole in our phone conversation. He was an investor. Dom Marchetti was going to become the chief financial officer. I didn't know that Dom was under suspicion of fraud at Hercules Investments until the news reports. When I read of the murders and Kash running off like that, I started freaking out."

"What was your concern?"

"I don't know..." Jazz flipped her silky black hair over her shoulder. "Your mind wonders, and I was worried that someone that was involved with killing the Marchetti family would chase him or that, like in my wildest dreams that he might somehow be remotely involved with their killings."

"Why would you say that?"

"I don't know. He has never shown any violent tendencies. He has always been nothing but a gentleman and kind to me."

"Did you invest in LymRX Technologies or help him with the business, perhaps in marketing or publicity?"

She gave a short laugh. "Me? Not a chance. You have seen where all my money is. The car parked out front, this place and my furniture. Yes, I enjoy blowing off some stress on 7th Avenue, but I don't have those financial resources. I understood the overall concept of his business, but I was a business major and barely made it through freshman biology. When he started talking about compounding plants from the rainforest and their uses, I would glaze over. He was very intelligent. He was working on his PhD at Stanford in bioengineering. Me? I could barely recite the Greek alphabet from the sororities, but I am an expert in the real estate market."

"How did you meet?"

"Like most millennials, on Tinder. We hit it off, and he was financially stable."

"Do you know where he may have gone?"

Jazz shook her head, "No. His parents live in Houston. But they are not very close as far as I know."

"I went to his apartment on Harbor Island, but he was not there."

Cody asked, "Do you have a key?"

"No. I just knocked on the door and I walked down to the garage and his Range Rover was gone."

Kate leaned in and clasped her hands together. "Jazz, I want you to listen to me. I am going to be very honest about Kash. Some people put up a façade to project an image that may not be entirely accurate."

Cody interrupted, "Like on Tinder. Often the photo or the description presents an image, and it is not representative of the reality when you meet that person."

Jazz nodded in full agreement, "Yes. Absolutely. The pitfalls of online dating apps."

Kate continued, "Cody, thank you for that comparison because that is very similar. Kash is not what you believe. He never made it past his freshman year of his local college. He was involved up to his nose with a fraudulent business that was shut down by the Feds and the owner jailed. In fact, Kash cut a deal to avoid going to jail. The office of LymRX Technology is currently vacant, and all the fancy equipment is rented. His apartment furniture was rented from a staging company. It was a façade built on an illusion."

"No, that's not true. I was there for the open house. I arranged for the caterer. I saw the researchers, the lab and I personally met Woodruff, the doctor who developed the drug."

"Dr. Alan Woodruff Spencer?"

"Yes."

"A fraud as well. He surrendered his license for abuse of painkillers and was charged with insurance fraud. As far as the researchers, those were actors hired through a local casting company. He was running a con. He fooled a lot of people that may have resulted in the murder of an entire family."

Jazz's hand moved over her throat, "There is no way he would have killed them. Why would he?"

"To conceal his crime or to cover his exit like a magician. While everyone is looking over here, he is slipping out the back door. That's why we want to talk with him."

Cody asked, "Was he into fitness? Like running or biking?"

Kate recognized Cody wanted to determine how fit Kash was and how far he could pedal that bicycle from the airport parking garage.

"Not really. He was more a treadmill and gym type of guy. He was in decent shape, but the gym was not a focus of his life."

Cody stood up. "I know you are going to go through the various stages of grief at the loss and violation of trust by Kash. You met someone and trusted them enough to allow them an entry into your life. When you conclude he abused and violated that trust, you will start hating yourself for being so trusting, and you may even think you were stupid. I've seen a lot of things, but this was this guy's life. Scamming people. He was a professional. His life is a charade. He is the rarity. Don't hate yourself. You are too smart, successful and pretty to allow this conman to define your life."

She looked up with ocean blue eyes as tears leaked across her delicate cheeks. She nodded and sniffed and quietly said, "Thank you."

Cody patted her shoulder. "If you hear from him, please contact me. We want to help him. Here is my card. Call anytime."

Chapter Fifty-Six

Once they had left Jazz's condo, they climbed back into the car. Kate grinned and looked over at Cody, shaking her head and said, "You are smooth."

He snickered. "What?" as he extended his arms out from his body.

Mocking him, she said, "You can call me anytime. Here is my number. Let me give you some therapy."

He gave a half laugh and said, "I know she feels used. I merely wanted to leave the door open for her to call us."

"Empathy is a critical component of a good homicide investigator. It allows you to develop rapport with victims, families and even the suspects. It is also the foundation of harmony in the family."

"And an outstanding character trait for genuine leaders."

"Absolutely essential for bosses. Compare Sarge to our Lieutenant. Back to Jazz. I applaud your efforts to console her with that devastating news."

"I hope she understands she can call me." Cody said.

"I witnessed a therapy session. If she is going to call, she will call you. Like I said, you two would make pretty babies."

"Not going there."

"You wouldn't be the first that started true loving a witness, victim or even an informant."

Cody looked at her and said nothing as he drove back to the Blue Monster.

Kate smiled and said, "Oh, by the way, I just received a report from the lab rats on the analysis of the vehicle at FDLE. No traces of blood. I'm not surprised as clean as that car was. If he committed the murders and with the potential blowback spatter on his clothing, there should have been some blood traces in the car. But hell, as bad as the rain was that night, it could have washed it off or encased the blood in mud. We know he had the car detailed, but I am skeptical that they could have removed all the traces of blood. Ugh. Where is Kash!"

Chapter Fifty-Seven

Where is Kash? Sitting at her desk, she thought about everything that mattered to him and most people he abandoned. He left his business, his apartment, his car, his cellphone and now his girlfriend. He had ridden a bicycle out of the airport with no belongings. Since he wasn't an experienced biker, he probably did not ride far. Even five miles from the airport, would provide a lot of territory and a lot of places to park his head for the night.

She knew he had the crypto and the availability to purchase gift cards. A lot of gift cards. He could stay at the finest hotels in Tampa and eat at the most exclusive restaurants. For a man trying to avoid discovery, it would be foolish to go to those places because someone could recognize him. Most fugitives can't avoid old habits and haunts. If Kash was being serious about staying below the radar, and by every sign that was indeed his plan, he would avoid the obvious places and stay in places that he might consider roughing it.

How was he getting around? On his bike or foot? Rideshare using gift cards? They would still need an account. Despite her doubts, she prepared a subpoena for the rideshare companies. That would not cover the local taxis or if he bought a used junker and kept the plates.

She went to Craigslist and put in the search parameters rooms and homes to rent for a five-mile radius around the airport zip code. Eighty-four listings came up.

Kate called Cody over. "Here is some real detective work for you. I have a list of listings on Craigslist for places within five miles of the airport. I'll take half. Find out if they have a new tenant checking in Monday with his description and wanting to pay in cash or exchange in gift cards. You can eliminate the apartments. I would think that would be a little too public for him."

"What about Airbnb?"

"You have your thinking cap on. I would say no because they don't do cash and you have to establish an account. Too trackable."

"Good point."

One after another, they learned the listing was still vacant or was no longer available and filled by someone that did not fit the parameters. Of course, Kate also considered that he could have used a straw purchaser to act as his representative. Jazz would have been the person to use, but it didn't seem like he wanted her involved. Unless she was lying. There was a possibility that she was harboring him in one of her listings, but that would be difficult in today's vibrant market. Agents showing listings, even those only by appointment, would cause high enough traffic that would be more than a man on the lam would want to endure.

After an hour with no joy, Cody hit pay-dirt. He turned towards Kate with the excitement of a child with straight A's on his report card. "I've got a winner. The landlord had turned the garage into a mother-in-law suite. The renter was a little darker skin in his twenties. He paid with Visa gift cards and after dropping off a suitcase and duffle bag in a silver SUV, he left. Later, he returned on a bike. That is all he has been riding until a yesterday. He showed up driving an older maroon Saturn."

"Where?"

"Carver City."

Chapter Fifty-Eight

Cody drove out of the parking garage and headed north towards I-275 and took the ramp towards the Airport. They exited at the Lois Avenue ramp and drove a few blocks north, turning right into Carver City. An island of working-class smaller homes around 1,000 square feet that were built in the early 1970s. High-rise office buildings and upscale shopping at the International Plaza surrounded them. Investors were rapidly buying up the homes and flipping for profits, driving up the prices and driving out the longtime homeowners.

The home that they parked in front was a single level white block home with a roof that barely had a peak. A thin black gentleman was sitting in a rusted metal chair smoking a cigarette. The front yard was paved with patio bricks, creating one large parking lot. There were no cars.

Cody squinted into the sun and said to Kate, "He may have parked around the corner or somewhere else."

"We'll see."

Cody smiled and said, "Hello. Are you Mr. Wilson?"

"Yes sir. You must be the police."

"Yes, we are."

"Like I told you on the phone. I enclosed the garage years ago when my mother got ill, so I could keep an eye on her. It's just me and the lady friend. The neighborhood is changing and her son told me I could rent that out for money. This fellow calls me and shows up on Monday. Said that he would pay me what I was asking. He comes and goes. He didn't talk much. He looked around and said that he could only pay in Visa gift cards. He gave me three. That was $1,250 for the month. That was $250 more than the rent. I thought it was a scam. He said that I could take them to the bank before he moved in. He dropped his stuff. I got my buddy to drive me up to the bank and confirmed the Visa cards were good. When I heard him come back, he was riding a bicycle."

"You don't drive?"

"Epilepsy. I have friends give me a lift. Although there are fewer and fewer. They all dying or moving from the neighborhood. Taking the money and running."

Kate held up a picture of Kash on the phone. "Yep, that's him. I don't know if he is coming back."

"Why do you say that?"

"He got no stuff in there right now. Have a look. Starting yesterday, he only had a backpack in there. I saw him down the street at the Korean BBQ. He came back and left. I was sitting right here, and he waved at me. Got in his car and left. I don't know if he will be back or not."

Kate asked, "What about the car?"

"He parked a red Saturn right there." He pointed at the ground. "Left a few spots of oil. Nothing like his other car. You know one of those fancy SUVs?"

"Do you know where he got the car from?"

"Nope."

Cody said, "Okay Mr. Wilson. If you don't mind, we will have a look inside."

"Nope, I don't mind at all. Help yourself." He stubbed his cigarette out in an ashtray next to his chair.

They walked inside the small garage apartment. The room was tiled and had a microwave sitting on top of a mini fridge. The room had a queen-size bed that had been made. They looked through the room and the adjoining bath. There was little evidence of anyone having been there other than a floss stick in the trash and the wrappings from the BBQ.

Kate pointed to the toilet seat. "It's up."

"It's a guy. A single guy. Only married guys put the seat back down and probably only half of those dudes because they are constantly nagged by their wives." Cody winked at Kate.

"Okay. You're probably right."

As they walked back outside, Cody squinted into the sun and shielded his eyes with his hand. He slid his Oakleys over his eyes. "Mr. Wilson, if this fellow returns, would you mind calling me?"

"As long as I can keep the money."

"You entered into an agreement with him. That's yours to keep."

Mr. Wilson broke into a wide smile. He flicked the ashes off a new cigarette and took a celebratory drag. He smiled and coughed from the lungs.

Once inside the car, Kate looked over and said, "Where is Aakash?"

"He may come back."

"I just wonder why he is still lurking about. It's not his girlfriend. Unless he plans to take out another person. This is just a little messy. He kills the entire family after Dom figures out they rigged the financials? Then he sticks around.

Was it revenge or an argument with Dom and he staged it to look like a suicide after the murder? If he is confident that the story would hold, why hide at all?

Cody shrugged his shoulder. "I don't know. Maybe he figured by parking at the airport and the ATM withdrawal from DFW, he would stay under our noses while we chase these other leads like chickens in the farmyard."

"Perceptive. Time will tell."

Kate sped up onto the entrance ramp of I-275 North, heading back to the Blue Monster. Traffic almost immediately slowed to a crawl as the motorists slowed down, gawking at a trooper conducting a traffic stop. Cody engaged their emergency lights and pulled in behind the FHP black and tan SUV. The trooper gave a thumbs up and flashed the 10-8 code that all was good. Kate saluted back and Cody eased their car back into traffic.

She turned to Cody and asked, "Do you miss being a trooper?"

"Nope. I enjoyed stopping cars and finding what that might lead to as far as contraband or warrants. One time, I stopped a car for expired tags. He was driving his mother's car. He didn't know that he was wanted for murder out of Massachusetts."

"Your first homicide arrest!"

"Indeed. Working traffic crashes and low pay? I don't miss any of that."

"Let's call it a day. I'll drop you off. I'm going home to Brittany and my mother."

"No more glow in the morning."

Kate put her hand up and said, "Stop." She smiled.

Chapter Fifty-Nine

Kate answered the ringing on the car's Bluetooth, and heard the comfortable voice of Trent. "Well, hello. I thought this was going to be one of those no kiss goodbye and the ultimate walk of shame of never hearing from you again."

Her face cringed. "I know. My bad. It was a super busy day. I'm heading to the house now."

"I saw the Papa's Pilar Rum sitting on the counter when I came home. It brought a smile to my face."

Now smiling, "Mine too. Thank you for being there for me last night. I needed that, and it made me realize I need to make room for someone special that can provide ballast in my life. I've got the cop world, and I've got my home life, but no me time."

"So, you want a little something on the side? A friend with benefits?"

"You know better. I want us together."

"Are you sure? You're not going to get a puppy instead?"

"Too much training. I've already got you a collar and your shots. You can be my therapy animal."

"I promise I do not have fleas."

"I'm glad you don't. I may still get a puppy. It might be good for Brittany."

"Dogs are agreeable companions, depending on the breed."

"Well, what is your schedule this weekend? Maybe we can get together. Will you help me find a puppy?"

"I don't know. I have a very busy social calendar. Oh, I just checked and I have a cancellation for whatever time you want to get together."

"Excellent. Okay, I'm pulling up to the house now. Let me check our schedule and I'll ring you back."

"Sounds good."

"I really had a good time. Thank you, Professor."

"Purely my pleasure."

Guiding her car into the driveway of the house, Kate let out a sigh of relief. It would be nice to unwind with the family, and she smiled at her companionship with Trent.

It was always her problem. He was a keeper, and she almost screwed it up by casting him off because of guilt and loyalty to Brittany and the memory of Jake. She knew she needed to open her closed circle of trust. She had once cracked it open for Trent and then quickly closed it again. The loneliness was tugging at her like an anchor on a boat. She saw what Frank went through after Bridget died. She did not want to fall into that same despair and end up alone.

She walked into the house and was greeted with the smell of chicken and yellow rice. Kate inhaled and held that scent in her nose, while closing her eyes and smiling. She dropped her backpack and walked into the kitchen.

"Hi everyone."

Brittany ran to her mother and gave her a big hug. Kate held the embrace as she tried to push away the tragic visions of Ethan and Megan Marchetti.

"Hey sweetie. Have you finished your homework?"

"I didn't have much."

"As in, you have completed it?"

"Yes, mother." As she rolled her eyes.

"What do you think about puppy shopping with Trent this weekend?'

The enthusiasm almost exploded like the cork on a champagne bottle. "Yes!"

"Okay, you'll have to come up with a name and get used to potty training the pooch."

"I will." Brittany gave another hard, gripping hug to her mother. "Can we get a Frenchy?"

"We'll see. Okay, well after we have this delicious meal, why don't we watch a movie?" Kate lifted the lid on the slow cooker and inhaled the aroma and looked at the bright hues of yellow rice, peppers and peas.

"That is a lovely idea. I'll go check and find something to watch."

As Brittany ran off, Kate turned to her mother, "Thanks for dinner, mom."

"I knew you could use a good comfort meal. How are you doing?"

"I'm tired, but keeping my nose above the waterline."

"That is good to hear. How is Trent?"

"Good, I spoke to him on the way home. We are going to get together this weekend, as you probably heard."

Her mother bounced with excitement and clapped her hands. "I am thrilled. He is good for you. You need this in your life."

"I agree, mom. Now let me have a taste of this fabulous meal."

Chapter Sixty

The next morning in the squad room, Kate was already shuffling through files and updating the murder book. She sat alone and paused as she looked out the row of windows overlooking downtown Tampa.

She was convinced Dominic was a murder victim, but she really was no closer to identifying who the killer was, except for possibly Kash. Was the motive of covering a fraud strong enough to execute an entire family? Why kill them if you planned to run, anyway? Jazz gave the impression that her boyfriend was running not from the law but from others. Who were the others? His business partner, Doctor Spencer? Someone from Blackpool Investments? Or one of the Krewe of Kingsmen? She knew the CEO of Blackpool was in federal lockup. Perhaps, an investor or an associate. Blackpool had no relationship to the Marchetti family. She crossed that possible nexus off the list.

Cody walked in and looked at Kate. "No glow today?"

She batted her eyelashes. "You missed it. I had the glow of family time, but that has lost its brightness as I contemplate our case."

"Well, I too am engaged with the case. I called the Craigslist guy, Mr. Wilson, and asked if he had any sightings of Kash."

"Yes?"

"No dice. I also asked the patrol unit for Carver city to keep an eye out for the maroon Saturn. Few on the road since GM shut them down in 2010."

"You'll get your honorary Sherlock Holmes pin before too much longer if you keep conducting that investigative work."

Cody's phone chirped. He said to Kate, "Maybe Mr. Wilson is calling back already." He accepted the call. "Hello?"

"Detective Cody?" A female voice asked.

"It's actually Cody Danko" He winked and nodded at Kate.

"I'm sorry. I am a little nervous. This is Jazz."

"No problem, Jazz. How can I help?"

Kate smiled and gave a thumbs up and winked back.

"You said to call if I heard from Kash? He just called and said that he had borrowed a phone. He said that he was at a library, but wanted to know if he could come over later and that he was sorry. I don't know what to do. I still care for him."

"You did the right thing. We just want to get his version of what happened. Did you tell him we had been there?"

"No. He asked if anyone had asked about him. I feel awful, like I betrayed him."

"That is natural. But you understand he began the betrayal when he created a fraudulent company and invited you to take part as a pawn in that fraud. I'm sorry to say, with your intellect, good looks and easygoing personality, he loved having you to distract potential victims. He used you to sell them on the concept. He could show that he was in a committed relationship and worthy of trust."

"I guess you are right. I just feel terrible."

"This will take time. I can tell that you cared for him. For your sake, it's best to learn at this stage about it, then much further down the path that he was planning to travel. I am so sorry that this happened to you. You don't deserve this. Did he mention which library?"

"I don't believe he was at the library. He showed no interest in reading, let alone going to the library. He was always researching online."

"Okay, I'll be in touch. I assure you he will not find out that we were talking."

"Thank you, Cody. You are very kind."

"Call if there are any changes. If he shows up, don't answer the door."

"Okay, thank you."

Cody turned to Kate and said, "As you could tell, that was Jazz. She said Kash called from a burner or a loaner. He said he was at the library and planned to stop over sometime today."

"Excellent. Many a fugitive's downfall is a woman. He is thinking with the little head instead of the big one. That is probably why he hasn't blown town. If we miss him at the library, we can wait on him to come to Jazz's place."

"Which library do you think?"

"Let's start with the Ybor Branch. It's smaller with free parking in a lot. If I was a bad guy, that's where I would go. The downtown John Germany Library is big and parking is challenging. And with the Straz Center next door and the Art Museum across the street, he is more likely to bump into an investor or a fellow member of the Krewe of Kingsmen."

"I like it."

"Me too. He is probably doing research or using their computers to access email and stuff."

Kate grabbed her backpack and Cody followed her as she half ran in the hallway towards the stairs and bypassing the wait on the elevators. She knew this was a solid lead. Kash had fallen for Jazz and he had no reason to give a false story about being at the library. She told Cody to drive, and they hustled to his car in the parking garage.

As Cody pulled out onto North Florida Avenue, he turned right on the one-way street and floored the gas, trying to catch the roll of green lights headed north.

Chapter Sixty-One

Cody turned their car off North Nebraska Avenue into the parking lot of the Robert W. Saunders Public Library. The newer two-story red building had a glass atrium main entrance and was adorned with a multicolored stone and ceramic mural saved from the previous library called "Symbols of Mankind." The mural depicted the diversity of the community and various symbols representing the knowledge discovered inside the walls of the library.

They circled around the parking lot and spotted a maroon-colored Saturn backed into a parking space. This matched the description of the new wheels described by Mr. Wilson.

She instructed Cody to stop under the portico for the book drop. She stepped out and walked back across the parking lot, staying close to the building, hoping to conceal her movements. She approached the rear fence line for the elementary school next door. She could hear the sounds of kids playing on the playground. Kate turned right and walked around the bushes until she passed the Saturn with the fading paint. She snapped a photo of the license plate and then retraced her steps.

Once she was back in the car, she pulled up the photo and called communications to run the license plate. The car came back to a white Toyota. Kate assumed he stole the plates off of a parked car. Probably in a parking lot like the airport or one of the long-term lots where the owner would not notice.

"Okay, how about you stay here? That is probably his new ride."

"Or old ride." Cody said.

"Quite a step down from his Range Rover."

"One day you are the king, and one day you are the pauper."

"Yep, some people take their wealth for granted. I'll look inside the library and see if I can spot him inside. He is less likely to pick up on me being a cop. You scream cop."

"You hurt my feeling."

"Truth. Keep an eye on the car in case I miss him. The front entrance is on the other side at the atrium on the far side of the building, so in all probability, he would walk past you here. If I see him, I will come out and we will set up near his car and call for some reinforcements."

"Sounds like a plan."

Chapter Sixty-Two

Stepping out of the car, Kate walked towards the front entrance of the library, passing the bus stop with folks waiting for the next bus. Kate eased past the atrium to look at the north side of the building for any other entrances. She could only see windows and no other exit doors.

She pulled open the door to the atrium vestibule and looked at the man pushing out the other door. Their eyes locked on each other. His thicker head of hair had been cut close to the scalp. Kate immediately recognized him. At first, the man's face flashed in bewilderment. Then panic gripped his face. He froze momentarily as his eyes darted side to side.

Kate yelled, "Don't think about it!"

It was too late. Kash darted out the door. Kate had to navigate around an elderly patron with a walker and pushed out the door, following Kash. She knew he would run right to Cody parked at the portico.

Unexpectedly, Kash looked to his right and darted out towards Nebraska Avenue and through those waiting at the bus stop for the number 12 HART bus. He had reached the street and was in a full sprint across the street. Kate was pumping her arms and legs. She knew that if she did not catch him, this might be the only chance to catch him. She vaulted over the park bench like a track hurdler, and as she ran across the asphalt street, she yelled, "Police! Stop!"

Kash continued running and looked over his shoulder at Kate, as he made it to a vacant grass field next to the Vibe Lounge. There were no melodies today. He stumbled just a bit and caught his balance. He was surprisingly fast. But not as quick as the pursuing detective, who was closing the distance.

Kate reached up and grabbed his shirt collar, which acted like a tethering dog's leash. His body lurched forward as his head and neck came to an abrupt stop. His knees buckled and Kate rolled him to his belly and put her knee into his back.

She looked up to see Cody handing her his handcuffs. Kate applied the cuffs and patted Kash down for weapons. She found no weapons, but two bulges in each sock. It was $5,000 of cash rubber banded together. All hundreds.

"Kash McCool, you are under arrest for resisting arrest."

Breathing heavily, Kash was silent.

Cody looked at Kate and said, "Now I understand what Ruth meant on your speed. If we were in the NFL, they would have thrown a flag on you for un-sportsman like conduct, a horse collar tackle. Fifteen-yard penalty."

"A full tackle would get my pants dirty. I just got them back from the cleaners."

They walked him past the gaggle of the folks waiting for the number 12 bus. Some people smiled with respect, while others were in shock. Several had their phones recording the incident.

The detectives placed Kash in the back seat of Cody's car. The trio drove around to the abandoned Oldsmobile. Kate looked back at Kash and said, "Do you mind if we take a look inside your car?"

He shrugged. "Is that a yes, or no?"

"Lawyer."

"Sure, no problem. We are going to have to tow the car because you have the keys to it, it has stolen license plates on it, and we need to conduct an inventory of the contents for safe keeping. As far as a lawyer, I don't want to break the news to you, but you cannot call Melvin Storms because he has a conflict of interest."

Kate called communications to dispatch a wrecker to tow the car and a patrol car. A few minutes later, Officer Doug Pasley rolled up in his blue, black, and white patrol SUV. Doug stepped out with a big smile. He waved his arms to the side of his tall frame. "Two of my favorite detectives. How are you, my friends?"

Kate said, "We are good. Just chased this desperado down."

"Which one of you caught him?"

Cody answered, "Who do you think?" As he hiked his thumb towards Kate, "Kick ass."

"Oh, I've seen her chasing speed in the past. She is a legend."

"Well, it didn't take long. I was barely out of the car when she horse collared this guy. It was impressive."

"Indeed. How can I help you?" Doug asked.

"If you don't mind, the wrecker is on the way. Could you standby and inventory the contents? Here are the keys and his information is on this paper."

"Sure, no problem. I'll meet you at the Blue Monster."

"You are a pal."

Chapter Sixty-Three

In the dank, claustrophobic interview room, Kate tossed a dog-eared and well-worn yellow pages book that had been passed from one criminal to another over the years into the lap of Kash. The shrinking yellow pages from years past still had a sizeable section for attorneys and bail bondsman.

"You can tell your lawyer that we will charge you with murder." It was a bluff. Kate knew she did not have enough evidence to support a murder charge.

"Murder? Whoa. No, no, no. Absolutely not."

"I'm sorry. After you invoked your right to speak to an attorney, I can no longer speak with you. I just hope you find a talented attorney. I would stay away from the ones who also have a bus stop sign."

"I want to clear this up. I haven't killed anyone. As God as my witness!" He held up his hand like he was being sworn into court."

"If they paid me a dollar for every criminal who found God in this interview room or swore on their mother's grave, I would be rich. Tell your lawyer."

"But it's the God's honest truth. I swear." His head leaned forward, almost spitting the words.

"I'm sorry, but I still can't talk to you." She pulled the door behind her.

"Wait!"

Kate paused and stared at Kash.

"What if I said that I don't want an attorney?"

"You have to be very clear in your waiving your right to an attorney and willing to speak to me."

Like a bobblehead shaking his head, "Yes. I want to waive my rights."

Chapter Sixty-Four

Kate summoned Cody to return to the interview room. They sat down and faced the suspect and turned on the digital recorder. They both identified themselves and stated the time and date.

Kate said, "You previously invoked your right to an attorney and to remain silent. I understand that you have changed your mind. Is it without any coercion that you have decided to change your mind and under your own free will?"

He nodded yes.

"For the benefit of the recording, I need you to affirm that is your desire."

"Yes."

"Yes, what?"

"Yes, I want to speak with you without an attorney, and no one has coerced me."

"Okay. I am going to read your rights again to ensure that you are under no obligation to speak to us without an attorney."

After reading his Miranda rights and confirming his desire to waive his rights, Kate begin the inquiry that she hoped would open the door into what had happened to the Marchetti family, and how three of them went to sleep and would never wake to see another sunrise.

"You moved here after testifying against the CEO of Black Pool Investors, while you were the top salesman in selling non-existent lithium mineral rights."

"I did not know they were non-existent."

"I'll have to admit that you are very creative and resourceful. You are one of the most challenging suspects that I have encountered and tracked. You are a smart man. And so are we. Let's not be cute. You would have been prosecuted but entered into a pretrial agreement." Kate was hoping to play his self-inflated ego, while also putting him in your place.

"Yes, I testified, and I knew the sales were most probably fraudulent."

"Not probably. They were nonexistent and you knew that you were ripping off retirees and those with expendable incomes."

He leaned back in his chair like a child disciplined by their mother. He nodded without speaking.

Kate continued, "So, you moved here. Why here?"

"Tampa is a great town. Great restaurants, nightlife, recreation, close to the beaches and lots of millennials."

"Now you sound like the chamber of commerce. Not just beaches but plenty of eager potential investors?"

"Yes."

"Did you target Brian Poole?"

"I knew he might be sympathetic to our business model."

"You say that he was vulnerable, and you exploited him and, as a result, you used him as a springboard to gain the trust of other investors."

"We had made remarkable achievements in research to treat Lyme Disease and were on our way to using that research towards ALS and M.S."

Kate laughed, held up her hand and said, "Stop. We are not potential investors." Kate thought, this guy can't tell the truth if they hooked him up to jumper cables. "A kid with a chemistry kit in his bedroom would have been closer to achieving a cure to Lyme Disease or ALS. Let me lay out my cards so that you understand I know everything. Okay?"

"Yes, okay." As he nodded.

Kate stared into his brown eyes. It was almost a staring contest before Kash finally averted his eyes. Kate continued, "I know that when you speak of "we," you are speaking of Dr. Alan Woodruff Spencer, who surrendered his medical license and was charged with fraud. I know you leased office space with no expectations of fulfilling the terms. You rented all the equipment, which was left abandoned. You paid an initial deposit and never paid the required amount on delivery. You hired actors to pose as lab workers. Your car was leased. Your apartment furniture was leased. Your life was leased. It was all an illusion."

Kash's head sunk as the curtain was being pulled back on his deceit.

"You borrowed a boat from other investors to give the illusion of wealth and produced this glitzy video, website and a business pitch deck. Your financials were all made up. You were planning to hire Dominic Marchetti as your chief financial officer. That was really your mistake. You had been running a magnificent con until that point. Marchetti saw through your three-card monte. He smelled the rotting fish in a red tide. He was going to expose your fraud. You had no choice but to silence him. You couldn't risk what he said to his wife, so you killed her and the children."

"What? No! I did not kill anyone."

"You spoke with him that evening"

"Yes, I did." He exhaled loudly and leaned back in his chair and shifted, trying to buy time for his response. Kate paused as she could see that Kash was weighing his options and the gravity of the situation.

"Okay. I want a deal. I will tell you everything that I know, but I want immunity."

"Not happening. Immunity from murder?" Kate shook her head.

"No. From LymRX Technologies."

"We are not overly interested in your fraud. As far as I am concerned, your investors should have done more homework. You exploited wealthy people who were more than willing to use money to corrupt and influence people. You essentially turned the tables on them."

Kash smiled as if he had gained praise from the boss at his success.

Kate asked, "Have you read Robert Cialdini, *Influence: The Psychology of Persuasion?*"

His eyes lit up and he said, "Yes."

"Well, I fully understand his thesis on the power of persuasion. Required reading in business schools and police interviewing. So, let me start with a little of my influencing. We will charge you with a one count of violating the Florida Communications Act in defrauding the laboratory rental company. We can add a lot more charges to that. I can promise the Tampa Police will only charge you with the one count. Now start talking. You have thirty seconds or no deal and we walk." Kate had already cleared this strategy through Fiona Quinn.

After contemplating his alternatives, "Okay, you are right. Dom was in trouble with Hercules. I offered to pay his debt to Hercules, and I agreed to hire him as my CFO. I thought his presence would increase our credibility with investors."

"Investors like Brian Poole? How did you target him?"

"When I worked at Black Pool, one girl became debilitated with Lyme after hiking in New England. After hearing the politics in the medical community and how desperate people were to be cured, I looked at it as an opportunity."

"An opportunity? People die from that."

"I know. I conducted internet searches for articles on family members. I found one on Brian Poole in a business journal. I focused on him and did a lot more research on Brian, so that I could befriend him and get close to him. I know this sounds creepy, but I did social media stalking and conducted surveillance on him to see where he liked to hang out. I learned his likes and dislikes. It was easy after that to get close to him and he introduced me to others. His seal of approval provided enough intrigue with his pals that we were the next best thing and jump on the train before it left the station. Time was running out. This investment would make them filthy rich."

"Okay, so let's get back to Dominic."

Kash swallowed hard. "When he realized I had been cooking the books."

"For the record, when you say cooking the books, you mean you had essentially set up a shell company with no viable assets, no revenue and no established product."

Kash paused and nodded. "Yes. I thought he would understand since he had committed a fraud himself, and I was buying his get out of jail card."

"He didn't buy in, did he?"

"He said that he could not betray his longtime friends and that he planned to come forward and report the company. I asked him for time to cover the debts and secure financing."

"Was he aware that this drug you were working on was a farce?"

"Those sponges from Tarpon and plants from the Amazon have medicinal purposes and..."

Kate interrupted, "Kash... please. Those wool sponges you ordered from Tarpon are the bomb for bathing. They have no medicinal qualities."

"No, he did not know. He only knew the financials were off and he was going to give me until the end of the week before he disclosed the financial irregularities."

"Who was he going to report you to?"

"I guess because we received incentives from the State, County and City, he was going to report us to them and the FBI."

"What happened after that phone call?"

"Nothing. I spoke with Spence or Dr. Spencer and told him we were going to have to come up with something since Dom was pulling the thread to unravel us. I had a couple of drinks, and I went to bed. The next morning, I was having breakfast, and I read the news alert on my phone that they were dead. I panicked. I feared I would be next."

"Why did you think that?"

"Whoever killed them would likely target me."

"Did you not think it had to do with Hercules?"

"No. He was very concerned that a lot of people would be very upset at the embarrassment of LymRX Technologies and that he had already spoken with one person exploring the depth of their concern, and he said they were livid."

"Did he say who?"

"He said that he didn't want to say. That person wanted to go into damage control and preserve their integrity."

"Can you prove to me you were at home?"

"I called Spence while I was in my apartment. My car never left the garage. I would have used my key card to come back up in the elevator."

"You have shown a unique ability to go off the grid. You could have used a cab or used the stairs. Why run?"

"I was terrified! If his *ENTIRE* family was executed, I could be next." He pointed at himself. "I wasn't going to stick around for negotiations. I took the money and ran."

"Why not leave town?"

"I thought if I stayed close that they would look at the far end of the search beams, thinking that I ran. Besides, I wanted to see Jazz. I hoped to convince her to go with me."

"Where were you going to go?"

"I knew the FBI was going to come for me. I thought maybe I could hire a private charter to Ecuador."

Kate smiled knowing that she had already anticipated that move.

He continued, "I figured I could leave after the fuss died down. But if people were concerned with public humiliation, how best to conceal it then to kill me and throw a blanket over the fire? If they will kill an entire family, including kids, I would have meant nothing to them."

"I'm curious. You appear to be a dazzling guy. Why engage in fraud that you know is going to end in failure?"

"My parents worked for a company that never recognized their talents, meanwhile the owners were having a good time on the proceeds and backs of their employees. My parents expected me to be a conformist like them. I felt college was a waste of time and money. It disappointed them in my decision. Then I had outstanding success at Black Pool, but they were disappointed again when it collapsed. I wanted them to see how resourceful and resilient I was, while proving to them how intelligent I am. I also wanted to disrupt the powerful elite and prove how a college dropout could outsmart them and take their pants to their ankles."

"Remember, the longer that you circle the fire, the more likely that you are going to be burned." Kash gave a one shoulder shrug. He didn't quite buy that theory. Kate continued, "Okay, we are going to take a break for a few minutes. I want you to think and give me the names of every investor, both public and private."

Chapter Sixty-Five

The two detectives stepped out into the hallway outside of the interview room. Kate looked at Cody and asked, "What did you think?"

"He is a rotting piece of garbage and wouldn't know the truth if it was on the fangs of a rattlesnake. But I don't like him for the murder."

"I agree. He has no scruples and had no intentions of telling the truth. I could tell that he felt he could give a little to get out from under the murder. I think he is legitimately scared of someone coming after him."

"What are we going to do with him?"

"Charge him with the fraud. We can make the case that he is a legitimate flight risk and should be detained without bond. He admitted to us his intention to flee the country. That should work until the FBI can get charges on him. I sent all his account information to the white-collar squad. They were salivating. But you know the Feds are never in a hurry. With the Feds, their motto is what we don't do today, we will start on tomorrow and what we don't finish tomorrow, we can work on next week."

"So, I have heard."

"Apparently, his fraudulent scheme violates his pre-trial diversion and U.S. Probation can put a hold on him. The FBI is going to call his probation officer. The FBI wants to interview him. I told them we are not running a daycare and they need to hurry. The U.S. Attorney's Office never likes to charge folks until they have their case stitched up tight. I told them that once he is gone, he is probably long gone."

"But we found him."

"Especially you, pretty boy, and your rapport with Jazz."

"She would have called you as well." Cody said with an easy grin.

"Mr. Hallmark." They both laughed.

Kate said, "Okay, let's charge him and then once the Feds put a hold on him, we can drop the charges and let them roll our case into theirs. Once we drop him off at the Orient Road Jail, we have some work to do."

After returning from the jail, they discussed what they had learned. Kate knew that people with power had been deeply offended and embarrassed at being victimized by a fraudulent and worthless company. She agreed with Kash's assessment that Dom was about to blow the lid off the top and expose their vulnerability.

Kate asked, "Let's make a list of everyone who stood to lose money, prestige or power. We will start with the list that Kash provided. What about Brian Poole?"

Cody wrinkled his mouth. "I don't see him. He has a lot of money, but I gather he is laid back and not as concerned with his wealth as some might be."

"I agree. Of course, he might put up a front, but he provided an alibi. The same with folks on the Rob-Her. They had just returned from Europe."

"Most everyone else we looked into also had good alibies. We will have to look into the rest of the investors that he provided."

"Let's look at the politicians that were sucking up on the open house video. A lot of them can never pass up a photo op. If they were behind tax benefits and grants, there could be political fallout."

"I understand the tax incentives, but grants as well?"

"Yep. And Loans. Everyone wants to be the next Silicon Valley. What's next? Green renewable energy and biotech. That is the new shiny objects of the future. If they can secure the next big new future deal that could become the attractive anchor for future businesses in the same field, they will open up the coffers. Clean business with high-paying jobs and attracting the right kind of people."

Chapter Sixty-Six

Kate reviewed the phone records for the deceased victims. All four of the phones were pinging from the house all night, which, considering the weather, was to be expected. The kids chatted via text with friends and all texts concluded with silence after 9:00 pm.

Carol had a few chats with her mother and a friend. Nothing juicy or showing what might occur later in the evening. Kate reviewed Carol's social media posts. Again, there was nothing to show any discord. The same for both kids who had Facebook and Instagram accounts. Typical youthful banter and sharing photos.

Dominic's phone showed one brief call from an unknown number, one from Kash McCool at 8:30 pm and another from Rodney Upton, Senator Thorland's straphanger at 9:05 pm. Then the text went out to Melvin Storms.

Cody sat down with Kate at the round conference table at the front of the homicide squad room. He pulled out a file and began explaining what he had found on LymRX Technology and the politicians.

Cody said, "You were right. I did not know the political intrigue that goes into luring businesses into town."

"The problem is that money and power have a corruptible influence. What did you find?"

Cody explained, "Kash McCool assured county commissioners that LymRX Technology had deep pockets from private investors, a pocketful of patents and was considering re-locating from Houston. The county provided hundreds of thousands in loans."

"They bought his story, hook, line and sinker. McCool is a born salesman but with no history of success outside of Black Pool. I wouldn't necessarily put that on my resume as a marquis builder."

Cody continued, "He admitted, in a filing with the SEC, that LymRX Technology had significant deficiencies in business practices with record keeping, contract management and financial controls."

"That is where Dominic comes in."

"Exactly. Kash advised they were hiring a new CFO to tighten the business side and that they expanded faster than expected and outgrew their control methods and record keeping."

"What about the state?" asked Kate.

"They required a proposal for job creation prior to approval for the granting of incentives to ensure a return on investment."

"Providing the company remained solvent." Kate said.

"Yes. Otherwise, they are on the brown side of the sod at a cemetery. So, the director of economic development was previously chief of staff to Senator Thorland."

Kate's eyebrows lifted. "Ahh, the plot thickens. I can imagine all the finger-pointing when the media becomes aware that this was a shell company and essentially stole money from the taxpayers. It will be like a bunch of people holding their noses while running from a skunk. This is great work, Cody. I wonder what kind of political donations that Kash made to these oxygen suckers."

Cody held up a sheet of paper. "Great minds. I wondered as well. Senator Thorland, who helped steer the money to LymRX Technology, received a $5,000 campaign contribution and McCool also donated $5,000 to the Party as well."

Kate said, "Unbelievable."

"But wait! There is more. Thorland's son-in-law, George Harrelson, was appointed to the LymRX Technology company's board with a salary of $20,000. Harrelson, whose previous experience was selling real estate, has also opened up a consulting business focused on assisting companies looking to relocate to this market and explore funding opportunities."

"Wow. This is like a den of snakes."

"You would think that they would learn their lesson. A few years ago, Savtira defrauded a bunch of investors and the State. I think they were into cloud computing of some sort. They were moving to Ybor and promised hundreds of jobs. They went belly up and their CEO is doing a long stretch in the federal penitentiary. Next on deck is Kash McCool. I could see how embarrassing this could be to these morons, especially Thorland."

"With a thoroughbred list of local investors, who all gave the wink and secret handshake along with Thorland's blessing and influence, the County and State were tripping over themselves to hand out cash. They became Kash's personal ATM."

"Most of the investors, including the State and County do not know that they have closed up shop. Then, when they try to reclaim assets, all they get is equipment that belongs to someone else. That's why our charges will never stick. Fiona will never go to court on this. She would look at this case as more a civil matter between Kash and Pyramid Lab Rental, because the company has all their laboratory equipment returned and barely used, minus the half money deposit they get to keep. This has the Feds' name all over it."

"Yeah, this would take time to build this case."

"The Bureau has certified fraud examiners to dig into the bottom of all these records. Now we have to see if one of these folks had the balls to kill an entire family."

"Or hire it out."

"Yes. I have a suspicion as to the who."

Chapter Sixty-Seven

Kate's phone rang and she could see it was Marty Garrison on the caller ID. Kate worked with Marty in the district two patrol. Marty was the size of Paul Bunyan and had a heart the same size. He also had an encyclopedia memory of names and events.

"Modee!"

Marty's enthusiastic voice said, "You still single? My marriage proposal still stands."

"What would Lisa say about that?"

"She understands there is enough of me to go around and that's why I have an all-girl Modee fan club."

"Well, I will have to consider that proposal. What is going on in D-2?"

"Bob Wortham and I were lurking about and saw a car creeping around without any lights well past dark. We figured he was either DUI or up to no good. Either case needed a legal intervention. As we turned on the lights, the driver wanted to skedaddle.

Bob and I buckled up and gave chase. This dude could see I had been playing Grand Theft Auto and knew how to drive, so he bailed and started running. He had this cute little ponytail, but he was running so hard the mane fell out and he looked like Fabio with his beautiful golden locks bouncing."

Kate laughed at the imagery and said, "No one can tell a story like you. Continue because I know somehow this will involve me."

"Kate, we miss your runner's speed out here. I don't think anyone could outrun you. The next best thing was to roll Bob out of the car and unleash him like a rabid dog. Bob may be a few pounds lighter than me, but he can run a lot faster."

"I hate to be pragmatic, but neither one of you is going to win a gold medal."

"We have slowed with age, but I remember a kick ass young officer with your initials said to work smarter, not harder."

"Guilty. I may have been faster, but sometimes I outran the headlights, and I could always count on you and Bob bringing the beef and bailing me out."

"That didn't happen too often. So anyway, while Bob jumps out of the car and yells at this fool to stop, I drive past him with my window rolled down and tell him to stop or I would have Bob shoot him. Ponytail stopped."

"Thank goodness you didn't even have to get out of the car."

"Right? So anyway, this Mr. Ponytail, whose name is Byron Honeywell, had some weed in his pocket. Probably not enough for the State Attorney to file on him. All we have is traffic violations. He doesn't know any of this and starts pleading with Bob that he has information on the Marchetti murder-suicide."

"I don't think there is a suicide in this."

"Really? Wow! Okay, so Byron said that he was talking with a friend of his, who lives close by the Marchetti home, and he is willing to serve her up like a Thanksgiving turkey, all basted and stuffed full of my favorite cornbread stuffing. And yes, a little cranberry sauce on the side."

"Who is this person?"

"He said her name is Sarah Cornish. According to him, she heard gunshots and then saw a car pull away a little while after. To be honest, it sounds legit. He is scared of jail and his parents finding out. Now, she may be mistaken about the events, but he is being an Honest Abe to get out from under the charges. I told him if he was telling a tale, I would track him down like Dog the Bounty Hunter."

"Modee? Thank you, hon. If I were there, I would give you a big kiss right on the lips and make you leave, Miss Lisa."

"Kate, stop. You are making me weak at the knees."

"Tell Bob the same for me."

"I hope this pans out for you."

"Thanks, I'll let you know."

Kate called Lester Rollins and asked him if, during the neighborhood canvass, they had spoken to Sarah Cornish. Rollins went through his notes and said that they had not, but had spoken with a Roy Cornish, who in fact lived down the street. Roy said that he had heard nothing besides a little rumbling from the thunder. After the recent installation of hurricane impact windows, he heard little if anything outside the house and no one in his family said anything.

Kate called back Marty Garrison and told him that Lester Rollins had spoken to the family and said they didn't hear anything and everyone slept through the incident. Marty said he would ask Byron for more details.

Marty called Kate back and said, "According to Ponytail, he is knocking boots with Sarah and she said that she couldn't sleep because of the storm. Sarah went out onto the front porch and lit up a joint to calm her anxiety. She thought it was fireworks or a quick succession of thunder. After hearing the sounds, she saw a car driving down the street. Not thinking anything was wrong until the morning when the cops were all over the place. Because she was out getting stoned, she didn't want to share that with Daddy-O. He screenshot the convo and sent it to me. I'll send it to you now."

"You are the best."

"My legs are quivering right now."

"Take a seat. I don't want Bob to have to resuscitate you."

"Amen, sister."

Kate thought of her times in patrol working with Bob and Marty. They were great street cops and always seemed to be a magnet towards the action. If there was a big arrest or chase, they were usually involved. They were always there to back you up.

Chapter Sixty-Eight

Grabbing Cody, they drove to the Cornish home, which was at the opposite end of the block from the Marchetti home. The yellow brick craftsman bungalow contrasted with the size of the Marchetti home. It still would have a hefty price sticker.

The two detectives stepped up to the wood decked porch and rang the doorbell. A teenage girl answered the door. Her black hair had purple highlights and was short enough to expose multiple piercings around her ears. After she identified herself as Sarah Cornish, Kate explained why they were there and that she could provide a little more clarity to the interview her father had provided to the police.

Normally, Kate would be a little coy and develop rapport and gain cooperation through her interviewing prowess. Not this time. She was not in a patient mood and went for a throat punch.

"Hi Sarah, I understand you are withholding pertinent information concerning a homicide?"

Sarah looked behind and stepped outside. "My brother is in the kitchen and I don't want him to hear me. Yeah, Byron told me you guys twisted his nuts, and he had no choice but to drop me in the grease."

Kate nodded. "Byron is right. He was looking at some serious time." Kate looked at Cody and winked.

"Like I wish they invented thunder blankets for people like they have for dogs. It really stokes my anxiety. I have my card for anxiety, but my dad doesn't want me to smoke inside. For real, this will keep Byron out of the gulag?"

"For real. Girl Scout honor" Kate held up her three-finger honor symbol.

"Really?"

"I lead my troop in cookie sales."

"Okay, so I was getting stoned."

"No, you were administering a medical dosage to ease anxiety."

Sarah beamed a smile brighter than headlights. "I like you Detective Kate. And you, mister quiet one, you're hot."

Cody smiled and said, "Thank you for those revelations. Could you fill us in on the what you saw that night?"

Sarah's thumb began rubbing the webbing of her left thumb. "So, like I thought, it was fireworks or thunder in the distance. I heard four booms. Then it was quiet and another boom of thunder for sure right above me. Scared the crap out of me. Then I heard a car start, and I saw the headlights come on. I heard the tires on the wet pavement and the car drove past and around the corner."

Cody asked, "What kind of car was it?"

"SUV."

Kate asked, "Big, small, old, new, color? Help us out. Feel free to fill in the blanks here."

"Like I said, I was stoned and not knowing like the whole family was zeroed out. I really didn't pay much attention. It was raining hard. It was just an SUV. Like maybe a jeep or an Explorer, but not as big as a Suburban. Dark. Black or gray."

Kate asked if she knew what time it was.

"After midnight, but before morning."

Kate rubbed her forehead, and her mouth twisted with frustration. She was now out of patience with the Sarah, the stoner.

Sarah said, "You might check with Looney Loomis."

Kate's eye right brow arched up. "Who?"

"Looney Loomis." She pointed to a house across the street. And then gave a middle finger salute directed at the one-story home. "He has cameras all over the place. He acts like he has the crown jewels in there. My dad says that you can pick your spouse, but not your neighbors. He is bat-shit crazy. He used to run out and yell at cars until someone called the cops on him. He retired and even his wife left him because he is so crazy."

"Thank you, Sarah."

"Did you get a look at the driver?"

"Hell no. Could have been one of those driverless or autonomous cars for all I know. Not to mention, I don't want to be the next victim on the assassin's hit list. Are we like close to being done? All this trauma is causing anxiety. I need to take a gummie."

"Just about." As Kate gestured with an open hand in a calming motion. "Did you know the Marchetti family?"

"Nope. They could have been in the Congo as far as I am concerned. That is like a different country down there."

"In what way?"

"Look at their house. My dad does okay, but not that okay. That's like a Kardashian size home. Like that's messed up. Tapping out the whole family." Her lips tightened and her head shook slightly. She looked at Cody and said, "This is like straight out of TMZ."

Cody said, "Tragic."

Kate said, "Okay, if anything else fires across your synapsis, give us a jingle."

Sarah pointed at Cody. "Mr. Quiet, I'll give a shout for sure."

Chapter Sixty-Nine

Calling Rollins again, Kate asked him if he had interviewed Loomis. Rollins advised he had a patrol officer help on that one, and he said that the homeowner was not cooperative and had nothing to share.

Kate could see the outside of the house could use some bleach and fresh coat of paint, but she could also count six cameras affixed to the trees or to the exterior of the home.

Kate called one analyst, Sheila Compass. Kate recognized the voice immediately from high pitch and fast talking. Despite her speaking annoyances, she was good at her job. After her to run Loomis, Kate could hear Sheila tapping on the keyboard and paused. Sheila mumbled to herself as she read through whatever was on her screen.

Sheila said, "Looks like a crank. Nuisance caller. At least a dozen calls reporting cars speeding, unleashed dogs, dogs defecating or urinating in his yard, kids trespassing in his yard. No arrests or weapons issues. Just an angry man."

"Any place of employment on the reports?"

"Either listed as self-employed or retired."

"Okay thank you, Sheila." Kate turned towards Cody. "Well, you heard that. This place looks like he is keeping the Secrets of Dumbledore."

"Harry Potter?"

"10-4. Let's go."

As the team walked up on the walkway to the house, a speaker from the door barked, "Who are you? State your business."

Kate looked at Cody and rolled her eyes and held up her badge. "Tampa Police. Detective Alexander and Detective Danko."

The angry voice said, "Don't come any closer until I confirm your identity."

Kate ignored his command and continued towards the front door. "I told you to stay where you are."

"And I told you who we are. Now we can continue yelling to the speaker like you're the Wizard of Oz behind the curtain and all of your neighbors will know your business, or we can have a discussion at your front door like adults?"

Kate pounded on the solid wood door with her knuckles. She stepped to the side in case he started shooting. They heard the deadbolt flip open and the door slowly cracked open. A hotel style security bar kept the door from being opened more than a few inches. A shaved head and one brown eye peered through the opening. Now she understood what Sarah meant by Looney Loomis.

"We understand that you may have recorded a vehicle driving past here just after midnight, early Monday morning. A dark SUV?"

"I don't want to get involved. My recordings are for my personal protection and safety and are my personnel property."

Kate leaned towards the door. "Actually, they could be material evidence of a crime. Once again, we can take a look, or I can come back with a search warrant and have the tactical unit knock your door off the hinges."

Before Loomis could respond, Cody leaned towards the opening and said, "I noticed on your car, the sticker Army Proud. I was in Alpha Company 2nd battalion 27th Infantry."

Loomis' eyes shifted up and down, assessing Cody. "Afghanistan?"

"Yes sir, Kunar. FOB Bostick. You?"

"516th Signal Brigade. Hawaii and Japan."

"We had to rely on the signal corps for all our comms. Take a look." Cody unbuttoned his cuff and rolled up his sleeve and displayed a tattoo of a wolf's head. Under the head was inscribed Nec Aspera Terrent.

Loomis looked at the Army logo and asked, "What's the translation of the Latin inscription?'

"No fear on earth. We called ourselves the Wolfhounds."

Loomis looked back at Kate with a subtle sign of contempt and with a softer tone directed exclusively to Cody, "I suppose we could take a look and see if my cameras caught the vehicle."

Cody said, "Well, with you being former signal corps, I know this equipment is solid." Cody looked over at Kate and gave a lone nod. Cody continued, "We really appreciate your help."

Loomis closed the door and unlatched the safety latch and opened the door the rest of the way. The two detectives stepped inside the doorway. Loomis pushed the door closed and twisted the deadbolt.

Cody said, "If you don't mind, I get a little claustrophobic spending too much time in the bunker. My PTS gets agitated in unknown places with the doors locked."

"Oh, sure, no problem. I guess with the police here, I should be okay. The control room is back here."

Kate lingered behind, realizing that Cody, her understudy, was taking the lead. He had connected with Loomis and was developing rapport. She was like bad whiskey on a sore throat, and it was best to stay quiet and observe.

Loomis may not have qualified as a hoarder, but his living room looked like a landmine had detonated. Stuff all over the place. Dust bunnies bouncing about with every movement. He had collected enough hurricane supplies to last through the next decade.

Kate looked into a bedroom that had been converted into the control room. Six video monitors provided constant input from the cameras monitoring the outside world. There was a twin bed that looked like he made it to prepare for inspection. Tight corners and crisp. Kate wondered if this was the room that kept him hostage and fueled his obsession with a normally quiet neighborhood.

Loomis looked at Kate and said to close the door. Kate looked at him in bewilderment. Cody nodded in encouragement to Kate to follow the orders.

Cody looked around and asked, "Is this a Ferriday cage?"

"Yes, it is. You never know who may listen or try to corrupt my collection methods with an EMP."

"Sure. An electromagnetic pulse would destroy everything. How is it configured?"

"Mylar sheathing around us 360 degrees. The raised floor is built on top of the sheathing and it's grounded by rebar drilled into the ground. I have the conduit shielded to the living room, where I have the router setup."

"Impressive." He looked at Kate and they both rolled their eyes.

If there was a secret handshake for the Army, Cody had just used it on Loomis. Cody was asking the right questions like feeding chum to the shark-infested waters. He had reeled Loomis in and they were new best buds. Loomis was like a kid on Christmas morning, extolling his knowledge of the cameras and recording system with battery backup. Loomis droned on about the megapixels, millimeters, degrees, terabytes and A.I. Enough to make your head explode.

After nearly 10 minutes of nonstop chatter, Cody finally broke in and asked the question of the day. "So, Larry," they were now on a first name basis. "Back to the other night. Do you think this fabulous system captured the image of the SUV?"

Loomis almost seemed offended. "Absolutely. The AI." He looked at Kate, "Artificial intelligence."

Kate smiled. "Mr. Loomis, thank you for the clarifier." She tried not to roll her eyes.

Loomis turned back to Cody with his excitement. "My A.I. is programmed not to alert me to passing vehicles." He held up his index finger. "That is, unless they come to a stop. However, I can view the entire street and I archive all activity on the NVR."

As Kate looked at the monitors, she thought about how creepy this was. The cameras were like a Peeping Tom on the street. Anyone walking down the street was recorded and archived. Including their personal conversations with their walking partner or phone conversations. Despite her personal objections to the intrusive nature, she knew there was no expectation of privacy walking or driving down a public street to carry on any activity in full view of the public.

The view of the street was as good as standing in his front yard. With the ability to zoom closer to the digital image like enlarging a picture on your phone, the viewer from the control room could identify if the driver was wearing lipstick or not. If they had shaved or not.

The system recorded Sarah across the street flipping the bird, which was identified as a person by the artificial intelligence. This was the society in which we lived. The only privacy was in your own home. But she wondered if Loomis was perv enough to hear conversations or sounds from inside a home. She didn't ask.

She watched from a distance as Loomis and Cody scrolled through the digital footage from the night the Marchetti family was executed. Loomis was enthralled with his newfound friend, Cody, who encouraged Loomis's slobbering love of technology, spying on his neighbors and anyone else that happened into camera view. He was a voyeur at heart.

Finally, the camera canted to the left of the house and picked up approaching headlights. The car's lights shined on the precipitation. Just as Sarah had described. In fact, the camera could see Sarah sucking on the joint as the glow illuminated her face from the doobie.

The SUV appeared to be black. There was nothing distinguishing about the front of the vehicle, aside from the distinctive grill. The speed of the wipers was clearing rain off the windshield, showing how much rain was coming down. As the car slowed to make the right-hand turn, the image of the driver became clearer. Despite wearing a ball cap, the thin beard of the driver was clear. Kate thought she actually recognized the driver, but not with certainty.

They shifted from one view to another as the SUV moved through the various camera fields of view. The rearview of the vehicle, now identified as a BMW X3 displayed a Thorland for Senator campaign sticker.

The camera also captured the license plate. Kate knew before running the plate that the car would come back to Rodney Upton, Senator Thorland's Chief of Staff. The same Upton she had met that morning at the Marchetti house after the homicide. He had acted like that was the first time he had been at the house. He did not say anything about being there earlier in the evening. A new suspect had emerged.

Chapter Seventy

Kate smiled with satisfaction. It was all making sense. Thorland and others were going into damage control. They knew with an election coming up, the exposure of the depths of the financial fraud that involved stolen money from the taxpayers at the behest of Senator Thorland would be damaging. Especially with a new young maverick contender that was a threat to the stability of the old guard power elite.

Would they murder an entire family and potentially Kash to maintain their grip on power and control? She tried not to follow the daily political discourse, but she knew politicians were often beholden to interest groups, lobbyists, and donors. Voters only mattered in the direction of polls.

If it became known how easily Kash McCool and LymRX Technology had scammed the distributors of the taxpayer's money, they could get torched at the voting booth. Many people would stand to lose their influence with a new senator that might have a different path and newer influencers.

She now had a witness and corroborating video that placed Rodney Upton at the Marchetti residence about the time of the murder and yes, she could now comfortably say that the family were innocent victims of homicide.

Kate headed towards the front door. Cody lingered just a bit too close out of his rapport building session with Looney Loomis. Feeling liberated from the claustrophobic Ferriday cage, she closed her eyes and looked up towards the sky and felt the warmth upon her face while inhaling the fresh air. The humidity had not appeared yet in the early spring. She almost felt like she was back hiking in the Blue Ridge Mountains of North Carolina. Her mind drifted to the beauty of the mountains. When she opened her eyes, she looked at a palm tree in need of care. She had returned to reality.

They said their goodbyes to Looney Loomis and thanked him for his help. Kate could see the excitement in Loomis as they left. She knew he was now enthralled with the idea that he had captured a key piece of evidence to a murder inquiry. He knew everyone probably thought he was crazy, but he was not. He had been vindicated.

It thrilled him to have made a new friend in Cody. They were no doubt the first visitors to enter his home in a very long time, if at all. Kate had to agree with Sarah's description of Loomis.

She would prepare a subpoena for Rodney Upton's cell records, including cell tower tracking for the night of the murder. It would be key to determine what his movements were before, during and after the Marchetti murder.

Kate waited until they were sealed into the car and driving away. "You made a new friend back there."

"Hey, I feel sorry for him. He has some mental health issues. Paranoia is a scary place to be when you have no trust and believe enemies are all around. I saw an opportunity to develop rapport with that guy. We needed his cooperation, but you know, you could tell that he hasn't had much human contact outside of his trips to the VA hospital."

They slowed down in front of the Marchetti home. They paused for just a few moments in silence. Each detective quietly reflected on the recent development in their pursuit of justice.

Kate resumed, "Kunar Province? I remember hearing that in the news. Pretty intense, huh?"

"Yep. It sure was."

"How did you deal with it while you were at Bostick, besides hitting rocks with golf clubs?"

"Playing cards, smoking and joking, gaming and poetry."

"What, poetry? You're pulling my chain?"

He nodded, but bobbled with reluctance. "No. True. It was my jam to serenity."

"That's pretty awesome. Tell me one. I would like to hear one."

"Maybe later."

"What if a piece of Chinese space trash or rocket falls out of the sky and takes us out? I will never have heard the beauty of a sonnet by Cody Danko. C'mon?"

"Okay. Our secret?"

"My lips are sealed to the grave." She motioned a zipper across her lips.

"*Wolfhound Brothers*
We were once young boys and naïve
We were bold and strong
We landed on a dusty outpost surrounded by beautiful mountains
Those lofty peaks rained hostility upon us
We were rich and poor
Made no difference
We were brothers of camouflage
The brother to my right fell

The bother to my left fell
I fell to my knees and prayed
We need to leave
The generals said no
The politicians said no
We stayed
More blood
When we left, we were soulless men with fewer brothers
We were the brothers of camouflage
Memories and bonds of love and war wrapped us tight
We are The Wolfhounds who survived battle
No fear on earth."

Kate's eyes welled with tears. She thought briefly of her husband, Jake, and his deployments. She sniffed and said, "Wow. I'm speechless. That was powerful."

"Thanks."

After a long period of silence, Kate said, "You see, you are empathetic. You have a heart inside that chiseled body."

"I feel like I'm getting soft. I haven't really had a good workout since we started this case."

"That makes two of us."

"What are you talking about? You ran after Kash."

"I barely increased my heart rate. Probably more so after we collared him and the exhilaration of the ending the hunt."

"Okay, sure."

"That was a nice tattoo. You mentioned tattoos to Brian Poole. Anymore?"

"A few. Besides the Wolfhound, the other forearm is a cemetery with the tombstones of the guys that I knew killed. Also, a blue rose wrapped with a thin blue and black ribbon. I also have the proverbial heart with mom on it." They both chuckled. "How about you?"

"One. On my upper left back it reads, "My husband traded his combat boots for angel wings." It has army boots and wings."

"Deep. I like it." They both nodded, recognizing each other's ghosts from the past that influenced their lives.

Kate looked over at Cody and said, "Okay, here is our game plan. We will get a warrant for Upton's phone location. I want to prove that he was here and track his movements leading up to the murder. We need all his background. You know that as a political strap hanger, he has a vast assortment of look-at-me photos on Insta and other sites. I could tell that in my one brief interaction with him, it is all about him and Senator Thorland. He seemed like a first-class suck-up."

"Do you think he is capable of murder? An entire family?"

"I learned a time ago not to underestimate someone's motivation. A chance meeting, I would say no. When we add that his future success is tied to Thorland and to help conceal a crime, an embarrassing career-ending crime? You and I and 99 percent of the rest world would say hell no."

"Well, he can't get to Kash in jail unless he finds someone that owes him a favor and gets a shiv into Kash."

"I agree. Kash is as safe as he has been since the murders. There is one idea that I have."

Chapter Seventy-One

Kate drove the car down the six-block chic shopping and restaurant area known as Hyde Park Village. To the left was a two-story shopping plaza encircling a 3-tiered fountain. Kate was able to find an open spot on the street without going to the parking garage.

"C'mon follow me."

"Sure. What do you have in mind?"

"I remember this place and it's close to the Marchetti's. The medical examiner said they all had a strawberry substance in their stomach contents. He thought maybe ice cream or a shake. Well, how about a smoothie? Fit-n-Full Smoothie here may have sold them the lethal smoothies."

Kate pulled the door open and held it open for Cody. The smell of fruit and ice cream was a treat to the senses. The young girl behind the counter looked like a high school student with her ginger hair pulled back in a ponytail. "How can I help you?"

Kate leaned in and asked, "Do you have an app?"

"We sure do. You can download it off the app store. Apple and Android."

"Can you look up a name on your computer?"

"Oh sure. What is your name or your phone number?"

"No, it's not for me. It's for one of your customers."

"Oh, I'll have to ask my manager."

A fit blonde with her hair pulled back walked out through a door drying her hands and looked over at the detectives and broke into an enthusiastic smile. "Hi Cody."

Kate's head snapped back to Cody.

Cody said, "Hi Olivia."

Olivia asked, "What's going on?"

Cody said, "We are working a case. We suspect that the person of interest perhaps stopped here on Sunday and purchased some smoothies."

"Okay, what's the name?" She looked curious.

"Rodney Upton."

"Yes, he was. I waited on him. He is one of those memorable people. Not like you Cody, but a bit of a..." She looked around and continued, ".. a dick."

"So yes, he has an app. He actually checked the box, allowing us to send emails and share with other affiliated vendors. So that removes his privacy, right?"

Cody and Kate nodded at each other. "Ahh, yes, I would say so. Not to mention that you already acknowledged that he was in here. You are merely confirming your business records."

"Oh sure. That makes sense. In the meantime, can I fix you anything? Like your usual Cody, the Caesar chocolate and how about you, ma'am?"

"I'll take the Zena Wild Berry."

"We are on it. Mary, would you take care of them while I look up the information here?"

"Sure, no problem."

While Mary started configuring the smoothies, Olivia pulled up the computer information and began scrolling with her finger. She waited for the whirl of the blender to come to a stop. As Mary began pouring the contents into the cups, Olivia said, "Okay, here it is. He came in right before we were closing. So annoying. The sale was made at 8:55 pm. He ordered four wild berry strawberry smoothies. I also have video that covers the transaction if you would like to see?"

Kate sucked on the straw to her smoothie and said, "That would be fabulous, Olivia. If you could take a screenshot of his purchase and make a copy of the video for that transaction."

"Sure, no problem."

"You can send it to Cody. I'm sure you have his email."

"Sure do. No problem. Those are on the house."

"You have been so helpful. Thank you, Olivia."

"Sure. Goodbye Cody. Give me a call."

"I will. Good to see you again. I haven't had time to work out lately. I'll be back soon, unless this one doesn't give me any time off." He pointed at Kate as she shrugged.

Kate sucked again through the straw as they walked outside towards the fountain. A group of children were chasing each other and having fun.

"Oh my gosh, you've had sex with that woman, haven't you?"

"Why would you say that?" As his mouth gaped open.

"Guilty. If she was a dog, she would have been drooling all over you. She all but wanted you to mount you there in the store."

"I work out at the gym up the street. I stop here for a smoothie, post workout."

"I think you've had more than a smoothie."

"We may have gone out a couple of times." He flashed a cute grin.

"I knew it." She punched him in his hard bicep.

"By the way, if you and Trent want an enjoyable meal, Timpanos on the corner is a great place. Good food, drink and atmosphere."

Kate said, "And a great night cap of sex?"

He shook his head from side to side.

"Wait, are you blushing?" She pulled on his arm.

"Nope."

"Okay fine. Anyway, we got the information that we needed. Good job, Fabio."

Chapter Seventy-Two

Arriving back at the Blue Monster, they stopped to speak with the analysts. They requested a deep dive on Rodney Upton, while Cody and Kate prepared the affidavit for a search warrant to request the cellphone tracking of Rodney.

One analyst, Dainta Vickers, called Kate. "Hi Kate, I went to school with Rodney Upton."

"Really. Which one?"

"Both. High School and College."

"Do tell. What was he like?"

"He was a lizard. Like a born politician. I figured him to be in the yearbook as the most likely to be a used car salesman. He was always acting like he was the most popular kid, but was never accepted in those groups. Always sucking up to the teachers. He was in the student council. He was like the treasurer or something. Never could get elected president."

"How about in college?"

"Big frat guy."

"Of course he was."

"I don't remember which fraternity that he belonged, but he was always heavily involved with Greek life and the student government. I think he was a poly sci major."

"Dainta, let me ask you. Do you think he would be capable of murder?"

"I would say no, but I would say he would do anything to get ahead and protect that ascension."

"Sounds like most politicians. What about his home life?"

"I think he grew up in humble beginnings. His parents were divorced. The port was where his dad worked. I don't think his dad was in his life. His mother was essentially a single parent struggling to keep a roof over their heads and food on the table."

"I wonder if he recognizes the sacrifices that his single mother made for him?"

"Probably not. He seemed too entitled to appreciate anyone other than himself."

"I have to say, Dainta, it was always a joy hearing your voice on the radio when you were in communications, and I was in patrol. I always felt confident knowing you were my lifeline for help."

"Aww. Thanks. That seems a century ago."

"Feels like it too." As they both laughed.

"Anything else, Dainta?"

"He was always a sharp dresser. I never figured that one out because I knew where he lived in West Tampa. Let's just say that a shoebox would have been palatial. I don't think HDTV could do much with his house. He was pretty quiet about his upbringing. One of my friends lived a few doors down and we would pass his house. My friend Monica knew his background. They were closer to elementary school. I can call her?"

"No, that's fine. I don't want to start the neighborhood gossip to be the primary conversation at the West Tampa Sandwich Shop." Known for campaign stops for every politician, the sandwich shop was an institution in the neighborhood. "I gather that you did not stay in touch with him?"

"Nope. He wasn't in my circle. I knew him in school as Rod."

"Rodney fits with his blue blood image that he is trying to project. Thanks again, Dainta. This is very insightful. Sounds like he is trying to overcompensate."

"Yep, I would agree with that."

"Okay, thank you."

Kate looked at the analytical reports on Rodney. He had a lively social media presence, striving to be a political influencer and never moving past his Greek life at Theta Phi. Many people posted about their vacations, kids and children. This guy was all about who he was associating with and where he was hanging out. Being the gatekeeper for the Senator allowed him a certain amount of power. For a kid from humble beginnings, he was hiding his past for the sake of hailing his current associations.

He had a shoplifting arrest when he was sixteen at a high-end clothing store at the International Plaza. This was probably how he was acquiring his dress to impress wardrobe. He was in a lot of ways like Kash McCool. Creating and living an illusion.

She read his bio on LinkedIn. He said his love of politics had been fostered in high school with the student council, nurtured in his participation in college student government, as a campaign worker and internships for politicians, and matured in his service for Thorland. Kate scrunched her face, thinking, what an ass wipe.

Kate looked up his mom and called her landline, which was archaic in today's world.

"Hi, Mrs. Upton, this is Kate from the high school class of 2010 reunion committee. We are trying to get in touch with Rod to invite him to the celebration."

"Well, that makes two of us. If you get in touch with him, tell him I need some help to replace the hot water tank. I'm sure you can get in touch with him at Thorland's office."

"Thorland?"

"Yeah, you know Senator Thorland? Rod is some political muckety-muck with his office and moved uptown."

"Oh, thank you so much. It's nice to hear one of our classmates has earned so much success."

"Okay, whatever you say."

Kate evaluated that quick call. She did not want to go see the mother for fear that she might give the heads up to her son. After speaking with his mother, the distance was noted. She looked down on his success, as much as he probably looked down on her and his upbringing. She thought this was sad. A single mother, who may have had her faults, provided shelter and food. Perhaps there was abuse, regardless, he was not celebrating a rags to riches ascent. He was disavowing the existence. That might be a nice backstory if he ever ran for office himself.

Chapter Seventy-Three

Kate called Fiona and requested to draft an affidavit for Rodney's phone. She needed everything on his phone. Text messages, phone calls and certainly the cell tower tracking. Most important for the case was determining his movements. After talking with Fiona, Kate decided she had enough to claim exigent circumstances in this case. Considering the murder of the Marchetti's and Kash being in fear of life, who knew who else might be on the target list.

Anytime you claimed an emergency or exigent circumstance, you were required to provide the search warrant with 48 hours. The provider's legal compliance team forwarded the current location of Upton's phone. Not necessarily where he was, but the current whereabouts for the phone for which he was a subscriber.

Not surprisingly, his phone was in the area of Senator Thorland's Tampa office. Kate was more concerned with the tracking on the night of the Marchetti's murder.

She reviewed triangulation of the cellphone data to see where he was from Sunday until Monday. He was on Davis Island for part of the day and then at 9:00 pm he was in Hyde Park Village to pickup the smoothies. From 9:30 until 2:00 am, he was in the vicinity of the Marchetti residence. Ding ding ding.

Kate was encouraged that she had him surrounded with circumstantial evidence. The cell location data and the smoothies along with the video of his car leaving the area described by a witness during a timeframe that shots were fired. She was hoping to bring Rodney in for a face-to-face interview. She was eager to strategize about his narcissistic tendencies. Who would be the chess master?

She and Cody drove to Senator Thorland's office in the Timberlake Federal Building. She still had Upton's number on her cellphone from when he called her. He picked up immediately.

"Hello detective, how can I help you?"

"We are going back over friends of Dominic. We really didn't have time to chat at the crime scene that night. I wanted to know if you would mind answering a few questions?"

"Oh sure. Fire away."

"Actually, we had business in the area and we parked outside of the Timberlake Building. We didn't want anyone worrying about two detectives coming to the Senator's office. You know how gossip starts. I'm sure being the chief of staff is very important. In fact, your job is second only to the Senator." She made the kissing gesture to Cody, followed with the gagging gesture. Cody smiled back.

"I stay busy. It's a great deal of responsibility to look out for the people that we serve. As you know, there is no greater calling than to serve the community."

"Great, well, I'll see you downstairs."

She turned to Cody and said, "I hope to bluff him into a corner. The interview room at the Blue Monster might knock him off his stride."

"You're going to bring up the toilet seat, aren't you?"

She flashed a coy smile, "You know it." She pointed at the door. "Here he comes."

They watched Rodney walked out the front door held open by a security guard. Dressed in a light blue suit and a white oxford shirt. He exemplified a professional appearance. He looked around and saw them wave towards him. Kate smiled and waved, like she was motioning to an old friend. He came over to the car and jumped into the back seat.

"Hey, Rodney, this is my partner, Cody Danko. Listen, the security guards have already rousted us by being parked here. They have their orders. They don't want a repeat of the Oklahoma bombing and have some mad bomber parking in front of the building. I told them we were just picking up a staff member from the Senator's office and would leave. So, our office is a just a few blocks away where we can talk without being disturbed. Besides, we like to record all interviews of witnesses. The recording equipment is in place there, then we can bring you back. It shouldn't take very long. In fact, look at the lobby of the police department for a potential photo op if the Senator ever has a speech on any law enforcement issues. Besides the memorial to fallen officers out front, they have an airplane suspended from the ceiling of the lobby."

"Really?"

"Yep. I wish I was there when they got it inside. It's pretty cool."

"I have lived here all my life, and I never knew that."

"Well, most people would not know unless they had business inside the building. Unfortunately for most people coming into the building, they are wearing handcuffs. You are free as a bird."

Kate hoped that statement would not be true by the end of the evening. He was all smiles in the back seat as they drove the few blocks down the bus lane of Marion Street to circle behind the police department and enter the garage.

Chapter Seventy-Four

The trio each had a seat in the interview room, and Kate engaged the recorder and announced their presence, date, and time.

Although being free to leave and not being detained, she chose to advise him of his rights. She was concerned that if Rodney made damaging comments, that a judge might view his statements inadmissible because of the appearance that he was encouraged to accompany the detectives. Despite no handcuffs, the ride in the back seat and being questioned in an interview room with the door closed could be up for discussion in hindsight of whether he was free to leave. Better to be safe than sorry.

If they had conducted the interview in the car parked outside his office, they would not have read him his rights. It all came down to the impression if they were free to leave. Being in the police department diluted that appearance. She excused away the reading of the rights as just routine for those being interviewed.

Kate looked at the relaxed and in control Rodney Upton. "So, Mr. Upton, I want to thank you for coming in today. Like I said, we are interviewing as many folks that we can concerning the Marchetti's. I know you are busy as the Chief of Staff for Senator Thorland. That is quite an accomplishment for your age. You must be a special talent to achieve his approval."

Kate didn't mean a word of it. She had enough dealings with politicians and their brethren that she had little use for them. She also knew that they all thought they were special. How many times had she been berated for stopping these self-important and entitled politicians for a traffic violation? She wanted to suck up to him and then slowly turn the heat up like a frog in a pot of water. Before they realize it's boiling, it is too late. They are cooked.

Rodney leaned forward with a smug smile. "Thank you. I work hard. My life is devoted to the Senator and his constituents."

"What was your relationship with Dominic Marchetti?"

"We were in the same social circle. We were members of the Krewe of Kingsmen that takes part in the Gasparilla parade."

"I just don't know how you find the time between running the Senator's office, his campaign for re-election and donating your time to the charity of the krewe. Do you have time for yourself or to sleep?"

"I keep a calendar in order to stay focused and to prioritize for planning."

"Old school. How about your Apple watch?" as she pointed to his wrist.

"No, that's what I meant. My calendar is on my watch."

Kate answered, "I have one also, but I don't wear it at night. I don't need a watch telling me I had a dreadful night of sleep. You?"

"I take it off for showering, but I'm addicted to it."

Kate nodded in agreement. "Talking of politics, at one time in college, I considered running for the student body. I had actually been on the student council in my high school. Just the secretary, but I have to be honest, I had considered going into politics. But marriage, and kids, kind of changed my idea."

"It's funny you should say that. I was the treasurer in my high school."

"No kidding? I was nothing but essentially a note taker as the secretary. But you know, it made me understand how often your constituents take you for granted. It's a thankless job that you have."

"It can be." He turned the tables on Kate, which she expected. "Look at you. A successful detective and you said the other night that you went to Duke."

He was listening. She knew she needed to swallow some pride and lower her social standing. She did not want to seem like a blue blood attending a private school versus Upton attending a state college.

"It was my running to school that was my platform. From the doublewide trailer park to the high school was five miles. With no car, it was good training to escape my life. Duke felt pity and gave me a jock ride. You know most of us jocks were P.E. majors. Playing flag football and tossing medicine balls."

She could see that he was calculating the level of competition.

Kate continued, "Otherwise, I would be flipping burgers and smelling of French fries." The relationship deepened as kindred spirits from a rough upbringing. "I don't know where you came from, but you tend to work harder when you have nothing." Kate knew exactly where he came from. Nothing.

She had developed rapport with him, as she continued to ask questions concerning his rise in the political field. He started as a campaign worker and then landed an internship, which was followed by a paid staff position. He had only been the chief of staff for a short time replacing Marc Dorcius, who became the director of economic development for the State.

"Now, when was the last time that you saw Dominic?"

"Oh gosh, probably a week or so. I saw him at Four Green Fields with a couple of other Krewe members."

"So that was the last time that you saw him? That must have been traumatic, knowing the last time you saw him, you probably did not know that would be the last time you would ever see him."

"That's why when I came over to the house the morning of their deaths, I was stunned at such a loss of life."

Kate thought he did not seem too stunned. More about who he was and less about what had happened. "Devastating. What do you think happened to them?"

"I don't know exactly. I leave that up to you folks, but I would assume homicide-suicide. So sad about the children."

Kate noticed a lack of warmth to his reply. "Horrible. You mentioned that morning the suicide of a friend had impacted Dom?"

"Yes. I don't recall the name, but he felt terrible for the widow, who was devastated. He hired a caretaker to help her out of her depression. I think he thought of the impact on his family with his planned suicide."

"Planned?"

"I am sorry. I misspoke. I just know that he was facing some scrutiny at work over finances."

"How did you know that?"

"Melvin told me that night."

"Was he depressed?"

"Not that I noted. But I'm not a psychologist. I am a political scientist." He flashed another smug smile.

Such arrogance. "Indeed, you are. Apparently a very good one in a coveted and trusted position. When was the last time that you spoke with him on the phone or text him?"

"I speak to so many people on a daily basis, I couldn't say with any certainty."

"I can only imagine between emails that you have to deal with and phone calls, along with all your meetings. Could you go over your movements on Sunday evening into Monday until we met? Despite your hectic schedule, I would assume that the small time frame would be fairly memorable."

He rubbed his chin and looked upward as he contemplated his answer. Kate knew that his cocky narcissism and diminished opinion of the police would be his undoing as he walked into a trap and never saw it coming. She was enjoying this.

"So, I mostly stayed at home. I caught up on emails and watched some TV. I went out in the early evening and walked around Hyde Park Village to get some fresh air and went back home before the rain started."

"You stayed in the rest of the night?"

"Yep. From 8 or 8:30 pm on."

"Did you meet anyone at the Village?"

"I did see the owner of the Smoothie shop. Olivia. She is like really into me, but I just don't have time for a social life."

Kate wondered if this pompous ass ever had a date or made it to second base. One night with him, and she would claim a sudden onset of a bladder infection or hemorrhoids, "You didn't get a smoothie?"

"No. It was getting too late."

"Okay, so you stayed home until you got the text from Melvin Storms and never left your residence?"

"Yes, that's true."

Kate thought this was really going to be fun. Better than catching beads off a parade float at Gasparilla.

"See, I told you this was no big deal. Are you about ready to go back?"

"Sure."

"Okay, we'll be right back."

Chapter Seventy-Five

Kate and Cody stepped out into the hallway. She wanted to give him a minute to adapt to the temperature and feel comfortable that he had outsmarted the cops, who he no doubt felt were inferior to him.

Cody said, "This is entertaining. You had a future in politics. I had no idea."

"Total lie. I gave him the secret handshake that we had the same aspirations. Me? I was a total jock in high school. Cross-country to volleyball to track. I had no desire for politics. It was all about developing some rapport. I did drive by a trailer park on the way to school but never lived in one."

"Duke and a P.E. major?"

Duke, yes. P.E. no. I never actually said what my major was." She crinkled her face. "I was actually a business major and psych was my minor."

"Impressive. I never completed college."

"College is overrated. Your experience and no student debt is much better."

Cody nodded as they walked back towards the interview room.

This time, Kate was carrying a folder. She smiled at Rodney.

"Oh, I almost forgot. Is there any reason you would have been out driving at about 2:00 am Monday morning near the Marchetti residence?"

He lied so effortlessly. "No. I was in bed."

Kate looked at his feet as they hiked-up under the chair, showing an involuntary discomfort to the question. "Hmm. Really?" Before he calculates his exposure to danger and starts spinning, she hit him again. "The cellphone data shows your phone was not at your house but at the Marchetti home."

"You know, with that storm, it probably interfered with cell service, just like satellite TV."

"You bring up a good point. I'm sure that satellite TV was adversely impacted that evening. Cell towers are stationary and affixed to the ground. They triangulate the location with surprising accuracy." Kate pointed to his watch. "You know your watch will tell us exactly where you were, your heart rate, and if your lying-in bed or simply lying." She let that last statement marinate for just a moment. Just long enough to pick up some flavor. Then she brought out the meat clever. "But we also have a witness that was outside on their porch and heard gunshots and watched your car drive away."

"Probably heard thunder and saw a car like mine."

She thought, this guy is like a trained seal. He immediately barks at a stimulus. He had been so engrained to spin tales into believable responses that it was natural. Almost without thinking.

She nodded, almost in appreciation for his ability. She held up one finger and opened up her cellphone and leaned toward Rodney, turning the screen toward him. "Isn't that your car?"

"Looks similar. I'm not sure that it is."

Kate paused the video. "Isn't that your car with the bumper sticker for Thornton?"

"We hand those out all over town." Upton proclaimed.

"Okay, Rodney. You may think that we are stupid, but we are not. That is your license plate. If we look at the enlarged still photo from the video, that is you correct?"

"I'm not sure." He stroked his light beard.

"It's you." Kate lasered her eyes at Upton.

He leaned forward in his chair and said, "This is a political ambush. The opposition has friends in the police department. This is a ginned-up frame."

Even when he faced direct evidence, he was going to deny and then make counter accusations. He would not easily admit that he was in trouble and needed a parachute for a soft landing.

Kate continued, "Believe that if it makes you feel better. This video taken from a home down the street corroborates the eyewitness testimony and the cellphone tracking along with your watch activity. Your boat is taking on water."

He folded his arms, sat back and flashed contempt at Kate.

"One more thing. You bought a smoothie that night."

"Oh, that's right, I forgot. Sure did."

"Actually, you bought four. Guess what they found inside the stomachs of each one of the Marchetti family during the autopsy? You got it. A strawberry smoothie that had been spiked with sleeping pills."

"Coincidence."

"Well, sport, you left the toilet seat up in the master bath. Most single men wouldn't think of that. Your urine splashes and grabbing the seat and flushing the toilet will prove that you were in that bathroom. Did you wash your hands?"

"I may have used that in the past when Dom was showing me around."

"I see. Are you saying that they have never cleaned the bathroom since the last time you were there?"

He gave a shrug and twisted his mouth. His right arm reached back to his neck and rubbed it. Another display of discomfort.

She continued, "The two drink glasses in the kitchen sink. I hope you remembered to wipe down the faucet, or your DNA will be there. Oh, and the keyboard where you typed the letter or the cellphone when you sent the message to Melvin will also be examined for DNA."

Kate could see Rodney had pushed the reverse button to recall if he had wiped the sink. He probably cleaned the glasses, but now he wasn't sure about the faucet. She knew this was why he wanted inside the house that night to get his DNA and prints throughout the house.

Kate steepled her hands on the table and said, "Okay, well, right now we are conducting a search warrant of your residence. Are we going to find anything more incriminating?" She could see panic flash across his face. "Your boat is taking on a lot of water. In fact, it is sinking right now. You have a choice. You can go down with the ship, and we all know how this story ends or we can give you a lifeboat to save you. We know a lot more than you think?"

"No. No. No." Upton was shaking his head and closing his eyes.

"You are looking at the death penalty."

Cody made his first interjection. "That only comes after ten years of appeals to the inevitable. Sitting on death row in a jail cell at Starke Prison with all the most violent and badass convicts for ten years. That is before they give you an injection of a life altering juice. You killed an entire family, including two children. No jury will give you compassion. Nor will the jail population. Especially considering you are a former politician."

They watched as he contemplated his world collapsing. His boat was being tossed at sea and he was considering his options. It had become so quiet that they could hear footsteps walking past the interview room and the air-conditioned air blowing through the vent.

Kate's phone buzzed. She read the message from Lester Rollins and smiled. "I have some news from the team searching your home. In addition to finding sleeping pills, they found a black raincoat hanging in your laundry room. It has high velocity blood spatter like what you get from shooting someone at close range. We will analyze the blood. I'm certain it is Dom's. They also found your muddy shoes. Oops. Yes, the lab can also match the soil to the Marchetti residence. I'll guarantee that your shoes have blood spatter on them. We are going to unleash CSI on your BMW. The positioning of the gun and handling of the firearm are also inconsistent with a suicide. The buzzer has just blown in the third period of the hockey game. You are going to the penalty box."

The smug look was gone from Upton. He knew the curtain had closed on his performance.

Kate spoke, "Here is your only chance to avoid the death penalty. It is to cooperate. Admit your guilt and tell us who else was involved. We know you were looking to cover for the Senator and his vulnerability once the depth of the LymRX Technology fraud is made public. Especially with the influence of Marc Dorcius to get the grants and tax breaks. The political donations from Kash McCool to the Senator. We know that Dominic Marchetti was going to notify the authorities. You couldn't allow that to happen. You were the faithful servant protecting the Senator and the Party."

She watched as his mouth twitched about and it looked like the inside of his mind was on the spin cycle of a washing machine, contemplating his choices. He was way off kilter. Totally unfamiliar territory for the previously confident political mastermind.

Kate spoke, "You know they will all throw you in a tank filled with piranhas ravaging your carcass. They will describe you as a psychopath. They will interview your mother and describe how you should never have been let into the aristocracy. You were a juvenile offender. An imposter. You can take the lion out of the jungle, but you can never turn a lion into a pet. You are an outlier. A despicable murderer."

That was the nudge off the ledge that he needed because he knew that was exactly what would happen. "Okay. I'm not going down alone. Brian Poole was also involved. You can check and see he was the first phone call I made. It was his idea."

"Okay. We are making progress. Tell us what happened?"

"You are right. I gave them smoothies with sleeping pills. That was Poole's idea. I had pleaded with Dom not to go to the authorities. It would have ruined everything we had accomplished and would achieve after the next election. He would not listen. I had no choice. I knew where he kept his gun in his desk. He fell asleep after the smoothie and a couple of drinks. I shot him. I was afraid he had discussed everything with Carol. I figured it would be chalked up to a homicide-suicide by killing the entire family. I saved the kids from a life of despair. Dom was losing everything. His career and fraud charges."

Kate wanted to choke the life out of him. No remorse. He killed the children to save them despair? No, he killed them to extend the coverup. She paused to maintain control of her emotions. With the recording ongoing, she did not want to lose her temper. Her rage simmered. There was a special place outside the gates of hell for people like this evil piece of rubbish. Even the death sentence would be too kind. She wanted a tortuous death for him.

"Any more proof on Brian Poole?"

"I have text messages from him."

"How did you get to know him?"

"We were in the same fraternity, The Teepee's. Theta Pi. That's how we met and then he contributed to the campaign and the party. Eventually, he became a primary investor in LymRX Technology. He was pissed that he was bamboozled, and that Dom had lost a lot of his money in an investment. He wanted to silence any opposition, including Dom and Kash, as well as to reduce his exposure to embarrassment."

"So, for his ego and pride, Poole wanted to kill an entire family and the guy that manipulated him into investing in a nonexistent company."

"Yes."

"Let's go over the details of the night at the Marchetti's?"

"I brought the smoothies over. I timed it close to bedtime, so they would sleep through the storm."

"And gunshots." She knew this was setting up his premeditation and intent.

"Yes." His voice trailed off.

"What about Dom?"

"I tried to reason with him that this would cost everyone, including himself and his family. He said that his family would stand by him, and he would stand by his friends. He would not let Kash destroy any more of his friends. He wouldn't listen. We had a couple of drinks, and he passed out." Then, with a hint of anger, Rodney said, "He forced my hand. I killed him and the rest of the family." He stared with defiance.

Silence hovered in the room as the two detectives digested what Upton had admitted to doing. Kate turned off the recorder and reached into her folder while standing up. She pulled out two photographs. One of Ethan and one of Meghan. "These are the two children that you killed. I am going to leave them here. You may have shot them in the dark like a coward, but their faces will always be in the light and haunting your dreams."

Chapter Seventy-Six

Stepping outside the interview room, Kate said, Let's go pickup Mr. Poole and see what he has to say. So much for fraternity brothers pledging allegiance."

Cody smiled and said, "Yeah, Rodney barely heard the bus toot its horn before he threw Poole under it. He would never last in a combat platoon, where you depend on each other to survive. You would do anything for your brother to protect them. Including jumping on a grenade. You were awesome in there."

"You know who the greatest salespeople are?"

"You?"

"Us." She motioned to herself and Cody. "Anyone can sell a timeshare to people on vacation in a tropical location. We are selling a lifetime membership to a ten-by-ten room with a stainless-steel toilet, sink and a horrible bed with no view. Every cop show tells the bad guys to scream for an attorney and seal their mouth. Our skills convince them otherwise. I read sales books all the time."

"Well done."

"Thank you, partner. You know, it's hard to celebrate when two children were murdered for a coverup."

"You brought a voice and justice to those children."

"Yes, we did."

Kate walked into Alfonso's office. "We have a cleanup on aisle four. Bring a mop. Can we have Arroyo take our prisoner to jail while we go out and talk to Poole?"

The big man leaned back in his chair and released his trademark deep and sustained laugh. He stood up and gave a high five to Kate and said, "Congratulations. If you don't mind, I would like to call The Caveman?"

Beaming, she said, "Be my guest. As long as I can listen."

"Stand by." He put the phone on speaker and dialed the number.

On the second ring, the officious voice answered, "Lieutenant Willard."

"Jack it's Alfonso. I just wanted to let you know you made the right decision in sticking with Kate Alexander on this investigation. I questioned your wisdom of changing dance partners in the middle of a song, but you obviously realized that it's best to leave it to the greatest detective. From the beginning, she was correct. She just obtained a confession for the murder of the entire family, along with a wheelbarrow full of circumstantial evidence. She knocked it out of the park along with Cody."

"Thank you for the call. Glad it worked out. I need to get back to my kid's game." The call ended and his disappointment was palatable. He would take credit with the front office for leading the investigation, but it was a stab to the heart to give credit to Kate and her new partner, who had fragged him at the golf course.

Alfonso said, "To be honest, I never knew he had kids. Not once did I ever have a conversation with my direct supervisor as to hobbies or family? Aside from golf, I know nothing of the man." He shrugged. "Well, you heard him. Good job."

"It pained him to say it." Kate said. "He was not congratulating us. He had as much enthusiasm as an undertaker."

"You're right."

"Now you can coast across the finish line into retirement."

"Thank you, Kate, for everything that you have brought to this squad. You have enriched my life as well."

"Okay, let's save the mushy stuff for your final send off."

The big man just nodded and smiled.

Chapter Seventy-Seven

Brian Poole answered the door in a loose-fitting tank top. His previously styled manbun on top of his head was now braided down the back of his scalp, dangling like a ponytail. Kate wondered if this guys' toughest decision each day was which novel way to wear his hair.

Kate asked, "Mr. Poole, would you accompany us back to the police department?"

"Am I under arrest?"

"No. Some information has come to light concerning the death of the Marchetti family, and we would like to provide you the opportunity to clarify a few concerns."

He placed his hands behind him and looked down toward Kate. "The short answer is no. Unless you have an arrest warrant, I am not leaving. Besides, I have a massage scheduled in an hour." As he looked at his watch.

"Would you mind answering some questions?"

He put his hands on his hips. "Again, the short answer would be no. Here is the deal. I have spoken to my attorney, and I am not saying anything. The only way that I'm leaving here is in handcuffs, and I am not answering any questions. I'll save you the oxygen from reading me my rights."

"Okay, we just wanted to give you the opportunity to answer some damaging allegations."

"So, no doubt, this has to be related to Rodney. The cheese-dick political suck-up. He has his head so far up the ass of the Thorland's, he would need a proctologist to pump light and oxygen into him. He is desperate to be something that he is not. By the way, I want to play a short recording that I made."

Poole walked over to a digital recorder and he already had what he wanted queued up. Kate knew Poole was expecting their arrival. She wondered if The Caveman had leaked the arrest of Upton to his puppet masters, who in turn warned Poole. He walked over to them and hit the play button as they listened to a male voice they recognized as Rodney Upton said, "Brian, our problems are almost over. They're gone. As soon as I find Kash, everything will be okay." He stared at Kate.

"Why did you not say anything about these the last two times that we came here?"

"I have the right to remain silent. I will forward a copy of this recording to you. Have a nice day."

Pool had called their bluff. Unlike Rodney Upton, he had heeded the advice rendered on every cop show. He was not going to cooperate and had his attorney on speed dial. He had provided another piece of evidence to seal the vault door on Upton.

Kate looked at Cody and said, "What a life. You may be rich and powerful, but you are always looking over your shoulder. These two couldn't stab each other in the back fast enough."

"You're right. It's the backstabbers club. No real friends. No trust or loyalty. It would be a scary world to live in."

"You got that right. One day you are the rooster and the next day you are a feather duster."

"So true."

Kate knew that the political and power elites would not let some commoner destroy their fiefdom. They were throwing Upton overboard. He would take the hit and they would survive making their deals. She actually believed Upton concerning Poole's involvement. The text messages between them were vague. As was the recording, but would be enough with all the other evidence and confession to close the freezer door. She was concerned that Poole would skate. Then a thought crossed her mind.

Chapter Seventy-Eight

Once inside the car, Kate explained she had an idea. She drove on Cleveland Street, paralleling the Selmon Expressway. She turned right on Armenia Street and then to Memorial Hospital. Next to the hospital was a boring medical arts building. They parked at the rear parking lot and walked into the aging building, past a pharmacy to the left.

They took the stairs to the third floor and entered the family practice office for Dr. Emily Dobbins. Kate and Cody walked into the waiting room that looked like nothing had been replaced in the past twenty years. Waiting patients filled most of the chairs. They watched a man struggle with a walker coming out a door. Kate scurried over to assist the older gentleman through the door and used that opportunity to step inside out of the listening ears of the waiting room.

The receptionist said, "Can I help you? You need to wait outside, please."

Kate said, "I'm sorry, we are not patients. We are looking for Krystal Lincoln."

A blonde in blue scrubs wheeled back on a roller chair and said with a big smile, "That's me."

"Hi Krystal, I am Kate. We spoke on the phone the other day about Brian."

Krystal lost her exuberance. "Yes, I remember."

"Would you mind if we talk in private?"

A shorter female wearing a lab coat and ponytail stepped out of a room and said, "I know, Mr. Philpot. Bless your heart. Well, Annie will be in a moment." She looked over at the three and said, "What's happening here?"

Krystal said, "These are police officers, and they wanted to ask me some questions about a person who I know. Is there someplace we could talk for a couple of minutes?"

"Oh, sweet Jesus. Sure, I reckon you could use my office."

Kate said, "Thank you Doctor Dobbins. It won't take long. Do I detect a North Carolina twang?"

"Indeed. Boone."

"App State?"

"You know it. UNC for med school."

"You?"

"Outside of Raleigh. I went to Duke."

"Ahh a Dookie. Okay, well, tap on this door if you drag Krystal out of here in handcuffs."

"No ma'am. That won't happen."

"Okay good. I'm off to see the next patient."

Once they were inside the meticulously adorned office with a host of framed pictures of family and vacations, they sat down around the desk.

Kate said, "Krystal, we wanted to talk to you about Brian Poole. I spoke with you by phone and you confirmed you spent the night with him?"

"Yes, that is correct."

"In light of the fact that a person closely associated with Brian, Rodney Upton, has now been arrested and charged with the murder of the entire Marchetti family, does that change your mind?"

Crystal covered her mouth in shock. "I did not know. Brian is a fun guy to hang out with, and he treats me well. We've been dating kind of casual for a few months. I stayed with him that night. I remember because it was raining."

"Do you remember anything else?"

"He received a phone call in the middle of the night. He stepped out into the hallway, and I got up to use the bathroom. I heard him say, "Dude, are we going to have any blowback?" Brian then asked, "We have to find Kash and eliminate him as well. We have to show people they can't do this and get away with it." That was all I heard, and I went to the bathroom. When I came back, he was in bed. I asked what that was all about and he said it was business and was sorry to wake me."

"How was his demeanor?' Kate asked.

"He was fine."

"Okay, let me ask an important question, and you are not in any trouble. I am only interested in the truth. Did you provide any drugs to Brian? Please be truthful. If you don't, then you could be in deep trouble, along with Dr. Dobbins finding out more than she probably would like to know."

There was a long pause. Kate could see Krystal calculating like a high-speed computer. "Yes. Zolpidem tartrate for sleeping. I told Doc I was planning a trip to Europe, and I always had trouble sleeping on long flights and adjusting to the time zone. She offered the prescription."

"And you gave it to Brian?"

She nodded and said, "Yes. I am so sorry. He asked me for some sleeping pills."

"Did he say why he needed them?"

"He said that he needed them for anxiety that his new business venture was keeping him awake, and he didn't have time to go to the doctor. Please don't tell Doc I got those under false pretense."

"I'm not. But you are going to have to. You are going to have to testify on this and that he used you."

"Oh, my gosh. I can't believe this." The waterworks began.

Kate patted Krystal on her shoulder and they walked out of the office towards the exit.

Chapter Seventy-Nine

Kate called Rollins, who was conducting the search warrant at Upton's residence, which was in Gray Gables, a small community just west of the outskirts of Hyde Park. He lived in a taupe and white craftsman style home. Probably close enough to the prestigious neighborhood that he could claim that he lived there. It fit his always wanting to be something more.

Rollins answered, "Kick ass. How many have you got in jail?"

"Only two. How is it going?"

"Fabulous. I'm calling this the house of mirrors."

"Why?"

"This cat must have a love affair with himself. He has at least one mirror in every room."

"I don't doubt it."

Rollins said, "To cover the backstory of my text to you, eagle eye Dee found the blood spatter on the rain jacket. It was hanging up like a trophy waiting to be selected. The shoes were covered in grass and mud. Dee believes there is also blood in the shoelaces. We also found his other clothes in the dryer after being washed. He probably didn't realize Tide doesn't remove all the blood in the wash. I guess this cat hung up the raincoat and forgot that it might have evidence on it. We searched his trash and found a ball cap in it. We bagged it and tagged it."

"That is awesome news. Let me ask you? What about the medicine vial for zolpidem tartrate?"

"Yep. Thirty pills made out to Krystal Lincoln from a Dr. Dobbins. I knew he wasn't Krystal, so I figured we would take it. We took a photo of it as well."

"Bingo, we can send the bottle to FDLE for DNA analysis."

"That could take a while."

"It could. I am hoping to call in some favors or have Alfonso do his magic. We had a good circumstantial case, but once you found evidence linking him to the crime scene, he gave up and confessed. Thanks for the excellent news."

"It brings joy to my heart. Those babies needed justice, and you brought it to them."

"Amen."

Chapter Eighty

Kate knew the Senator and his cronies would insulate themselves from being called to answer for the corruption and murders surrounding the LymRX Technology debacle. They had plausible deniability. Thorland would be quick to be the engineer driving the locomotive that would run over Rodney Upton. Yes, he would face some scrutiny because of the actions of a staff member who chose violence because of his upbringing in a dysfunctional family. Violence was this poor person's acceptable alternative to using diplomacy.

She knew how the spin doctors would pose a creative rendition. Dominic Marchetti's fraud from Hercules was his undoing, and that he had an argument with Upton that resulted in his death. There would be no mention of LymRX Technology. If that was uncovered, most people would gloss over the details of a fraud and would quickly slip away from public scrutiny. She knew with the shrinking cadre of investigative journalists, the chances of a front-page political news scandal news was remote.

However, if it became released by the opposition during a contested political campaign, that was something that could gain traction. Like a four-wheel Jeep in a winter storm. The opposition would release information, something like the Senator used his influence to secure millions in grants and tax concessions to a non-existent company with no assets or employees. He used the taxpayers as a personal piggybank, while also receiving campaign donations from the company and investors. His chief of staff, the most important person on his staff, resorted to a cold-blooded murder to conceal the fraud. That would be much more salacious and provide more attractive clickbait to read.

Kate wondered how to create her own spin. Then a thought started rumbling through her brain like a battalion of marching soldiers. She called Chuckles, the old informant of Frank Duffy. He answered on the second ring, "Hey beautiful. How are you?"

"I'm good. How is Jerome?"

"He is being a bit of pill right now. He wanted to go out last night. Me? I just needed some Chuckles alone time. His feelings are hurt, and he is a bit pouty today. He'll feel better after the gym."

"I wish this was a social call, but I have a little subterfuge in mind if you are game, and I need your help."

"Girl, I love covert operations. Just say the word, and I am all over it."

"I need someone to speak to the campaign manager for Lori Dennison for Senate and provide some damaging opposition research."

"Political intrigue, my cup of tea. Let's have the details."

"After the story is disclosed, it could give Dennison a substantial boost in the polls against the incumbent Thorland. I have to remain at arm's length. I will send you the details."

"I can hardly wait. I'll be Sergeant Schultz on my source. I know nothing."

"Thank you."

Chapter Eighty-One

By the end of the week, the news broke from the leak that Chuckles provided. The Dennison campaign held a press conference detailing the scandal and all the juicy tidbits. The media smelled a wounded animal, as in Senator Thorland. He quickly became roadkill. Squished under the weight of an eighteen wheeled media machine going after an institutional politician that had betrayed his electorate.

The polls showed Thorland's campaign was hemorrhaging profusely and unlikely that a tourniquet could stem the flow. Marc Dorcius, the former chief of staff and current director of economic development resigned, as his signature was on the grants.

Kate drove to the Orient Road Jail. She walked through the front door and approached the young deputy with a crew cut posted at the curved booth. She identified herself and asked the deputy to retrieve the prisoners, Kash McCool and Rodney Upton, and that they both be brought up front for two different interviews.

After waiting about fifteen minutes, the deputy stood up and told her, "Your first customer, McCool, is ready. Interview room two." He motioned her towards the blue door that opened to the interview suites.

She heard the buzz and pulled on the door. Once that door clanged closed, echoing the sound of the heavy door in the empty corridor, she walked towards door number two. Once again, she was buzzed in. She pulled the heavy door and stepped inside a room with a table and two chairs.

She stood and waited for a dark haired Hispanic looking deputy to open up the door separating Kate from the jail. He opened the door and in walked Kash McCool. He still looked afraid.

Kate motioned for him to sit down. "How are you doing?"

"Surviving."

"I'm not here to ask questions. As I promised, Florida will not be adding any charges. In fact, they will drop the one charge against you. You will now be transferred to the U.S. Marshals and returned to Texas to address your probation violation. In all likelihood, they will sentence you for your role in the Black Pool Investments fraud scheme, since you had not completed the terms of your pre-trial diversion. The FBI is also moving forward on potential wire fraud charges relating to LymRX Technology."

His shoulders dropped along with his head. Kate viewed the submissive pose as realization that it would be a very long time before he was walking as a free man. The memory of Jazz would comfort him on his lonely nights in jail, but that's all she would ever be was a memory.

Kate stood up and patted him on the shoulder as she nodded to the deputy through the window in the door. The heavy steel door opened. Kate could hear the chatter of the jail population coming through the door.

Kash stood up and looked at Kate with his eyes welling up and said quietly, "Thank you."

"Good luck."

The door banged closed, and she waited and her mind thought of what a horrible place to be confined. Many of these prisoners knew they had a slim chance of freedom for years to come. Some would never have freedom. Dying inside the walls of some penitentiary or death-row. All jails looked the same and sounded similar. Never quiet and the sterile surroundings of block construction with steel door and bars. Hope is choked out of you day by day.

The door opened again. In walked Rodney. The orange jumpsuit he wore was a far cry from his high-end fashion attire. The wingtips were now replaced with sandals. His cockiness was muted, but he still had a smug smile of contempt.

"Rodney, have a seat." He sat in the hard plastic chair.

Kate looked at him and said, "I'm not going to ask you questions. Your attorney would not appreciate my visit. I just wanted to give you an update. Well, we talked with Brian Poole. He threw you under the bus. He played a recording of you that implicates you. I just wanted to let you to know that he stabbed you in the back. All your friends just gave a huge stiff arm to you."

"That's bullshit."

"Sometimes, you really don't know who your friends are, and who will plunge the knife between the shoulder blades. You were just never really part of the club. Have they sent a high-priced attorney to represent you?" Kate let that linger for a moment. "Keep an eye out for an orange jumpsuit armed with a shiv."

Kate stood, and once again nodded to the jailer. The door opened and Rodney stood without a word and walked out.

He paused in the doorway and said, "Poole gave me the sleeping pills. He got it from his girlfriend, Krystal. I'm not going down alone." He stepped out of the doorway and the heavy door jolted closed.

Kate thought about how Rodney must feel. The hurt of betrayal from people he once considered friends and allies had now turned their backs on him. A wannabe preppy kid, who had now been thrown into the swamp with societies most treacherous villains, would no doubt have problems in the jail's general population. He would have to change his high and mighty attitude to survive. He had no marketable skills to trade with the other inmates.

As Kate escaped the sadness of the jail and reentered the bright sunshine, FDLE called Kate from the lab to say that Brian Poole's DNA was discovered on the pill bottle of sleeping pills that was used in the smoothies. Alfonso's last favor with FDLE had pushed the pill bottle to the front of the line.

Along with the DNA and the testimony of Krystal Lincoln and Rodney Upton, the State Attorney would now have enough evidence to charge Poole with conspiracy to commit murder. She knew Poole would claim that the bottle had been stolen from him and that Krystal had left it behind by accident. There was one additional lead that she wanted to explore.

Kate drove to the block that Brian Poole lived on. As she was getting out of the car, her phone rang. It was Ron Markham from the medical examiner's office. "Hi Ron."

"Hi Kate. I wanted to know first that I'm ruling Dominic Marchetti as a Homicide. The toxicology on blood levels of sleeping pills just came back. The levels of sleeping pills along with the alcohol would have incapacitated him. He would never have been able to shoot himself. He had enough to have slept through lunch. I know you already have your confession and forensics, but I think this puts a bow on top for all the naysayers and proves you right."

"Ron, I would give you a hug if you were in front of me. Thank you!"

She paused and felt the final vindication that she had been right from the beginning. The pieces did not fit. Now the puzzle was nearly complete. Just one last piece was lacking. She resumed walking and starting with the house directly across the street. It was a simple red brick ranch home with a well-manicured yard. Although not on the water, multi-million-dollar homes surrounded the older home, and it was still worth a million dollars.

She knocked on the door. The white wood door opened and a middle-aged man answered the door. His hair had the texture of a shoe brush with a tinge of orange. He had a beard that covered two chins. A warm smile presented a welcoming acceptance.

"Hi, I'm Detective Kate Alexander with the Tampa Police Department. I noticed that you have a doorbell camera. We were investigating a suspicious vehicle in the neighborhood on Sunday evening and I wanted to see if you could check to see if your camera may have captured an image."

"Oh sure. I'm Dave. Come on in." He motioned to her to have a seat on the black leather sofa. She stroked the cool smooth padded arm.

He plopped down in the recliner as his black AC/DC T-shirt stretched to its limits. He picked up his tablet, adjusted his black-rimmed glasses and said, "So the doorbell camera really is only good at capturing an image to the front door. But I have another small camera in the window that covers my entire front yard and street. So, let's see what we have here. You said Sunday?"

"Yes. It would have been in the evening before 9 o'clock."

"Surprisingly, we get a fair number of cars down the street."

"We are looking to see, maybe a BMW SUV."

"Bingo. We have a winner. Here you go."

Kate stood up and walked to the recliner as Dave showed her the video on his tablet. In the camera view was a black BMW parking in the circular driveway. Rodney Upton stepped out and walked up to the door. Brian Poole answered the door and handed something to Upton. They spoke a little over a minute and Upton left. This would confirm the time that Upton said he had received the sleeping pills from Poole.

"That's great. Could you send me that video, please?"

"Oh sure. Was that a drug deal?"

"Why would you say that?"

"That guy that lives there, Brian. He never works and lives in that enormous home. He has parties, but I never get invited."

"That is a shame. Sometimes it's better not to be too close to your neighbors."

"You might be right." He pushed up with both hands and stood in front of Kate. "If there is anything else that I can help with, you let me know."

"I will. Thank you, Dave."

She called Cody and updated him on the FDLE findings. She told him about the camera recording from Dave's house.

Cody said, "That is great news. I think that's the last block that topples the stack."

"Fingers crossed."

Kate was now going to call Fiona and hope that they would have enough evidence against Poole. He might still make his claims that the bottle had been stolen. With Krystal's testimony, along with Upton's and a recording showing the time to corroborate Upton's version, Poole could not escape.

Chapter Eighty-Two

Fiona listened to Kate described the probable cause that they had established on Brian Poole. They had the statement of Rodney Upton, whose testimony would be called into question. Upton's life was truly on the line. The death penalty or life in prison. They had Krystal's statement that she provided the sleeping medicine to Brian Poole, which was corroborated by Upton and found in Upton's residence. The DNA on the pill bottle proved Poole handled that particular bottle. The autopsy would provide evidence that the sleeping medicine was the same type found in each of the four victims that made them unconscious and unable to resist their murder. They now also had the camera recording from Dave, the across the street neighbor that provided further corroboration to Upton retrieving a package at Poole's home.

Krystal's statement that she overheard Poole talking on the phone at the approximate time that aligned with phone records. She heard him ask the caller if there would be blowback. Poole also said that they had to find Kash and eliminate him. Poole's motive was now disclosed that he had revenge in mind and to target Kash and the Marchetti family for retribution. These conversations sounded more like a mobster than a tech millionaire.

Fiona discussed with Kate the elements and required proof of charging a person with Florida Statutes titled Attempts, Solicitation, and Conspiracy. Fiona said that she felt confident they could show Poole had knowledge and intent that the crime would be committed. As well as that, he agreed and confederated with Upton to cause the offense to be committed. She had the DNA results linking Poole to the pill bottle. Regardless, she told Kate that she had essentially a chain of evidence from Krystal to Poole and to Upton. The revenge motive would be easy to prove in showing the financial losses to Poole.

Fiona told Kate that they could prepare the application requesting an arrest warrant. Once the judge signed the warrant, Kate would be in good standing to make the physical arrest. That brought a smile to Kate. She felt exhilaration at the idea of putting cuffs on Poole. She had no idea how pleasurable it would become.

Kate's phone rang, and she answered, "Hi Trent."

"Congratulations on wrapping up the big case. All the political intrigue brought to a close."

"I still have one to coral and that will happen soon. I'm just at a loss of how Rodney Upton without any previous history of violence, is able to kill an entire family of four while they slept and have little remorse."

"Without knowing all his history, aside from the news accounts, past trauma often influences the later infliction of pain on other victims. Besides having his status quo and success toppled by the potential exposure, he may have looked with vile contempt at the Marchetti's wealthy upbringing, standing in the community and harmonious family. All that he lacked growing up in an unloved, dysfunctional and lower socio-economic environment bubbles to the surface. The inner rage was there. It became a waterfall. He planned this with premeditation. This was not some person that snapped. He was already broken. With the total lack of remorse, he could be diagnosed with psychopathy. Of course, I could never assess him because of our conflict of interest."

"Very interesting, and sounds reasonable. Thank you for that insight. I could use a few more shots of rum and a long hug."

"I'm there for you."

"Thank you. Speaking of being there for me, are we still on for puppy shopping?"

"Absolutely."

Chapter Eighty-Three

On Friday evening, Kate and Cody navigated through the streets of Davis Island. The quiet streets had become congested with cars parked on both sides of the street as they approached Poole's residence. A few houses away, traffic came to a standstill. A young man in khaki shorts and a black polo ran past them with keys in his hand.

Kate looked over at Cody and smiled. "This is going to be awesome. I think the party is at his house."

Cody flashed a smile of white teeth, nodded and said, "Epic."

They pulled up to the portable valet stand, being supervised by an athletic-looking mid-twenties fellow with short blonde hair. Two teenagers descended upon the car and opened the car door. Kate asked her attendant to call the supervisor over. He shouted over the car to Billy that they wanted to speak to him. He rolled his eyes and jogged over. Have to keep the traffic moving.

Kate flashed the badge to Billy and explained that they would not be staying at the party. They were there to pick something up of an urgent matter and would leave in less than ten minutes. Billy scrunched his face like he was mulling over the next move in Tetris. He relented and had them back up into a spot in the grass next to the driveway.

The guests, mostly unloading from high end sports cars and luxury models, were all prepared for a themed party reminiscent of the Gasparilla pirate invasion. Like a grownup costume party for pirates.

Cody looked at Kate and said, "Did you bring your corset and stockings?"

"No, but I brought my gun and shackles. How about you? Puffy shirt and pantaloons?" They both chuckled. "You know, they may recruit you to fill some vacancies in the Krewe of Kingsmen."

Cody scoffed.

They approached the front door of the home. There was no doorkeeper. People were walking in and sharing handshakes, kisses and introductions. Lots of laughter and storytelling. It reminded Kate how uncomfortable she was swimming in these waters. In college, she attended a couple of these soirees.

She hated them. She didn't like large parties either. She always felt that she was on display and being judged by those around her. How did she look? How did she sound? Was she smart? Was she the focus of the conversation after she left?

The two detectives captured many looks from the curious party goers. They weaved through the crowd as Kate spotted Poole holding court among a group of pirates and wenches. They were all focused on his smiling face as he lavished at being the center of attention.

He spotted Kate, and his smile dropped like a boulder off a cliff. She could see that he was looking to put out the fire, with no one noticing. But everyone watched with attention to see what had diverted his focus. He excused himself and hurried to the detectives.

"Can I get you a drink? Something to eat. I have a crab and a prime rib carving station."

Kate said, "Brian, we are not here for the buffet. Would you mind stepping outside where we can talk to you?"

"Actually, I do mind. I am having a party and you are intruding. You can call me in the morning and we can schedule an appointment with my attorney."

"Well, you will definitely need your attorney. You can call him from jail to set up that appointment." Kate said, staring into his eyes.

His right eyebrow lifted, and his head tilted slightly like a dog processing a command. Kate noticed that the laughter had stopped and most of the talking had quieted to a low dim. The two detectives and Poole were now the focus of everyone's attention.

Kate leaned in and whispered. "Brian Poole, I have a warrant for your arrest for Conspiracy to Commit Murder. Turn around and put your hands behind your back. You don't want to make this any more embarrassing for yourself."

He returned the hushed tone, "Miss Alexander, this is a charity function that I am hosting. There are a lot of important people here, including politicians. Can this not wait until the morning?"

Her voice no longer hushed, "Do you think I am going to wait until morning? You have two choices. We can handcuff you now or outside in your front yard."

He looked at Kate and then at Cody. Both detectives stared with defiance into his brown eyes. He was weighing his options. He finally nodded in capitulation.

"Outside. You will pay for this. I will have your job."

She ignored the threat and smiled with satisfaction. "Since you are going to the brig, who is your first officer to take command of your listless ship?"

He looked over at another pirate and said, "Jackson, would your take over for me and call Melvin Storms for me? He couldn't make it tonight."

The pirate nodded.

Kate put her hand on his elbow to guide him toward the door. He pulled his arm away. She leaned towards his ear and said quietly, "Don't get bold. I will beat you like a scalawag rag-doll."

Poole looked around at the mostly speechless guests and said, "This will only be a brief respite, my fellow pirates. Continue ravaging yourselves on the bounty and drink."

Outside, as they passed more arriving guests, unaware of what was happening, they were all enthusiastic about saying hello. He asked for forgiveness and urged them to go inside. But onlookers jammed the door like they were watching a car wreck on I-75.

Cody put his hand on Poole's shoulder to stop him. Kate looked at Cody and said, "This would not have been possible without your help. Your cuffs, your arrest."

Cody pulled the stainless bracelets out and tightened them around Poole's wrists behind his back. Each detective grabbed his elbow and guided him to the valet stand. They placed him in the back seat of the unmarked car.

Kate turned to the valet supervisor and said, "I told you no more than ten minutes. Have a good night."

As they drove out of the driveway, Poole said, "I'm not speaking with you."

Kate looked at the sullen pirate. "In the buccaneer days, they would merely line you up and execute you by firing squad or hang you within days. Now you will languish in a penal institution for years to come. But we may arrange adjoining jail cells with Upton and Kash McCool. I am not asking you anything. We are taking you straight to the Orient Road Jail. Please say hello to your fellow conspirators."

Kate turned around and turned up the radio and began humming to *If I was a Cowboy* by Miranda Lambert. Kate's glowing face looked back at Poole, who clenched his mouth.

Chapter Eighty-Four

After dropping Poole off at the jail, the detectives made their way back into the mostly deserted garage for The Blue Monster. Cody circled around the garage.

Kate asked, "How about a celebratory drink?"

"Raincheck please? Sorry. Jazz called me and asked to meet for a drink at the Safire Lounge in the Floridan Hotel. She wanted to thank me for being so kind and helping her to reframe her relationship and betrayal from Kash. I figured that she really was not a witness, that it would be all right. And she initiated the call. But I changed the location to Buddy Brew for a cup of coffee. I figured that would be harmless enough."

"Just be careful that someone does not accuse you of leveraging her vulnerability. You know that the Safire Lounge was once called the Surefire Lounge back in its heyday during the 1940s for easy hookups. I think Buddy Brew is a good choice."

"The Surefire Lounge, really? I had no idea. Just one cup of coffee and no discussion of the case, I promise. I will proceed with caution. I don't need any headaches."

"Well, you are the one that seems to have a happy ending. Good for you. You can wish me luck puppy shopping with Trent and Brittany."

"We all need a little love in our lives. See you on Monday." Cody said with a sly grin.

They high-fived and separated. Kate picked up her phone and called Brittany, "Hi, sweetie."

"Hi mommy."

"I am in a celebratory mood. What flavor ice cream would you like?"

"Mint chocolate chip!"

"I know grandma likes it too. Mint chocolate chip times three. See you in a bit. I love you."

"I love you too."

She now made a business call. She dialed Carol's parents. She called the Swoboda's number and waited. She knew the Swobodas would never get closure. They lost their only child and grandchildren. At least Kate could provide some answers as to the why.

The why was very shallow. People have been killed for less. A car, a purse or wallet, a gambling debt and, yes, pride. Now she had to tell the parents that their loved ones were sacrificed to conceal corruption and greed. Kate could at least share that some of those responsible would face justice, while others would merely face condemnation. The FBI was going to open a public corruption inquiry into the politicians, but that would take time.

Dominic's mother, Valerie McCormick, was the last official call to be made. After providing McCormick with the final update, there was a long pause. Kate asked, "Are you still there?"

"Oh yes. I was just contemplating my revenge."

"I have to warn you..."

"Not physical revenge. I am going to make them a project. I have quite the platform to use. I am going to have a huge press conference and name names. I am going after every ass wipe politician and strap hanger involved in this financial debacle that led to the death of my grandchildren. They are finished in this town and in politics. That Krewe of Kingsmen will not be throwing beads off parade floats anymore."

Kate thought it was strange to hear Valerie planned to seek revenge for her grandchildren, but no mention of her own son. Sad.

Kate ended the call and dialed Frank Duffy. "Hello stranger, how is my favorite partner doing?"

"I'm good. Kate. I'm in a good place. I am going to the Franciscan Center next week for the Operation Restore PTS program and then back to work."

"Sounds like a plan. I am happy that your foundation has been propped up and secured."

"Like a house built on rock."

"I need a plus one to go to Alfonso's retirement party."

"What about the Professor?"

"Okay, a plus two."

"You mean a third wheel? I'm there. How have you been doing?"

"I could have used you. Big case and big problems, but all tied up in a neat bow. I had to go toe to toe with The Caveman."

"Oh boy. Do tell. How did it go?"

"Have you ever heard of fragging or manscaping?"

The end.

Thank you for taking the time to read this book. If you liked this book, I would be extremely grateful if you would be kind enough to leave a brief review on Amazon. This will help to enlighten other readers and spread the word. My Amazon Author page is: https://www.amazon.com/Mike-Roche/e/B00BHEIF78?ref=sr_ntt_srch_lnk_1&qid=1661706928&sr=8-1 I am humbled that you spent your time with Kate and Cody and my fictional tale. Please stop by https://mikeroche.com/ and join my email list for a free Kate Alexander short story and upcoming news on the future release of *Dead Cadillac*.

Thank you!

Cheers, Mike

Also By Mike Roche

The Blue Monster
Coins of Death
Karma! (Young Adult Fiction)

Non Fiction:
Mass Killer: How You can Identify Workplace, School or Public Killers Before They Strike 2nd edition
Face 2 Faces: Interviewing and Rapport Building Skills: an Ex-Secret Service Agent's Guide

About The Author

While working as both a local cop and a federal agent, Mike Roche has spent four decades chasing bad guys and conducting behavioral threat assessments of stalkers and assassins. A frequent guest at writers conferences, homicide conferences and podcasts, he was also an adjunct college instructor and law enforcement trainer. Mike enjoys the serenity of his retirement home in Florida, while watching the sunsets and sunrises surrounded by nature.

Afterword

Ticks are nasty little buggers!

I write about Lyme Disease and a fictitious treatment and company in this book. In 2008, I became afflicted with Lyme Disease. I initially felt tingling in one hand and then the other. I knew a Tampa Police officer who had died from ALS. His disease started the same way. I was naturally concerned. The doctor eliminated both Lyme and ALS and said it was probably a virus.

That started a two-year journey of a succession of doctors in search of answers as to why my body was slowly betraying me. None could provide an answer. From a person who enjoyed caring for my own yard and working out five times a week, I now could not do any of the aforementioned. I experienced increased neuropathy and weakness in my extremities, diminished lung function, body aches, fatigue, and significant brain fog. I would often count the hours until I could return to bed. Stairs were out of the question, and I was restricted from walking distances greater than a trip past the mailbox.

Some doctors questioned my condition. "How could it be Lyme?" "Did a tick bite you?" A poppy seed size of a bug is easy to miss. "Did you have the bullseye rash?" I can't see through my hair or on my back. Besides, only fifty percent of bites cause the rash. "You had a negative Elisa and Western blot Lyme test." Yes, but they are not overly accurate. I found out later that many had negative tests. "We don't have Lyme in Florida." Oh, but I travel a lot. I also have deer in my backyard in Florida. Guess what? They carry ticks. "But not all ticks have Lyme." Okay, I give up. I'm sick and I need help. The CDC denies the existence of Chronic Lyme.

One Christmas, which I thought would be my last, I barely had the strength to walk to the Christmas tree. There were many false diagnoses and costly treatments along the way. No one could provide a definitive answer. A neurologist told my wife that I had ALS and six months to live. I prepared my will and reflected on the many blessings of my life.

One day, I was teaching a class at Saint Leo University, and I sat down inside the chapel and prayed to God for help. A prayer that I had repeated many times in the past. When I returned home, my wife told me she was flipping through TV channels and happened upon a program of interest. *Mystery Diagnosis* had an episode about a teenage girl, who was very active and now restricted to a wheelchair. They diagnosed this young girl with Lyme. My wife, the tenacious nurse, tracked down the physician in New York, who treated this girl. He referred my wife to a Lyme literate doctor in Tampa.

Dr. Michael Cichon, who is now retired, took me on as a patient. He warned me I was not in good shape and may not survive the treatment of IV antibiotics. He confirmed his diagnosis of Lyme with an analysis of my blood that he sent to a lab in California.

The treatment was a long process. My bosses at the time were not very sympathetic. I think they viewed me as broken and unable to contribute, which was true. Fortunately, my safe harbor was home with my family. I slowly improved. The journey on the road to recovery was years long and grueling. I have had a few episodes of relapse, but I never feel comfortable saying I'm cured. I am always in fear of a return.

The political aspects of the diagnosis and treatment of Lyme in the medical community that I discuss in the book are real. As we witnessed during Covid–19, there was much disagreement on treatment protocols. Lyme is and was no different. Many doctors trying novel approaches were branded heretics and disciplined if they spoke out against the crowd. I was surprised at the number of physicians that were not well educated concerning Lyme. Many have little understanding past the initial ten days of antibiotic treatment and the onset of the symptoms. I am not a doctor. All I know is that if it were not for my wife and Dr. Cichon, I would not be here today. I am now over twelve years past that wrongful six months to live diagnosis and thrilled to embrace life every day.

Those that are suffering from ALS suffer from a cruel and tortuous existence as their bodies betray them. Their caretakers deserve all the respect in the world for standing by them.

"All truths go through three stages. First is ridicule. Second, is it's violently opposed and finally, accepted as self-evident." - Arthur Schopenhauer, German Philosopher

Printed in Dunstable, United Kingdom